Death
Eligible

Other books by Larry Axelrood

The Advocate
Plea Bargain

Death Eligible

A Darcy Cole Novel

LARRY AXELROOD

CUMBERLAND HOUSE
NASHVILLE, TENNESSEE

Cover design: Gore Studio, Inc.
Text design: Mary Sanford

Library of Congress Cataloging-in-Publication Data
Axelrood, Larry, 1960-
  Death eligible : a Darcy Cole novel / Larry Axelrood.
    p. cm.
  ISBN 1-58182-392-4 (alk. paper)
  1. Cole, Darcy (Fictitious character)—Fiction. 2. Capital punishment—Fiction. 3. Trials (Murder)—Fiction. 4. Chicago (Ill.)—Fiction. I. Title.
  PS3551.X45D43 2004
   813'.6—dc22

                                                          2004003948

Printed in the United States of America
1 2 3 4 5 6 7—10 09 08 07 06 05 04

For Anne, Claire, and Jack

Death
Eligible

Prologue

Christmas Day, eight years earlier

Stateville Prison looked exactly like a max joint should. It seemed like a set for a Jimmy Cagney movie. Outside, the place was a collection of ominous buildings all connected to one main round tower. Razor wire and high fences separated the buildings and their expansive grounds from cars traveling past on Joliet Road. During the summer months these same grounds were lush green lawns bordered by beautiful flowers. Today, the snow gave the same grounds a bleak, desolate feel.

Most of the inmates were enjoying a traditional Christmas dinner of turkey, mashed potatoes, and stuffing. Dewayne "Boo" Kirksey was not among them. Boo was in his cell in the segregation unit. Seg was for inmates who were vulnerable for one reason or another. Boo's problem was that he was a snitch, a rat, a trick. It got worse. He had snitched on a member of the Black Gangster Disciples, one of the most violent gangs housed in the Illinois Department of Corrections.

Boo was busy preparing his holiday feast. He pulled his mattress off his bed, exposing the metal slats that functioned as bed springs. Carefully, he tore the top off an empty milk carton. After assembling his ingredients—bologna, three butter pats, two slices of white bread and a plastic knife—he stuffed paper scraps into the milk carton and used his book of matches to ignite the paper. He held the milk carton under the frame and used the flame to heat the slats. Next, he tossed the bologna onto the heated slats. After forcing more paper into the carton, he began to toast the buttered bread. When both sides were browned, he assembled his sandwich, set it on a paper towel and cut it in half.

Inside the stainless steel toilet that hung from the wall of his six-by-eight cell was a plastic drink bottle, which contained a red liquid held in by a glued foil top. He used his little sink to wash off the bottle before wiping it dry. Boo had his sandwich, drink, and a bag of Cheetos.

It took a few minutes to finish his meal. Boo began to move the antenna on his small black and white television in an attempt to get a clear picture. He heard someone walking down the corridor in his direction. Holidays always left the prison shorthanded. There was a guard he had never seen before walking toward him. The guard had keys in his hand. "Kirksey, back away from the cell door." Boo did as he was told. Thickly built with short red hair, the guard looked like a shitkicker, the term the inmates gave to guards from the rural areas around the state who took the "well paid" prison jobs. After unlocking the door, the shitkicker walked away. Boo felt a wave of nausea sweep through his body.

It happened in a rush. There were three of them. The smallest of the three outweighed Boo by forty pounds. All of them had jail muscles, two of them had shanks, and the third had a nine-inch piece of metal that had once been part of a window frame. A solid blow to the side of his face forced Boo to the ground against his bunk. Pain shot through him after the window frame caught him squarely on the side of his face. Boo began to lose consciousness when the first shank tore into his eye. Blood exploded from his face. He looked up at the toilet before everything went dark.

1

As an evidence technician took photographs of the corpse, Detective Tim Kelly studied the body and guessed that it had been floating in the lake for a couple of days, maybe a week. Floaters were not uncommon. One or two were dragged out of the lake each summer by firemen. It used to be some poor kid who didn't know how to swim in the first place, but recently Lake Michigan's dangerous currents and unpredictable rip tides had been claiming the lives of even seasoned swimmers. But Kelly wasn't there for a floater; he was there for a murder victim. The corpse was naked, somewhere between fifteen and twenty years old. Her features were so badly bloated and distorted that he had trouble determining her exact age; he wouldn't have been surprised if she were substantially older. She wore a small gold necklace—a crucifix—and a ring on her right hand that had a translucent, milky stone in the center. A necktie was knotted tightly against her throat. There was a gaping hole in her chest and the skin around the wound had turned a light pink, which was in ghastly contrast to the chalky white of the rest of the body.

Kelly turned to survey the scene. Cops, firemen, paramedics, and the two divers, who were getting out of their diving gear, watched and talked as the people from the medical examiner's office unfolded the body bag. A small crowd of civilians gathered some distance away, separated by a length of yellow police tape. Kelly walked over to the evidence technician.

"How many more photos do you need?" Kelly asked.

"I've got what I need," he replied. "Do you want anything else?"

"Yeah, can you shoot the crowd over there?"

The ET leaned back and looked over his shoulder.

"No problem," he said. "Let me change lenses so I can do it from here, inconspicuously."

With arson cases, it's common practice to photograph the onlookers, because fire-starters apparently get off on seeing their creation to its end. Same thing with some serial killers, as if watching their victims take their last breath isn't enough to fulfill whatever sick power trip they're on. Since Kelly didn't know what he was dealing with here, a few snaps of the morbidly curious couldn't hurt.

The detective's attention was drawn to a man walking toward him. It was his partner, Virgil Johnson. Virgil was about six foot two, 250, with light brown hair, blue eyes, and a pale complexion. Virgil had grown up in a small town in the part of Illinois Chicagoans called "downstate." After high school he faced limited job options: factory work, the military, or farming. Instead, he attended Western Illinois University and ended up as a criminal justice major.

After graduation, he took a job as a police officer in DeKalb, another college town surrounded by farms, and went through the State Police Academy. In the academy, he met a couple of guys who were going to work in Evanston. Six months later, he applied to the Evanston Police Department and joined the force soon after. With its proximity to Chicago and its diverse population, Evanston was a challenging professional environment for Virgil. He enjoyed his job and felt far removed from his downstate beginnings.

"What's up, man?" he said.

"We got a murder."

Johnson looked over the corpse as the guys from the ME's office loaded it into a body bag.

"She's been in the water for a while, could have been thrown in anywhere," Kelly said.

"Yep," Johnson responded succinctly, when he was within the vicinity of the corpse. He looked away out over the lake. "And now we get to identify her," he said heavily.

"It's a good place to start," said Kelly. "They're going to autopsy her tomorrow."

"You know, I hate this shit," Johnson.

"Could be worse, you could be doing cow tipping cases in DeKalb," Kelly said.

2

Dr. Sally Fitzhugh walked into the autopsy theater with gloves and a mask on. An assistant nodded toward the two detectives.

"Doctor, Detective Tim Kelly, Detective Virgil Johnson, Evanston Police Department."

She looked at Kelly. "Hello, Detective Johnson."

"Uh, no ma'am, I'm Detective Kelly," he said.

"I'm sorry," she said, blushing. "I thought by the names . . ." her voice trailed off.

"Don't worry about it. Happens all the time," Kelly said.

Kelly was a dark-skinned black man, about five foot eleven, with an athletic build and a soft, deep voice.

Johnson stood back along the far wall to get as much distance from the body as he could. Kelly, on the other hand, was right up there at the examining table. Johnson preferred to view the body through the detachment of Polaroid images; Kelly was intrigued by all of the forensic sciences. While most cops had to work up a tolerance for an autopsy, Kelly was fascinated.

A city kid, Kelly grew up playing sports, going to action movies, and watching cop shows on television. After high school he joined the Marines, because in his mind the Marines were the toughest branch of the service. He excelled in boot camp and bounced through a few advanced training units before ending up in the military police.

For a nineteen-year-old from the south side, joining the Marines was an exciting adventure. He began in Germany, got promoted, and was shipped to Japan. It took him only sixteen months to finish his associate's degree through the military. Another promotion took him back to the states. He re-upped for two more years, finished his bachelor's degree, got another promotion, and opted to join the Reserves.

After his discharge, Kelly returned to Chicago and applied to the Chicago, Oak Park, and Evanston police departments. Evanston was the first to offer him a job and he'd been there ever since.

After Dr. Fitzhugh examined the obvious external points of injury, she began the internal work. When observing such procedures, Kelly couldn't help but think of a slaughterhouse. Of course he knew there was no need for delicacy, but he was always taken aback by the removed attitudes and rough manner of the examiners as they sliced through muscles, sawed through bone, hauled out organs, and pulled and pushed flesh as if it were slabs of beef.

The first incision was made across the chest from shoulder to shoulder, and then the body was cut from the chest down to just above the pubic bone, in a perfect Y cut. The doctor pulled open the body and noxious gases filled the air. An overhead fan failed to disperse the odor. The doctor continued her work unfazed.

The two detectives were relieved when Dr. Fitzhugh finished

the autopsy. They followed her out and tossed their masks into the receptacle where she had placed her mask and gloves. She washed up, and after toweling off began to talk to them.

"She was strangled and stabbed," she said. "Either one of these events would have killed her. What I suspect happened is that they stabbed her and as she was bleeding out they strangled her."

"You said 'they,'" said Kelly.

"'They' being the bad guy or guys. I can't tell you if it was one or more. There is significant vaginal trauma," the doctor said. "Some pre-mortem bruising. So I suspect that she had been raped. Any DNA evidence from the sexual assault has been washed away. However, I was able to gather some good material from deep under the fingernails. I have it bagged and will have that tested. But without having someone to match it to, it won't do us much good. So I suggest that you look for an individual or individuals who have fresh scratches."

"How old is she?" Johnson asked.

The doctor sighed. "It's hard to tell. I'm guessing she was eighteen or younger. With the bloating it's hard to tell, and girls these days don't look like they did ten years ago."

"How long has she been dead?"

"I can't be that precise," she said. "A couple of days. I know that all the medical examiners on TV can tell you within a ten-minute time frame, but I don't have that expertise."

"Well, if it's any consolation," Kelly said, "we won't have this solved by the end of the hour."

The doctor smiled.

"I'll have my reports prepared in the next day or two," she said. "If there is anything I can do, feel free to give me a call."

• • •

The headquarters of the Evanston Police Department consisted of a squat, two-story building near the train tracks that took commuters into Chicago from the suburbs. Kelly and Johnson pulled up by the front door of the station; Kelly jumped out and Johnson parked. Kelly jogged up the stairs, taking two at a time, and burst into the detective bureau. He always blew into the station with high energy. It was a holdover from his military training of moving "double time." He threw his brown herringbone sport coat over the back of his chair and turned on his computer to check his e-mail. There was a message from his nine-year-old daughter, who apparently still loved him despite the awful way he'd braided her hair that morning. After deleting various pieces of spam, he called the Chicago Police Department and spoke with a detective in the missing persons' bureau. Kelly ran down the stats.

"Female, white, approximately eighteen, thin to medium build, brown hair, weight probably about a hundred and a quarter."

He could hear the Chicago detective using a keyboard to enter the information into a computer. After a while, the detective spoke up.

"I typed in girls from the age of fifteen to twenty—that's our identification class on missings—but there are also hundreds of runaways that fit the profile."

"Let's start with the missings," Kelly said.

"Do you want them faxed or e-mailed?"

"Faxed," he said, then gave the number.

"Good luck," said the Chicago detective. "If you need anything, just give us a call. We'll help you in any way we can."

Johnson walked up and looked over Kelly's shoulder as he pulled sheets out of the fax machine.

"What do we have?" he asked.

"I called CPD for their missing. I also checked northern Cook County. Nobody else has anything close," he said.

They spoke with the cool detachment of cops doing their job.

They were trying to identify a murder victim who had been tossed in the lake, but their bland, all-business tone helped them keep a professional distance from the mayhem.

Kelly spread the faxes over a table.

"There are eight here," he said. "Let's split 'em up and make some calls."

Twenty minutes later, Johnson was standing over Kelly as he talked on the phone.

"Yes, ma'am. That would be great," Kelly said. "We really appreciate your help."

Kelly gave the woman the address of the police station and directions from the north side of Chicago. He placed the phone in the cradle and turned to his partner.

"We might have a hit," he said.

"No shit?" Johnson said. "That was quick."

"How did you do?"

"Struck out on two. One phone was disconnected, on the fourth I got no answer. Who did you get?" Johnson asked.

"A Vanessa Baldwin," Kelly said, leaning back with hands locked behind his head. "She runs a group home in Rogers Park. Had one of her girls go missing, Laura Martin. She never came home from work last week. Says Laura was basically a good girl."

"Gee, we've never heard that before," Johnson interjected. "How old was she?"

"Sixteen," he said. "And she was wearing a crucifix Ms. Baldwin bought for her one Christmas and a small ring, an opal that she had purchased for herself from her job at the mall."

"When's Baldwin coming in?" Johnson asked.

"She said she'd try to be here early this afternoon, depending on traffic. We can grab a quick lunch if you want," Kelly said.

"Doesn't have to be quick," his partner replied. "If there's anything you can depend on, it's traffic."

• • •

A uniformed officer escorted Vanessa Baldwin up the stairs to the detective bureau. Kelly had his back to the door and was on the phone. Virgil walked toward Ms. Baldwin, who stuck her hand out and said, "You must be Detective Kelly."

"No ma'am," he said. "I'm Detective Virgil Johnson. Detective Kelly, my partner, is on the phone," he said nodding toward Kelly.

She looked a little bit surprised.

"So Tim Kelly is black and Virgil Johnson is white," she said. "Your parents messing with you?" she asked.

"Maybe so, but it keeps life interesting," Johnson replied.

Kelly ended his conversation quickly and walked over to shake hands. Vanessa Baldwin was wearing a sweater dress, a bit heavy for the unseasonably warm November day. She had a sturdy, strong build and light brown eyes. Her hair was in small braids, pulled back away from her face.

"Seriously, though, I apologize. I always preach to my girls not to stereotype, and here I am stereotyping you on your names."

"No problem," Kelly said.

"Why don't you sit down, ma'am," he said, gesturing to an open chair.

Kelly removed two sealed plastic evidence bags from a large manila envelope.

"Ma'am, do you recognize this necklace?"

Tears formed in Vanessa's eyes.

"It looks like the one I gave Laura for Christmas two years ago," she said softly.

"How about this ring?" he said. She reached out and took the ring between her thumb and first finger, rotating it to catch the light.

"Laura loved the promise of rainbows in opals," she said. She looked Kelly in the eyes. "She's dead, isn't she?" she asked abruptly.

Kelly nodded and in a gentle voice said, "Maybe. We have a body we're trying to identify. A young woman pulled from the lake."

Vanessa's hands crossed her breasts, her chin rested on her chest. "She was a sweet girl, smart, pretty, but most important she had a positive attitude. She was striving for something more than most of the other girls I've worked with. I was afraid when she didn't come home that something terrible must have happened."

They sat in silence for a moment as the tears rolled down Vanessa's cheeks. Johnson handed her a box of tissue, then realized that it hadn't yet been opened. As he began to fumble with the top of the box, she gently took it from him and opened it effortlessly. She pulled a few out, dabbed her eyes and clutched them in her hand.

"She was a sweet girl," she said again.

"When was the last time you saw her?" they asked.

"When she left for work on October 30."

"And she never came home from work?" asked Johnson.

Vanessa looked at Kelly and then at Johnson. She looked down at the floor before finally glancing back up.

"No," she said. "She never came home. I know that she was going to get a ride home from her job at the Lincolnwood Mall from a boy she knew—Trip, she called him."

"Trip? That was his name?" asked Kelly.

"I'm sure it was a nickname. He's one of those boys from Longwood Prep."

"Longwood Prep," Kelly said, glancing at Johnson. "Okay, can you tell us where she worked at the mall?"

"She worked at one of those earring places. You know, where they do the piercing right there, with everyone watching."

"How long did she work there?" Kelly asked.

"Oh, about a year and a half. She got the job through one of the girls she goes to school with. She went to Mather High School."

"How long did you know her?" Kelly asked.

"About four years. I run a house in Rogers Park. Wards of the state live with me, girls, teenagers. Laura went to school, studied hard. She always had a job and never asked for anything. She never complained. She was all excited because she got her own room recently. We have a big old Victorian home and the senior girls get one of the two single rooms. She had just moved into it."

"Are her things in her room?" asked Kelly.

"Sure, everything she had is there."

"Would you mind if we took a look?"

"Not at all, whenever you need to."

"Can we drive you over there now? The sooner we get on this, the sooner we'll know what happened to Laura."

"That's fine," Vanessa said. "I want to help in any way I can. I am responsible for her; she doesn't have anyone else."

"Well, Ms. Baldwin, you must have played an important role in her life. Sometimes there's no explanation for why things happen. But we'll find out what happened and we'll make the people who did this pay for it." They made their way to the car.

Johnson parked the unmarked squad car next to a fire hydrant in front of a gray Victorian in between two multi-unit brick apartment buildings. He got out and opened the back door for Vanessa, who then led them up the stairs. The room was cramped. Amid a small twin bed and a dresser, there was just enough room to walk in and out. There was a tiny closet and one window.

"This is it," said Vanessa. "Anything you find in here that's nice, she paid for with her own money."

Johnson opened a plastic bag and, using a tissue, pulled a toothbrush out of a plastic cup on the dresser. He opened another plastic bag and, with the same tissue, picked up a hairbrush and dropped it in. They searched for and found a journal and a small address book but found no entry for anyone named Trip. They grabbed her school notebook and a couple of personal photographs, which they showed to Vanessa.

"Is Trip in any of these photographs?" Kelly asked

Vanessa took a quick run through them, about a half dozen, then went back through and studied them carefully.

"Nope, I know all these boys, but I've never actually met Trip."

"How do you know about him?" Johnson asked.

"Laura told me," she said. "We talked a lot. She told me he was an okay guy who treated her well, that he was handsome, and that he came from money. They'd met at the mall and had gone out a couple of times. Whenever they went out, it would be someplace she had never been, someplace exciting and new, usually expensive, of course," she said.

"Well, Longwood Prep costs a lot of money," Johnson said. "It's where kids go whose parents aren't happy with the public schools—you know, New Trier or Lake Forest."

"Well," Vanessa said, "money never made a big impression on Laura. But she did like getting to see places she could never go on her own. In fact, from what Laura told me, Trip's the type of guy who knows the cost of everything but the value of nothing."

"She seemed wise," said Tim. "It's a very telling comment, isn't it?"

"Laura was a good girl. She had the kind of dignity that only comes from being at the bottom, knowing you're better than the circumstances you're living through."

3

KELLY DROVE THE UNMARKED SQUAD car through the wrought iron gates and into a parking spot in a lot between two large buildings at Longwood Prep. He and Johnson walked to the building with four large white columns. They pushed through two huge oak doors and walked past two classrooms full of students before they found the dean's office.

After identifying themselves with their badges, they were introduced to a short, dark-haired woman who offered her hand.

"I'm Lesley Howard, Dean of Students," she said. "Gentlemen, what is the nature of your visit, if I may ask?"

"We're trying to locate potential witnesses in a criminal investigation," Kelly said.

She motioned toward chairs at a massive oak table that resembled the front doors of the building.

"How can I help you?" Howard said, looking as though she didn't want to help at all.

"We are trying to put a name to a nickname. A kid named Trip who goes to your school."

"I see," she said. "Well, I'm afraid that's a bit broad. Trip is not an uncommon nickname. You see, we have a lot of third-generation students here."

"At the risk of sounding unsophisticated, what's the connection?" said Johnson.

"Well, if someone is a John Brown III, he's third in line, hence Trip, short for triple."

"How many Trips do you think you have here?" Kelly asked.

"Oh, I can't say off the top of my head," she said. "Besides, the actual count seems trivial, doesn't it?"

"Okay, how many students are enrolled here?" he asked, trying a different approach.

"A little over three hundred," she said.

"And it's a co-ed school?"

"Yes, that's correct."

"So, if it's evenly split, we're talking about one hundred fifty boys in the whole school."

"Something like that," she said, shifting papers with no apparent purpose.

"Of that hundred and fifty, how many third-generation students are enrolled?"

"Really, I can't even venture a guess," she said. "Let me make it clear, gentlemen. We're much more concerned with our students' academic progress than with what their friends call them."

Kelly and Johnson exchanged glances.

"We don't doubt that, Ms. Howard. But it also seems clear that your multi-generational students are of particular importance to the tradition of such a fine school. Surely, you can think of a few."

Howard sighed, then glanced at her watch. She tore off a sheet of paper from a memo pad, wrote down a few names and slid it across the table

"These students come to mind," she said. "This is really all the time I can give you, and if you'll excuse me, I have some academic business to attend to."

"Can we talk to some of these kids while we're here?" Johnson asked, as she showed them the door.

"Absolutely not," she said petulantly. "This school prides itself on privacy. Need I say more?"

"No," said Kelly. "But let me advise you of the fact that we may need to come back with a warrant."

"And let me advise you of this," she said. "You are not going to be invited back."

She walked them to the front door.

As they walked down the front steps, Kelly said, "That woman is extremely worried about bad publicity."

"Or angry parents," Johnson answered. The detectives got into the squad car and set themselves up a block and a half from the school. BMWs, Mercedes, Jaguars, and Land Rovers filled the parking lot. The Ford Escorts and Camrys were borrowed from the housekeepers and nannies, who were slipped a few bucks by their charges for the use of the car. It was the end of the school day, and they watched as kids filed out of the buildings, lit cigarettes or flipped on cell phones, and began driving out of the parking lot. Kelly spotted a Lexus full of girls speeding out of the far exit.

"Let's stop the Lexus," he said.

Johnson put the car into drive and accelerated quickly, gaining behind them. When they found a nice stretch of the road with a sidewalk, he hit the lights and siren and curbed the vehicle.

Kelly approached the driver's side while Johnson stood off to the rear of the passenger side. The driver put down her window.

"Did I do something wrong, sir?" she said straightforwardly, without the usual desperate flirtation he received from teenage girls.

Her tone was respectful and polite.

"You seem to be having trouble staying on your side of the center line," Kelly said. "Can I see your driver's license?"

She looked puzzled, but reached for her purse under the front passenger seat. She pulled out a bulging wallet, and from a number of credit cards, produced a driver's license. She handed it to him and began to stammer.

"I'm really sorry. I didn't realize I was crossing the line."

Kelly let her words drift off.

"Where are you coming from?" he asked.

"From school."

"Is that Longwood?" he said.

"Yes," she said. "We just got out and I'm taking my friends home—"

Before she could finish, he interjected.

"How big is that school?" he asked trying to seem nonchalant.

"Not very big," she said. "A few hundred."

"Look, I'm not going to write you a ticket this time," Kelly said.

Her body softened with relief.

"My dad would kill me if I got a ticket," she said.

"Do us all a favor," Kelly said, "and pay closer attention when you're driving."

He leaned into the window and looked at the other girls. "That goes for all of you." They responded with a few faint "okays." As Kelly handed the driver her license, he started his real inquiry.

"Longwood Prep, did you say?" he asked the driver.

"Yes," she responded enthusiastically. "Right down the street."

"Yeah, I think I sat next to a kid from Longwood at a Bulls game a while back. Said his name was Trip something?"

The girls began to giggle.

"What," Kelly said, leaning back into the window, "you girls know him?"

"Well, that would depend on which one," the driver said.

"You mean there's more than one guy named Trip? This guy was a real goof."

The girls giggled again.

"There are a few, actually. But if you're talking about goofs, there's one who really stands out."

"Oh yeah?" Kelly said curiously. "Who'd that be?"

"John Phillips," someone yelled from the backseat. They erupted in laughter.

The driver smiled. "John Henry Phillips III. He's a major head case—totally in love with himself . . . kind of a scary guy."

"Hmmm," Kelly said, "he didn't seem that bad. I guess that's the leveling effect of a ball game."

The girls stared at him blankly.

"Okay, ladies," he said, winding up the exchange. "Please drive carefully, and thanks for your cooperation."

"Thank you, officer," rang out several sing-song voices.

The Lexus pulled away and Kelly walked toward his partner.

"John Henry Phillips III."

"Okay," said Johnson. "Shall we go scoop him?"

"Let's do a little homework first. I want to find out how old he is. If he's seventeen, we'll snatch him. If he's sixteen, we have to get a youth officer."

"But if he's sixteen, isn't he an automatic transfer?" Johnson replied.

"Hell, I don't know," Kelly said. "Listen, instead of screwing this up, why don't we contact the State's Attorney and find out what he wants us to do."

"And what if he tells us we can't grab the kid?"

"Well, then we can't. This kid comes from money. We can't make any mistakes because he'll have a great lawyer. I want to make this case stick."

4

LARRY STEVENS WAS THE HEAD of the prosecutor's office at the Skokie Courthouse, situated across the street from a lush and dense forest preserve that he could gaze upon from his window. On a credenza behind him were pictures of his wife and his three-month-old daughter, Megan, and seven autographed photographs of Ernie Banks. He had a Cubs hat on his bookcase, which contained a baseball encyclopedia and seven or eight other titles all revolving around the Cubs.

"So what do you have?" Stevens began.

"The floater we pulled out was stabbed and strangled," Kelly said. Kelly occupied the seat across the desk closest to the window, Johnson to his right.

"We got a tentative ID as a ward of the state from a group home in Rogers Park. Her name is Laura Martin. We're awaiting the DNA test—we got a hairbrush and a toothbrush. They're going to match it up to the victim, but the jewelry matches and the description matches. She was a little bit distorted for us to get a visual."

"Dental records?" Stevens asked.

"We are scrounging for them, but we'll have them. Working on the assumption that it is her, we started poking around and we have a pretty good lead. We believe she was last with a guy whose nickname is Trip. We think we have identified this character, John Henry Phillips III. He goes to Longwood Prep."

Stevens whistled. "Longwood Prep, that's some big coin. If his family is dropping that kind of cash on school, you can imagine what they're going to do with lawyers. What's next?" Stevens asked.

"We want to grab the kid, talk to him," Kelly said.

"How old is he?"

"He just hit seventeen at the end of October."

"Was he seventeen at the time of the death?"

"He was seventeen on the twenty-second of October," Kelly continued, "so I think we're good. Our victim was last seen alive on the thirtieth. ME thinks the cause of death was somewhere between October 30 and November 4. So he was seventeen."

"Okay, you've got to be careful," Stevens said. "It's got to be him coming in voluntarily to talk to you about some questions. If he squawks about a lawyer, that's it. We've got to move on. No thumb screws. No beatings. No suffocation, no threats."

"Hey, come on," said Kelly. "What the hell do you think we are, a bunch of amateurs?"

Kelly and Johnson had worked with Stevens before. They had a good working relationship. Three years ago Stevens had prosecuted their last murder case. They had waited for the verdict together at a nearby pub. Any police/prosecutor mistrust had vanished long ago.

"No, don't take it that way," Stevens said. "I'm just telling you to dot every *i* and cross every *t*. This could be something."

Stevens took a card out of a baseball-shaped cardholder and flipped it over. "This is my pager number; this is my home number. If you snatch this guy and he wants to talk, don't call Felony Review, call me. I'll do the review. Be careful. If this guy did it, I don't want his money to let him walk away from it. I want to nail the bastard."

Kelly pocketed the card. "If this works out, we want you to try this case, so you'll need to send someone else out on Felony Review."

It was a show of respect for Stevens. He suppressed a smile. "Just be careful."

5

AFTER TWO DAYS OF SURVEILLANCE with nothing more high-tech than binoculars, Kelly and Johnson found John Phillips and a teenage girl sitting in a car in a parking lot at a beach. They were parked on the ridge above the drive that led down to the beach. The weather had just turned, sending a cool mist off the lake. The temperature was in the low 40s, and they had the heater going as they watched their marks.

"What are they doing?" Johnson asked Kelly, who had the binocs.

"Nothing much. She's smoking a cigarette. He's drinking something."

Johnson sighed. "So we wait, huh?"

Kelly shrugged. "She looks young; we may have a minor

smoking. Maybe that's a beer he's drinking. Let's just yank them from the car and see what falls out."

"We can't. It's an ordinance violation, so we need someone local to do it," Johnson said.

"Okay," Kelly said. "Where the hell are we, anyway? These towns all look the same."

"Shit, we've followed this jagoff all over the north shore," Johnson said. "We could be in Winnetka, Kenilworth, Glencoe."

"Well, let's go figure it out," said Kelly as he put the car into reverse. "Maybe it says something on the park sign."

He was backing up when a horn was tapped to let him know a car was behind him. Kelly stopped, put the car into park and got out. He walked slowly toward the car. The driver looked to be in his teens. There were three other kids in the car. They were all rubber-necking like mad as they watched Kelly walk toward them. The driver put down the window.

Kelly anticipated their apprehension and held his hands up reassuredly, "Hold on, hold on, we're cops." Kelly pulled his coat apart to display the badge clipped to his belt.

"I just need to ask you something. What town are we in?"

The teenager was confused.

"Dude, you're a cop. Don't you know where you are?"

"I'm not sure," he said. "What, you don't know where you are either?"

"We're in Winnetka, dude." Kelly noticed the casual *dude*, confirming his belief that citizens in general are less respectful of undercover cops. It was the uniform thing, he guessed.

"Winnetka, okay. Thanks, guys."

He began to walk away, then stopped and pivoted. He didn't want the teens coming down to the beach.

"You guys don't have anything in that car you shouldn't have . . ."

"Nah, dude. We're cool," said the driver.

"Well, I tell you what: If you want to come down to the beach,

I am going to search your car. Or you can just turn around and leave."

"And how do you figure that works?" said the driver.

One of the passengers chimed in, "You need a warrant, man."

Kelly leaned into the window so that everyone could hear him clearly. "No, I don't. I'll search you illegally, and if I find anything, I'll place you under arrest, and then your lawyers will have to prove that I searched you illegally when you get to court. But first, you'll go down to Cook County Jail. What do you think, boys? You got anything to hide?"

"No, sir. We'll just leave," said the driver, suddenly humbled.

"Good idea," said Kelly. He noticed *dude* had been replaced by *sir*.

Kelly sent the boys on their way and rejoined Johnson in the unmarked car. He called the station, had them run down the license plate, told them what he needed, and waited for a Winnetka officer to arrive. About five minutes later a patrol car pulled up. Kelly got out and identified himself to the Winnetka cop. He was young, with a bright red crew cut and a face full of freckles on pale skin.

"I'm Detective Kelly, Evanston Police Department."

"Nice to meet you, Detective. I'm Maloney."

"Well, Officer Maloney, here's the situation. There's a car down there with two teenagers in it. The driver is drinking something, could be a beer. If that's the case I'd like you to go down there and shake them down. I'll confiscate the bottle, bag it for evidence and write him a citation. You up for it?"

The Winnetka officer looked pissed and puzzled.

"What, you don't think I have anything better to do than roust a kid for drinking beer?"

"Frankly, up here? You probably don't. But I need you to do this for me right now. It potentially has a lot more importance than keeping a kid from drinking."

The comment sparked interest in the young cop, as he saw the possibility of participating in serious police work.

"I'll go down and see what I can find," he said, sounding more enthusiastic.

The cruiser pulled up directly behind Trip's car, a BMW 750IL. Maloney got out of his squad car and crept up alongside the BMW. Neither occupant noticed him as he peered in and saw that the driver had a Miller Lite bottle in his right hand and a cigarette in the other. Kelly and Johnson had pulled up behind the squad and were getting out slowly as Maloney knocked on the driver's side window. It was locked, and the two teenagers were startled.

"Get out of the car with your hands where I can see them," Maloney said loudly but calmly.

Trip's left hand sunk out of sight so he could unlock the door, then he slipped out of the car. Cigarette in his left hand, beer in his right, Trip held his hands up about a shoulder's width apart. In the meantime, Johnson had pulled on a pair of rubber gloves. He snatched the bottle from Trip's right hand, poured the contents on the ground, and dropped it into a large plastic bag. He then took the cigarette out of Trip's left hand and crushed it out on top of the BMW.

"What the fuck?" said Trip angrily. "That's my car."

"Is it?" said Johnson. "I thought maybe it was your daddy's."

Before Trip could respond, Kelly instructed the girl to get out of the car. She had dark hair that hung over her heavily made-up eyes, and she sported the typical North Shore teenage uniform: jeans that were too tight and low and a T-shirt that was too tight and rode too high. She planted her hands on her hips defiantly, and to show she had nothing to hide.

Kelly looked her in the eye and said, "Honey, do me a favor and grab that beer bottle on the floor of the car where you left it."

She rolled her eyes, glanced at Trip and retrieved the bottle.

"Imagine that," Kelly said. "Now, pour it out and throw it in the garbage can," he said pointing to a can a few feet away.

"What, are you guys on litter patrol today?" she said, strutting over to the can.

"You wish," Johnson said as she tossed the bottle into the bag.

The girl and Trip watched in disbelief as Kelly took the crushed cigarette butt from Johnson and put it in a separate plastic bag.

"What's going on, if we're allowed to ask?" Trip said, folding his arms across his chest.

"We're doing an investigation and we just confiscated your refreshments as evidence. We'll get back to you," Kelly said.

"Evidence of what?" Trip said. "Are we under arrest?"

"I'm writing you up for ordinance violations," said Maloney. "Give me your driver's licenses, and don't screw around. Once I write you these tickets, you'll go to court and take care of them there. Give me any aggravation at all, and I'll place you both under arrest."

"What ordinances were we violating?" the girl asked as she and Trip handed over their licenses. Trip gave her a look and subtly shook his head.

"You ever read the park signs? Assuming these IDs are legit, you're too young to drink or smoke in the first place. And even if you were old enough, you can't drink on park property."

The two teens looked at each other.

"And our work here is done," Kelly said. "Thanks for your help, Officer Maloney. We'll let you finish your job."

Johnson and Kelly walked back to their vehicle and got in.

"So with this stuff," Kelly said, "we should get some good DNA to check against the fingernail scrapings."

"I'd like to just grab the fucker and sweat him," said Johnson.

"Know what I'm thinking?" asked Kelly. He didn't wait for a response. "We let the kid think about it for a little bit. Shit his pants, start worrying. Then we'll bring him in and tell him what's up. He's seventeen, so we don't need a youth officer."

"Yeah, but in the meantime, you know he's going to lawyer up," Johnson said.

"So we have to talk to him before he gets the lawyer," Kelly said.

"You know it's going to take weeks to get the DNA back," Johnson said.

"I know that," Kelly said, "you know that, but he doesn't know that."

"We'll have him 'voluntarily' come to the station to help us in the investigation of his friend's murder. Before he lawyers up, we'll sweat him hard."

"So we let it go for a day or two then we scoop him and tell him what we got?"

"Yeah, let's just hope we can nail him on something."

6

Judge Joseph Nicolau was seated at a table along the back row
of La Fontella, a small Italian restaurant a mile from the Criminal
Courthouse. As the judge tore a piece of bread from the loaf in
front of him, Darcy Cole walked in, pulled off his overcoat and
hung it on a hook on the wall. Joe stood and reached out to shake
Darcy's hand, clasping his left hand onto Darcy's bicep.

"Glad you could make it," said the judge.

Darcy rubbed his hands together. "It's always great to see you,
Judge. Even on a nasty cold day like this," he said.

The judge smiled. "You know Chicago. Two seasons, winter
and summer."

"I heard it another way," Darcy said. "It's winter and con-
struction."

"I suppose you're going to tell me that's why you're always late to my courtroom?"

Darcy and Joe went back a long way, but Darcy was surprised when the judge had called and asked to meet him for lunch, to talk to him about something important.

"Look, Judge, I'm a criminal defense attorney," said Darcy. "That means I'm on time only once a day, and that's the first courtroom I go to in the morning."

"Yeah, you guys, always chasing the money," said the judge.

The dining room was small and intimate. Along one wall hung pictures of celebrities, some Darcy recognized, some he didn't, none of whom you would call A-listers. A waitress came over with menus, but they didn't need them. From the specials board, the judge ordered chicken Vesuvio and Darcy ordered shrimp on angel hair pasta. They spent a few minutes in casual conversation before getting to the reason for the lunch.

"So, Joe," Darcy began, "you said you needed to talk to me. What's going on?"

The judge took a deep breath and cracked his knuckles. Darcy got an uneasy feeling, not because of the sound of popping bones but because of the meaning behind the gesture. He had known Joe Nicolau for thirty years and knew he was an honest, fair, hard-working judge. He didn't have any of the usual personality traits that could lead someone into trouble. Darcy had never seen him have a drink, didn't know of any affairs, knew he was a committed father and husband. But he also knew that when Joe was troubled by something—say, a difficult case or the well-being of one of his kids—he cracked his knuckles over and over. The habit stood out in Darcy's mind because he had always thought knuckle-cracking was a one-shot deal, that you needed refractory time before you went another round. The cracking continued without a word after the waitress dropped off the salads, and Darcy finally asked the judge if there was anything bothering him.

Nicolau picked up his fork and jabbed at his salad, then looked Darcy in the eye.

"Darcy, I've been a lawyer for thirty-eight years," the judge began. "The last eighteen years I've had the privilege of being a judge. I have always tried to bring dignity to the proceedings in my courtroom."

"That's definitely your reputation, Joe," Darcy responded.

The judge waved the compliment off.

"You ever hear of a guy by the name of Lavelle Macklin?"

Darcy thought for a second.

"It doesn't ring a bell," he said, shaking his head and taking a bite of his salad.

The judge looked around and leaned toward Darcy. There was only one other group in the restaurant, a three-top in the opposite corner.

"Darcy, this Macklin guy was accused of abducting a nine-year-old girl. He lured the girl to an apartment in the projects, then raped and murdered her."

The judge choked up a bit, his voice catching. He took a sip of water and continued.

"Now, you know I've been at this game a long time, and I've seen my fair share of murders, but the evidence on this one was horrendous. The suffering that little girl endured . . ."

Judge Nicolau leaned back and looked up to the ceiling, then looked back at Darcy. Darcy was starving but wasn't sure if it was appropriate to continue eating his salad.

"The police conducted their investigation. They grabbed Macklin and did whatever they had to do to get him to confess. There was a court-reported statement, twenty-two pages, detailed, and the case was assigned to me. We go through all the motions: motion to quash arrest, motion to suppress statements, motion to suppress evidence, and motion to suppress lineup identification. They did every motion known to man. I deny him on everything.

We go to trial, he takes a jury. The jury is out two and a half hours and comes back guilty on all counts."

Darcy, while listening intently, poured some oil on his bread plate and then shook out some cheese, dipped the bread into the oil and popped it into his mouth. It seemed less obtrusive than munching on carrots and lettuce while Joe poured his heart out.

The judge continued. "We do the sentencing hearing. Macklin had no real mitigation, and they brought in some aggravation—enough that I sentenced him to death. To tell the truth, I knew I was going to sentence him to death halfway through the trial."

His voice caught again. He reached for his fork and stabbed at his plate a bit, then set the fork back down. He took a few seconds to compose himself while Darcy waited.

"So, I sentenced him to die, completely convinced he was guilty. The evidence was overwhelming. They had a confession, circumstantial witnesses. The prosecutors did a good job putting it all together. I tell you, Darcy, it was a damn clean trial."

"Sounds like it," Darcy said, eyeing his salad, but sticking to the bread.

"But then Macklin drops his first appeal to the State Supreme Court, and he goes to the Appellate Court. They deny him. The justices were 3-0, no dissent and not much discussion. No trial errors; evidence was overwhelming. He goes to the Supreme Court again and they deny his petition. Federal District Court denies it too. Goes to the Seventh Circuit, gets denied. Appeals to the U.S. Supreme Court: denied."

"So he goes through all his appellate rights. Christ, how long did that take?" Darcy asked.

"About eleven years," Nicolau said.

Darcy shook his head while studying an insipid-looking tomato. "Yep. That's our legal system."

"Well, that's not all. It seems some investigative reporter at the *Tribune* digs up evidence that there was no DNA testing."

"Yeah, there have been a lot of those lately," said Darcy.

"And all the convictions before DNA are now subject to scrutiny because of the spate of cases that have come back exonerating people. I know judges all over the country who have gotten into trouble for denying post-convictions that requested DNA testing. The State's Attorney's Office has been agreeing to re-test post-convictions where DNA material was available."

"Macklin was one of those cases?"

The judge nodded. "The test was done and the DNA on the victim doesn't match Macklin's."

"So you got the wrong guy," Darcy said calmly, trying to downplay a judge's worst nightmare.

"Maybe," said the judge. "It looks bad. In any event, the case is on my call three weeks from today and I am going to grant his motion for a new trial."

"Okay," Darcy said, trying to draw out the point.

"I'd like to appoint you to be his lawyer. He filed the petition *pro se* and now he's going to need a trial lawyer. You'll be paid out of the capital litigation defense fund."

Darcy looked surprised. "Joe, I appreciate your consideration, but you know I don't take appointments."

"Of course you don't," Nicolau responded. "I know an appointment doesn't get you much. You make a lot of money, have high-powered clients. But you're the best trial lawyer I know, and I need you to do me this favor."

The desperation in Nicolau's voice made Darcy consider the situation. His experience with judges was that the majority called cases as they saw them. Few revisited cases in their minds or dwelled on possible mistakes. The job of a judge is to make decisions. They make dozens of life-altering decisions every day. If a fear of mistakes prevents a judge from making important decisions, he or she is through in the profession.

Nicolau continued. "Darcy, Macklin has to have the best legal representation. I failed. I was the judge. I was supposed to administer justice. I sentenced him to die. He sat on death row for ten years."

"If I agreed, what would I have to do?" Darcy asked.

"Simple. Show up to my court three weeks from today and file your appearance. You'll be the lead lawyer." Then he paused. "You did send in the paperwork for the capital litigation bar, didn't you?" he said.

Darcy had, so he didn't take the potential out.

"Yes, I'm pretty sure I'm on the roster."

"Good," Nicolau said. "So you know that under the present rules, a capital case requires a first chair and a second chair, both of whom are members of the capital litigation trial bar."

The first chair was the lead lawyer on the case.

Darcy nodded. "I have someone in my office."

The judge cut him off.

"No. It can't be from two people in the same office. When they created the new rules for capital litigation they required the first and second chairs be independent from each other. It has to be two individual lawyers. I'd like to appoint Justin Schachter as your second chair."

Darcy shrugged and raised his eyebrows.

"You don't know him?" Joe said.

"Doesn't ring a bell," Darcy said. "Can't I pick the guy?"

"No," Nicolau said emphatically. "Here's the deal. I've been watching this kid. He's been in private practice for three and a half years, used to be first chair in my courtroom. Good prosecutor, good kid, levelheaded, I like him a lot. He needs a break, and this could be it. I'd appreciate it if you'd take him under your wing on this."

"What kind of break is it to give him a pain-in-the-ass case at an hourly?"

"It's a hundred and twenty-five dollars an hour," said the

judge. "For him, that's a lot of money. He'll work hard, he's a good lawyer. I want him to work with you. I want you to meet him. He reminds me of you when you were young."

"Oh, God, this could be painful," Darcy said.

"I think you guys would be a good team, and I want to make sure Lavelle Macklin has a real opportunity for justice this time."

7

DARCY HAD BEEN ON TRIAL most of the afternoon, representing Eddie Jozwiak, who worked for Streets and Sanitation. Eddie was accused of being a ghost payroller. He was on the clock when the police videotaped him accepting money from a bust-out gambler who tried to get beyond his losing ways by snitching. Eddie was supposed to be filling potholes on a street six and half miles away at the time he collected from this loser. In spite of video and audio tapes, Darcy was representing Eddie on charges of syndicated gambling and official misconduct. The official misconduct was for committing the crime of syndicated gambling while working for the city.

The day had been spent fighting with the state in pre-trial motions regarding evidentiary issues. In light of the fact that the confidential informant was no longer available, having fled the jurisdiction with his whereabouts unknown, Darcy argued that the audiotape and videotape should be inadmissible because a proper foundation could not be laid.

After hours of witness testimony and legal arguments, the judge had come to a series of conclusions and made rulings that allowed most of the evidence in. But he left it clear that on a bench trial the judge would take into consideration that an important link between the tapes and a finding of guilty might be missing, so Darcy was pleased with a good day's work. The state asked for a thirty-day date in the hope of trying to locate their confidential informant. Finally the day had ended.

Darcy walked out of the courthouse. It wasn't even five o'clock, and it was dark already. As little ice pellets pummeled him—something most people call snow—a hard wind was blowing from east to west. He walked quickly to his car on the second floor of the parking garage. After starting the car and waiting for some warmth to permeate the frigid air, he fumbled through the CD case, found Pachelbel, and slid it into the player. Then it was a short drive back to the office building. With most people leaving the parking garage at that time of day, Darcy found a parking spot quickly and entered his building through Cavanaugh's, the restaurant and bar on the first floor. He surveyed the crowd. There were four lawyers in one corner, all of whom had once been state's attorneys. They were drinking and licking their wounds. One had a cigar going. Darcy approached the group and threw his coat onto a bar stool, propping his briefcase on top of it. He ordered Glenlivet, rocks, and bought a round for the others.

"Hey," Darcy began. "Any of you guys know a Justin Schachter?"

Without pulling the cigar out of his mouth, one of the lawyers smiled.

"You mean Shitty Schachter. Hell, yeah. Everyone knows Shitty."

Darcy looked at him.

"Shitty. That's his name?" he said, disappointedly.

"That's what we all call him. But he's a good lawyer. A mensch."

One of the other lawyers, short and balding with shirt buttons stretched to the limit, set his drink down. "Yeah. Shitty offices with me. Well, he gets his mail there. He's got a phone line there. He occasionally sees clients there, but he's never really around. He's either out working or at home."

"That's not true," another one said. "He's either out working, at home, or playing ball."

"Yeah?" Darcy asked. "Good athlete?"

They all laughed. "Oh, hell no, but he loves to play," said the cigar smoker.

"So how is he as a lawyer?"

The short, balding lawyer jumped in. "He's a great lawyer," he said. "I tried nine juries with him. No matter what happened he was on top of it. If I ever needed a lawyer, I'd hire Shitty." He picked his drink up and took a long pull. "Why?" he asked Darcy.

"Well, he got appointed to second chair me on a death case."

"No shit," said the cigar man. "They're paying a good dollar for that now. A buck and a quarter I hear."

"Yeah, that's what I'm told," said Darcy.

"That's chump change for you, Darcy," said the fat one. "But, you know, for shmucks like us, it adds up."

"Have any of you done one of these since the new rules went into effect?"

Three of them shook their heads, but the fourth, a guy Darcy knew as Dave, piped up.

"I did one. It blew," he said. "I worked my ass off, kept track of my hours and did interim billing. But every time I put in a bill the judge would cut it. No reason, just kept cutting it. Finally, I said, why do you appoint us to these if you're not going to pay us?

The son of a bitch had the nerve to say something about lawyers padding their bills. He had a huge boner for lawyers in general."

"Gee, that's unusual," said Darcy sarcastically, taking a sip of his drink. "How did you end up?"

"Natural life," Dave said, "it wasn't a real death case, they were just running it out for the press."

Darcy rattled the ice in his glass to get the drink cold and then took another sip.

"Well, I've never met this Justin. He's supposed to meet me here, so somebody point him out when he shows," he said.

"Absolutely," said cigar man.

"What are you smoking?" Darcy asked.

"Macanudo."

Then the four of them said in unison, "Ditka." Every beer-drinking, red meat–eating Bears fan knew that Coach Ditka liked Macanudos. Although since Ditka left very few Macanudos were being lit to celebrate a Bears victory.

After another round of drinks, the cigar guy yelled suddenly, "Hey, Nanook of the North, get over here." Lumbering across the bar was a big guy wearing a heavy winter coat and clunky boots.

He made his way over and pulled his coat off, throwing it on top of Darcy's briefcase, sending the stool and its contents onto the floor.

"Oh, Christ. Sorry, Mr. Cole. I'm Justin Schachter." He extended a large hand while trying to upright the stool and coats.

"Nice to meet you, Justin. Call me Darcy. I understand you already know these reprobates?"

"Yes, sir I do," said Justin. "You can't outrun your past, can you?"

"Hey Shitty, how's it going?" said the cigar man, shaking hands with him.

"What's up, Shits?" said the bald guy. "Haven't seen you lately."

"Ah, man, you know. I'm duckin' and weavin'. Working my ass off."

"That's what I like to hear," Darcy said, before calling a waitress over for a table.

"You hungry?" Darcy asked him.

"Actually, I had a pretty late lunch," said Justin. "But I could take a drink if you want one."

"Good call," he said.

Darcy ordered his third scotch and Justin ordered a bottle of Sam Adams and a glass of water. The waitress led them to their table in the dining room, away from the noise of the bar, and was back in a moment with the drinks. Darcy nodded at her, letting her know that he was going to run a tab. Justin drank the ice water in one quick gulp, set it down and picked up the beer.

"It's an honor to get to work with you," Justin said. "It was nice of Judge Nicolau to look out for me."

"He thinks very highly of you," Darcy said.

"I really appreciate that," said Justin. "I was his first chair for a while. His is the best courtroom I've worked in. Judge Nicolau likes hard workers, and I pretty much live my job, so . . ."

"When did you leave the State's Attorney's Office?" Darcy asked.

"Almost four years ago," Justin replied, feeling like a relative amateur. "Look, Darcy," Justin said nervously, "I know that you need a second chair like a blind man needs driving lessons, so I'll just do whatever you want me to do, or stay out of your way."

Darcy set his glass down.

"We're going to do this together. We'll sit down and analyze the case. We'll break up the witnesses, figure out what needs to be done. I got an investigator that I use, or if you have someone you like, we could use him."

"No, that's okay. We can use your guy," said Justin. "Like I said, I just want to be a team player."

"All right, we're going to be a team," Darcy said. "So, where do you want to begin?" Darcy said.

Justin tipped the bottle up and finished the beer. He set it down on the table and wiped his mouth with the back of his hand.

"Well, first thing we need to do," he began, "is get me another beer. Then, we've got to figure out when we're going to go over to Cook County Jail and meet Lavelle Macklin."

8

VANESSA BALDWIN WAS A WOMAN who got things done. She was standing next to an open grave watching the casket of Laura Martin being lowered into the ground. Besides the priest, who had never met Laura, and the girls from the home, there were only two other people present for the burial, Tim Kelly and Virgil Johnson. Neither Kelly nor Johnson had ever been to a funeral for a crime victim before. Kelly was watching Vanessa. Somehow, in spite of the tears, she looked stronger than ever. A light snow was falling as a couple of Mexican workmen lowered the casket into the ground. There weren't many murders in Evanston, although Kelly and Johnson had worked a few over the years. They were solved pretty quickly; they had simple solutions. This case was different.

Vanessa reached down and grabbed a handful of dirt and tossed it into the grave. Both Kelly and Johnson followed suit and then walked with her back to the car, Kelly holding on gently to her elbow. They made their way across the snow-covered grass to the car, and Johnson held the door open as Vanessa Baldwin got into the passenger front seat and buckled her seatbelt. He then closed the front door and got behind the wheel. Vanessa looked across the cemetery as the snow fell.

"It's a beautiful day, isn't it?" she asked.

Kelly did not know whether it was a rhetorical question, so after an awkward silence he agreed.

"Yes, it is a beautiful day and it was a beautiful service."

"No family was here for her," Vanessa began and then let her thoughts drift off.

"No family?" Virgil asked.

"Mother's dead," Vanessa said somewhat matter-of-factly. "Never knew the father. Didn't have any extended family. Her mother ran away from home when she was young, came to Chicago, began working the streets and became a junkie. Gave birth, dumped Laura off into the system and ran off until she needled and screwed her way to death."

"Pretty bleak," Virgil said.

"It is," said Vanessa. "But as pitiful as her mother's life was, Laura was still going to make it. You're going to make an arrest, aren't you?" she said.

"Yes, ma'am. We're going to get him. I promise you," said Tim.

"I believe you," said Vanessa. "Make him pay. Make him pay."

9

DARCY WAS DEEP INTO RESEARCHING the Macklin case when his longtime secretary, Irma, rang in to tell him that Paul Kern's administrative assistant wanted Darcy to go to Kern's office immediately for a meeting.

Paul Kern was the chairman of the board of Chicago's largest law firm, Grabow, Allard and Tendam. Besides bringing in millions of dollars in legal business to the Chicago office, Kern's job was to coordinate the offices in London, Paris, New York, Los Angeles, Miami, Boston, Munich, Tokyo, and Johannesburg.

Darcy had never met Paul Kern, but he just knew that he didn't like him or any of the lawyers like him. Although they all worked in the Loop, they lived in a different world from Darcy. Irma put the call through to Darcy, explaining that Darcy made his own appointments.

"I'm sorry, I don't know Mr. Kern," Darcy explained to the assistant. "And unless I know the nature of the meeting, I'm not taking time out of my schedule to run over to his office. In fact, if he wants to meet with me, he'll have to come here at my convenience."

"Excuse me, Mr. Cole, but do you know who Mr. Kern is?" she said, seemingly shocked at his irreverence. This only aggravated Darcy more.

"I still need to know the nature of the business."

"It's, um, a sensitive matter," she explained nervously.

"Okay, good start," said Darcy. "I need a little more, though."

"Well, it's a personal matter."

Darcy sighed. "We're really not getting any closer, are we?" he said.

"Okay," she practically blurted. "Mr. Kern is interested in interviewing you about perhaps representing a family member in a criminal matter."

"I see," Darcy said, glancing at his watch and the pile of papers on his desk. "I'll tell you what, I can see Mr. Kern at my office today at three-thirty."

"Hmmm," the assistant murmured. "Is that the only time you have available?"

"No," said Darcy. "I can see him pretty much anytime between three-thirty and four-thirty."

"I see," she said. "Can you hold a moment?"

"No," Darcy said. "I can see him between three-thirty and four-thirty. I am at the Monadnock Building, 53 West Jackson Boulevard. Just call and let my secretary know what time he's going to be here," Darcy said.

He hung up.

"Kiss my ass immediately," Darcy thought to himself.

He wheeled around and looked out over the lake. There were no boats out. The wind was creating whitecaps two to three feet high and making the old windows rattle and whistle. The phone rang again and Irma was on the line.

"Mr. Kern will be here at three-thirty," she said cheerfully.

"Good," said Darcy. "When he gets here, have him wait fifteen minutes and then bring him in."

At three-forty Irma showed Paul Kern to Darcy's office. Darcy met him by the door, shook his hand and motioned to a client chair. He then walked around and sat behind his desk. Paul Kern was impressive. A few inches shorter than Darcy, Kern wore his custom-tailored suit well. His short hair was razor cut with an elegant part. A silk pocket square jutted perfectly out of his breast pocket. He was in good shape, although he didn't seem athletic. Darcy thought he looked like a network anchorman who would be capable of delivering somber news in a compassionate manner before changing gears and showing the water-skiing squirrel.

"Thank you for seeing me," Kern said in a measured tone.

"How can I help you, Mr. Kern?"

"Well, it's a bit embarrassing," he stammered.

Darcy noticed that he hadn't brought a briefcase, meaning that this really was a matter of personal importance.

"I don't know where to begin," Kern said, squirming.

Darcy noted a distinct loss of poise.

"Mr. Cole, I'm sure you know I'm a good lawyer," he said. "But I'm a better businessman, chairman of the board at Grabow, Allard and Tendam."

"Now, I can't vouch for that first statement," Darcy said, hands in the air. "But I am familiar with your firm. The biggest in the city, isn't it?"

"Biggest in the world," Kern corrected him. "In any event, I'm not here as a lawyer or a businessman. I'm here as a father. I have a son, Brian, nineteen years old. He needs help."

"What kind of trouble is your son in?" Darcy asked.

Kern took a deep breath. "My son is charged with aggravated

criminal sexual assault and murder, and he's being held without bond."

"I'm sorry to hear that. It must be difficult for you and your family," Darcy said.

"Thank you," Kern said. "Why won't they let me bond him out?"

"That's a capital case," said Darcy. "You don't get bond in a capital case. The State has a hundred and twenty days to determine whether or not they're actually going to seek the death penalty. If in fact they elect not to seek death, you could do a bond hearing then."

Paul Kern's shoulders seemed to melt into his body as he sank into the chair.

"That's the problem," he said. "We have a lot of excellent lawyers at my firm. Some of them former prosecutors, former U.S. Attorneys, but I don't have anyone who has done a death penalty case. That's why I sought you out."

"I have done several, in fact," Darcy said.

"I also know that you are considered one of the best criminal defense lawyers in the city. You're the best, and my son needs the best now."

"I appreciate that," Darcy said. "Tell me what you know about his situation."

"Well," Kern said. "My son is a senior at Longwood Prep."

"He's nineteen?" Darcy asked. "And a senior?"

"Yes," Kern said. "You see, I was in London for two years, brought the family. Had a nice flat there. I was getting the European offices consolidated, getting a few projects online, coordinating everything. My son has an early birthdate, so when we came back, instead of trying to figure out if the credits from the school he went to in England would transfer, he just went back and did his senior year."

"Must have liked the school," Darcy said, jotting down some notes.

"Unfortunately, yes. So he meets up with an old schoolmate, a kid named John Henry Phillips III—friends call him Trip. Anyway, the police believe that my son and this Trip kidnapped a girl, raped her, and killed her. When Brian was arrested, he asked for a lawyer."

"Good thing," said Darcy.

"Right," said Kern. "But the other kid, Trip, sang like a canary when he was arrested. Isn't that the expression you criminal guys use?"

"No," Darcy said dismissively. "But anyway, what did the other kid admit to?"

Kern continued. "After he gave a full confession he had a lawyer show up, cut a deal. Now he's testifying against my son. Darcy, the State of Illinois wants to kill my son."

With that, the dam broke and Paul Kern broke down in tears. Darcy grabbed the tissue box and handed it across. Kern put his head in his hands while Darcy waited for him to regain his composure.

When Kern finally looked up, his eyes were red and he looked panicked. Darcy was deep in thought when Kern blubbered, "Darcy, I need you to save my son's life."

Darcy took a deep breath and blew it out slowly. Darcy tried to look for cases that offered more than just money. Seeing Paul Kern begging him to save his son's life touched something deep inside.

"Listen, Paul," Darcy said, leaning in toward Kern, "I'll represent your son. The new Capital Litigation Rules require me to have a second chair, another lawyer. I want to be able to pick that lawyer."

"Absolutely," said Paul. "All I ask is that I meet him."

"You got it," said Darcy.

"I suppose we need to talk money," said Paul.

"I suppose we do," said Darcy.

10

Division I of Cook County Jail was the oldest part of the facility. The basement had once housed the gallows for defendants sentenced to death, before the creation of the far more humane method of execution, the electric chair. Illinois now used lethal injection to execute their condemned. The chair was housed in a glass room in the basement of Division I. While the electric chair is gone, the glass room remains. It was there that Darcy and Justin were waiting to meet Lavelle Macklin.

"I have never been in the glass room before," Justin said, looking around. "Every time I come here, they put me in the law library."

"That was full," said Darcy.

"Too bad," said Justin. "This kind of creeps me out."

Darcy looked at him and smiled, then nodded toward the far

wall. Justin turned just in time to watch a rat scurry across the floor.

A shiver shot through Justin's body. "Oh, great," he moaned.

"This whole place is disgusting," said Darcy. "They need to tear it down."

"God, just take a whiff," Justin said. "How does anyone stand it?"

"The Green Valley Spa it's not," Darcy said. "You've got mice, roaches, and rats. Have you ever seen the mice running through the ceiling tiles?" Darcy asked.

"Hell yeah. In the law library, I saw a little herd of them running across the light."

They heard footsteps and turned toward the hall. Lavelle Macklin was short and built. His biceps reflected hours spent doing curls. Despite his stature, he had three Xs on his chest, for triple extra large. He walked in wearing the khaki uniform with CCDOC stenciled across the chest and down the pant leg. Darcy stood and then Justin got to his feet.

"Mr. Macklin, Darcy Cole," he said.

They shook hands. Darcy gestured toward Justin.

"This is Justin Schachter, my second chair on your case."

Macklin shook hands with Justin. They sat down around a steel table.

"First of all, Mr. Macklin," Darcy began, "congratulations on the *pro se* motions you wrote. They're pretty impressive."

"Yeah, well, you know, jailhouse lawyer helped me with it," Macklin replied. "He was doing everybody's. This DNA shit has saved a lot of lives."

Macklin wore his hair in corn rows, the ends of the braids wrapped in aluminum foil. He was dark skinned and had a deep voice. One of his front teeth was broken. Other than that he was well-groomed and well-manicured.

"I heard of you," Macklin said, looking at Darcy. "You're a good lawyer."

"So is Justin," Darcy said.

"Maybe so, but I heard of you."

"Well, the judge wanted to make sure that you had a fair shake. He's kind of concerned that maybe you sat on death row for a crime you didn't commit."

"Damn straight," said Macklin. "Motherfucker didn't care the first trial."

"First trial was a jury," Darcy said.

"Yeah, but my lawyer told me that the judge made it clear it had to be a jury trial."

"Well, I looked at the evidence," said Darcy, "and it seems to me that based on what they had, it was a strong case at the time. Thank God for advances in science, huh?" Darcy said.

Macklin smiled. "Yeah. If science would have waited another ten years, my ass would have been juiced."

11

In the Terra Museum on Michigan Avenue, in the heart of the magnificent mile, as the ads touted it, Darcy obediently meandered with Amy Wagner, feigning interest in the drawings of artists he'd never heard of. The thing that mattered to Darcy was the time he could spend with Amy, no matter where. As they looked at various drawings, Darcy remembered when he had first met her. It was in the emergency room at Northwestern University Hospital, where Amy was on duty as the emergency room doctor. He was working a case and she was a witness. It was dumb luck or fate that they had run into each other that way; it didn't matter, but for Darcy it meant far fewer lonely nights in his condo overlooking Lake Shore Drive.

After they'd viewed the current exhibit, they stepped out onto the sidewalk and walked up Michigan Avenue. The Christmas decorations, already up in mid-November, burned brightly, lighting the sidewalks packed with pedestrians—some shoppers, some tourists, and a lot of locals just trying to get home after a day of work.

Amy and Darcy walked into the face of a firm wind, passed the Water Tower and slid into Bistro 110. At the bar, waiting for an open table, Amy sipped a glass of Merlot in the time that Darcy knocked back a double Maker's Mark. They were seated at a four-top, which instantly became a two-top as a busboy removed two of the place settings. Seated next to them was a table of twelve, three women and nine men, various ages, all in business attire. Among the coffees and desserts were PDAs, laptops, and piles of documents. A couple of younger people furiously scribbled notes as the others spoke. They were approached by their waiter, who flashed them a smile with his harshly bleached white teeth. He gave them his name and began to run down the specials. Before he had finished the list, Darcy had forgotten his name, instead wondering if he knew his teeth were whiter than his apron, giving the work attire a dingy look. Amy ordered salmon and Darcy had the fire-roasted chicken, their comfort-food requests when they were particularly stressed. Considering their orders, they looked intently at each other.

"Okay," Amy asked. "What's going on at work?"

Darcy shook his glass before taking one last sip.

"I have two death cases," he said.

"Murders?" she asked with skepticism.

"Don't get excited," he said, amused. "They're death cases only because the government is seeking the death penalty against my clients."

"I thought Illinois wouldn't deal with any more death penalty cases," she said. "Didn't we end the death penalty with Governor Ryan?"

"No, they're still on the books, and the state's still seeking death in certain cases," Darcy replied. "Governor Ryan commuted all death sentences to natural life in prison before he left office. The death penalty still endures. As we speak prosecutors are trying to reload death row."

"So, tell me about your cases," she said with the look of concern that Darcy yearned for at the end of a crappy day.

Darcy thought about it. "You want the facts?" he asked, appreciating her interest.

"Just the facts, ma'am," she said mockingly.

Darcy smiled, leaned back and pulled his left hand through his hair.

"The first one started strangely enough," he began. "An old friend of mine, a judge at Twenty-sixth Street, called me and asked me to meet him for lunch. When I walked into the restaurant and saw him, he looked like hell, really distraught. Then he told me about the case of a Lavelle Macklin."

Amy interrupted. "Can a judge do that? Can a judge talk about a case outside of court with a lawyer?"

"Believe me," Darcy said, "Joe Nicolau has been a judge for a long time and he'd never do anything wrong. He's one of those guys who has dedicated his life to the law. He could have made a fortune as a trial lawyer, but he never liked the business of law. He only liked the facts of law, and he threw himself into it. He's a great judge, but he is torn up about this one case. Lavelle Macklin was charged with the rape and murder of a nine-year-old girl. The police managed to obtain a confession from him, and he was tried by a jury in front of Judge Nicolau. The public defender waived jury and decided to do the sentencing hearing in front of Joe. So, they go through the eligibility stage and they find him death eligible."

"He's eligible for death?" she said. "That makes it sound like a privilege."

"Yeah," Darcy responded with a smile. "Congratulations!

You're a candidate for death! Actually, it just means that there are certain factors in the case that make the person eligible to receive the death sentence. You then go into what is known as the death phase, which is a sentencing hearing where they bring in all the aggravation and mitigation."

Darcy held up his empty glass, trying to catch the eye of the waiter. Amy always shuddered at the gesture, considering it rude, so she gently touched his arm, saying, "Our appetizer will be here soon. Order another drink then, huh?" Then she gave him one of her melting smiles and said, "Besides, we're in no hurry, right?"

Darcy looked at her, then outside at the illuminated trees blowing in the cold wind. He felt a surge of warmth and contentment.

"No hurry at all. So back to my tales of woe, Joe Nicolau sentenced Macklin to die. But, of course, eleven years or so later, they do a DNA test and it's determined that Macklin could not have been the person who left the so-called DNA on the victim. So the case gets reversed and sent back for a new trial, and Judge Nicolau has asked me to represent Macklin."

"Some pro bono work, eh?"

"Not quite," said Darcy. "They created something called the Capital Litigation Defense Fund, and I get paid out of that. One-twenty-five an hour."

"Ugh," she said, smiling. "Poverty wages."

"Not quite," said Darcy, "but if it weren't a favor for Joe, I certainly wouldn't take on a case like this for that fee. Joe and I have been friends for thirty years. It's strange, but there is a sense of community at Twenty-sixth and California, and Joe is a leader of that community. He needs me to do this for him. Sometimes money doesn't mean anything."

Amy smiled. "So you couldn't turn him down."

"I couldn't," Darcy agreed. "If you had seen the pain in his eyes—he spent his whole life trying to be a great judge, fair, honest, compassionate, trying to do the right thing, and this is killing him. He thinks he sentenced someone to die who may not have been guilty. So he's damn sure he wants this guy well represented. He wants to make sure that whatever happens, it's done the right way. It's too important to him. I couldn't say no."

"So, is he innocent?" she asked.

"I don't know yet," said Darcy. "I'll look at the evidence and see. As far as winning the case goes, it really doesn't matter if he's innocent or not; it matters how the evidence lays out."

"That's a little cynical, isn't it?" asked Amy.

"Hey, it's an adversarial system, it's not a system that seeks the truth. It's about winning and losing."

"Oh, come on," Amy said. "Isn't that how he was sentenced to die in the first place?"

"That may prove to be true," he said, shrugging. "We'll study the hell out of the evidence. My job is to do the best I can for my client. If I can win it, that's great. If the evidence is insurmountable then I need to mitigate so he doesn't get sentenced to death."

At just the right time—they were both getting peckish—the waiter brought over their order of calamari, extra lemon, and promised to be right back with their drinks. In less time than it took to soak the squid in lemon juice, he'd returned.

They dug into the oversized pile in front of them, content to eat and not talk for a few minutes. When they took a break to sip their drinks, their spirits had picked up another notch.

"And how about the other case?" Amy asked.

"It's pretty simple," he said. "It's like Leopold and Loeb."

"Refresh my memory," she said.

It was Darcy's turn to smile.

"I keep forgetting! You grew up in Middle America."

She gave him a gentle punch to the arm. "Ohio and Wisconsin aren't exactly the badlands."

"A long time ago, the '20s or '30s, I'm not sure," Darcy began, "two rich kids who were attending the University of Chicago decided they could pull the perfect crime. They grabbed a young kid named Bobby Franks and killed him. These geniuses dump the body and one of them leaves his eyeglasses at the scene. The cops trace the glasses and learn that only four pairs of these glasses were made. In a New York minute they crack the case and these two lads—Leopold and Loeb—are under arrest. Two kids from wealthy families with every advantage and they decide to kill a kid for the thrill of it.

"Clarence Darrow was hired to plead for their lives. Darrow was the most brilliant lawyer of the day. It was a pretty famous case; they wrote some books and did a movie on it. The similarity is that I'm representing this poor little rich kid named Brian Kern. His father is Paul Kern, who runs Grabow, Allard and Tendam."

"Ah," Amy said, recognizing the name. "Your kind of guy."

"Right," Darcy said. "And, believe me, the apple fell *far* from the tree in this case. Anyway, his kid hooks up with a friend and they are accused of raping and killing a sixteen-year-old named Laura Martin, who was living in a group home in Rogers Park. So when the police scoop up these two, this other kid, Trip, cuts a deal and pukes all over Brian."

"Lovely," Amy said, just as she swallowed a forkful of calamari dipped in lemon.

"Sorry," Darcy said, wincing. "I mean he agreed to testify and told the government all about his buddy Brian.

"Brian, having a scintilla of a brain, told the police he didn't want to answer their questions until his father the lawyer got there. His father sent one of his boys down, so the police figure that since Brian's already lawyered up they'd cut a deal with Trip. Trip gave a full confession implicating himself and Brian, but making Brian the main bad guy. Trip has already confessed so once his lawyer shows up there isn't much he can do. So now they cut a deal with him and they're going to have him testify against Brian.

They decided since Brian was nineteen at the time and ole Tripster was only seventeen that they were going to try to kill Brian. They can't go after Trip because he's seventeen and you have to be eighteen in Illinois to get the magic needle."

"You know, Darcy," Amy interrupted, "I don't think I've ever actually asked. Do you believe in the death penalty?"

"Well, sometimes, yes," Darcy began. "I look at it this way. There are some crimes that are so barbaric that I really see no choice but to sentence the person to die. The problem is that the system is so screwed up that the death penalty is used when it shouldn't be."

"How about you?" Darcy asked. "What are your views on the death penalty?"

Amy smiled. "I'm a doctor. We work to save lives. There are no circumstances which justify the state killing an individual. It is barbaric and disgraceful."

Darcy chuckled. "Don't be so wishy-washy. Take a position."

"So now you know how I stand on that, so you better win."

"No pressure, huh?" Darcy said. "So what's on your mind?" he asked.

The salads had arrived. The waiter cranked some black pepper out of the large wooden mill and then left them.

"Thanksgiving," she said.

"What about it?" Darcy asked, salad fork in mid-air.

"Would you like to join the kids and me for Thanksgiving in Michigan?"

Darcy put his fork back down.

"You know I feel uneasy intruding on your family," he said.

"You're never intruding," she said.

"I love to be with you," he said. "Any time, any place, but I don't want to come between you and your children. It is important to me that I don't invade their territory. Besides," he said, "it's been a while since I had a Thanksgiving dinner."

"Well, you know, the basic menu hasn't changed that much. Turkey, stuffing, sweet potatoes?" she asked pitifully.

"One of the other lawyers in my office—you know Kathy. She invites me every year and every year I find a reason not to accept. One year I had Thanksgiving at the Union League Club, an absolutely absurd move because I ended up being asked to join this elderly couple who were also eating alone. He was a bigwig at the club, and they were very nice and all, but Christ . . ."

"What happened?" Amy asked.

"Well, nothing, which was the problem. They couldn't hear anything I said, and it took them about four hours to finish the meal. You know, I'm much better at just hiding out on holidays."

"I don't want you to hide," she said. "I want you to be with me and my family."

"I'm not sure," said Darcy. "Can I think about it?"

"There's nothing to think about," she said. "You're going to come. We'll have a good time."

Amy wasn't someone he could say no to.

12

DARCY ESCORTED JUSTIN INTO THE conference room. Kathy Haddon was cutting a bagel. Collata had his filthy cowboy boots on Darcy's desk while leaning back in the chair with his hands resting on his bald head. An unlit cigarette dangled from his lips. Collata had worked as an investigator for Darcy since his retirement from the Chicago Police Department. His shaved head and goatee gave him a menacing presence. He had thick forearms and an ample gut.

Patrick was apparently trying to figure something out on his laptop.

Collata didn't move until Darcy motioned for him to get his feet off the desk.

"Lady and gentlemen, I would like you to meet Justin Schachter," Darcy said.

"Shitty, how the hell are you?" Collata said, rising from the chair.

"Collata, good to see you," Justin replied, shaking his hand.

"Oh God," Darcy said warily. "How do you two know each other?"

"We've had a couple of cocktails together," said Collata. "You know, at the bar by the courthouse."

"Why doesn't that surprise me?" Darcy asked.

"Justin, this is Patrick O'Hagin, a partner here."

"Nice to meet you," Justin said as they shook hands.

"Shitty, that's quite a nickname," Patrick said.

Justin shrugged it off, which reminded Darcy that he'd never found out what it referred to. That, and the connection with Collata, gave him pause, but only momentarily.

"Kathy Haddon, also a partner," Darcy said pointing toward Kathy.

Kathy set down the bagel, rubbed her hands against each other then against her jeans and reached out.

"Nice to meet you. Don't mind the jeans," she said. "I didn't have court today and I'm only going to be here for a few hours so I didn't feel like glamming."

"You'll get no argument from me," said Justin.

Darcy motioned toward a seat and Justin sat down.

"Well, let's get this started," Darcy said. "As everybody knows, I got appointed by Judge Nicolau to represent Lavelle Macklin. The firm's going to get paid out of the Capital Litigation Fund. We also have the Kern case, another capital case. Due to the recent changes in the law regarding death penalty cases, a second chair must be appointed. Joe Nicolau appointed Justin. So my thoughts were that Patrick will work backup on one of the cases with me and Kathy, you will work on the other. So which one is it?"

Kathy looked uncomfortable.

"I was hoping that you would let me beg off on these," she stammered.

Darcy was a bit surprised.

"How does that sit with you, Patrick?"

"That's okay with me," he said. "I don't have a life anyway."

"Everything okay?" Darcy asked Kathy.

"Yeah, it's complicated," she said. "We'll talk later."

"Patrick, you're on board. You and Justin ought to figure out who's going to do what."

"So I'm not trying these?" Patrick asked.

"Sorry," Darcy said. "We have to have a first and second chair. I consider you my co-first chair."

"That's nice to hear," said Patrick. "But I've never done a death case," he said.

"Well, you'll get two in a row," Darcy pointed out.

Darcy turned toward Kathy.

"You don't need to stick around. We're just going to talk about these two cases. Do you have other work to do, or do you want to take off?"

"I appreciate it," she said. "I need to get out early."

She spread some cream cheese on half a bagel and put the other half on top. She then cut it and held out half.

"Anyone want it?"

Collata looked at it but didn't move. She held it out to him.

"How about you, big guy? You want it?"

He said nothing. She pushed it closer and closer until finally he pulled a paw out from behind his head and grabbed it. He pulled the cigarette out of his mouth with his left hand and took the bagel in one bite.

"Good boy," Kathy said. "Your water dish is over there on the floor."

"Sometimes we just throw marshmallows at him," Darcy said, shaking his head.

Kathy gathered up a few papers, waved goodbye, and closed the door behind her.

"What's going on with her?" Darcy asked Patrick, who only shrugged.

"No idea?" Darcy asked suspiciously.

"Hey, I'm just happy to get the two death cases," he said. "Even if it's only backup."

"It's a lot of work," Darcy pointed out.

"I'm ready for it. Besides since I'm only backup I can work in jeans."

Darcy turned back toward Justin.

"Why don't you hand out the documents, and we'll get started."

Justin unzipped his black ballistic-nylon briefcase and pulled out a file folder on the Lavelle Macklin case that contained four copies of stapled papers. He slid one across to Collata, gave one to Darcy and another to Patrick. Collata managed to lean forward and pick up the document. He studied it briefly, then threw it down.

"We need you to run down these old witnesses," Justin said to Collata. "We want you to talk to the medical examiner. Also, you should go over the police reports and the DNA reports. I want to nail down the cause of death. I don't want to give them any wiggle room so they can change the theory of their case. This was a sexual assault murder, and the theory of the case was that the perpetrator of the sexual assault committed the murder. I don't want them coming in with some double-victim thing, where she was raped six hours earlier, and then someone else killed her later. I want to make sure they're stuck with their original theory." Justin was talking in a fast, excited tone.

Collata leaned forward.

"Okay, we can do this," he said. "Jesus, Shitty, your undies are all bunched up. Settle down, man."

"Look, I'm doing a case with Darcy Cole," Justin said half-seriously. "I want to pull my weight."

"You're doing a case with Darcy Cole," Patrick said. "That means you have to pull your weight and half of his."

"Don't try to scare him, Tinkerbell," Collata said to Patrick. "You may be a partner, but you don't bring in the business. The old man does that."

"See the respect I get around here?" Darcy asked Justin. "I give you two days, and you'll be busting my balls too. I'm going to cover our cases at Twenty-sixth Street," Darcy said, "and then Justin and I will go to Division Ten and talk to Brian Kern."

Collata folded his reports over and over until they were small enough to slide into the pocket of his jeans. He then pulled a lighter out of the same pocket and lit his cigarette.

"Okay, boss, I'm off to find bad guys."

He patted Justin on the shoulder on his way out.

"Welcome to the team, Shitty. New guy always buys. Always."

• • •

Division Ten was one of the newer buildings in the sprawling Cook County Jail complex. Alone, it was bigger than most county jails in the United States and bigger than most jails in many small countries. Lobbies and hallways were configured like a college dormitory, but that quickly gave way to the oppressive isolation of tiers where the inmates lived. Justin and Darcy were buzzed through a series of steel doors into a glass-enclosed room with a stainless steel counter and three steel stools nailed to the wall. They watched Brian Kern make his way through a series of inter-locks until he was buzzed into the compartment with them.

"Brian, I'm Darcy Cole," he said, reaching out a hand.

They shook and then Darcy introduced him to Justin. Brian was in his stenciled tan hospital scrubs, with white socks and white shower shoes on his feet. He had a few pieces of paper in his shirt pocket and a white T-shirt under his scrubs. He had thin brown hair and a few freckles. His fair complexion was beginning to become more pale. He was thin in spots and doughy in others. Darcy had seen kids like this before. Kids driving their father's Jaguar convertible blasting thug-like rap music and talking wistfully about being able to bust a cap. Now Brian looked tired and scared.

"What if you tell me what happened?" Darcy said.

Brian pushed his hair back with one hand and glanced around nervously.

"Uh, yeah," he said. "Well, here's the shit, you know. You see, this dude Trip and I were close. He was my partner. Trip met this girl at the mall. She was kind of cute, tight body. No big deal. So he flirted her up and down. She went for it. He said she was hot enough to be a three-dater."

"What does that mean?" Darcy asked.

"Well, that he would go out with her three times and then if she didn't set it out, he was gone. Some chicks aren't that hot, so they're just a hook-up."

Darcy said nothing. Brian continued.

"So the night this all jumped off, we were down by the lake. We know where to go, kind of quiet so no one bothers us. So I sat in the car, doin' a one-hitter, while he takes this hottie into the woods. Turns out she was a freak, man, into kinky shit. So Trip just wants to get off, and they end up having some rough sex. At some point it breaks bad, because the next thing I know he comes back alone. I say, 'What's up?' He says, 'We're out of here, man. Let's go.' On the drive back up north, he lays it out for me. He says that early on, she loses her temper, or pretends to, and he starts smacking her around. One thing leads to another, she's dead."

"How did she end up in the lake?" Darcy said.

"He rolled her ass in there."

"But you didn't see him do it?"

"Nope. Never left the car," he said.

Darcy glanced at Justin, who picked up on it immediately. He stood and walked within inches of Brian. Then he leaned into his face.

"You know, Brian, I have been doing this a while. Not as long as Mr. Cole here, but the fact is that I'm closer to your age, and your bullshit smells fresher to me. So, let me tell you, that's a great story. Tremendous story. Let's stick to that story, okay? And then Mr. Cole and I will go to your execution and watch them stick the needle into your arm, watch them mix the chemicals, watch it all flow into your veins, and then gaze at you as you nod off to death."

Brian tried to push Justin out of his space, but the young lawyer wasn't moving.

"They've got you by the balls," Justin said. "And you don't want us walking out of here, left to use that trite bullshit. There are two people you don't lie to: your doctor and your lawyer. We're your lawyer, your doctor, your priest, your rabbi. Start telling the truth, or you're fucked."

"I just told you the truth, dude," said Brian.

Darcy sat back and let Justin go.

"You're full of shit," he said, practically shouting. "You're a rich suburban kid talking like you're a tough guy. What, did Daddy send you away for a session at some candy-ass military school? Wah, wah. Let me tell you something. You're not going to last ten fucking minutes in here. If you're going to talk that bullshit to some gangbangers you're going to wake up with a big-ass shiv stuck through your ribs. Keep up this attitude, there's nothing we're going to be able to do for you. And you know what? We come back in a week, and guess what, Brian Kern's been pumpkinheaded."

"What's that?" Brian said nervously.

"Okay, lesson one," Justin said. "Somebody is going to beat your head in. They jump off the bunk onto your head, they kick it, they hit it with books, rods, anything they can find. The idea is to get your head to swell up like a pumpkin so you walk around like a billboard. 'This cat's been pumpkin-headed.' Everyone knows. The next thing is, they start to sell you around as a sissy, and there's nothing you can do because you got only two choices: You do what they say or you get pumpkin-headed again and again. If you don't do what they ask of you, you know, be somebody's girlfriend, with your stupid-ass pumpkin head, then they got to shank you. Take a guess what that is, Brian."

Brian didn't answer. He just dropped his head and stared at his shower shoes. Justin continued.

"That's where they find some piece of metal or wood and they make it into a knife then they find a way to stick it in you. People die all the time in here. So keep up the bullshit, Brian, and you're dead meat. Do you understand me?"

Justin began pacing in the four-by-twelve room. Brian looked out of breath and frightened. Darcy leaned in.

"Look, Brian, I understand you have to put up this tough-guy facade because you're in Cook County Jail, but you have to let us help you. You've got to do what we tell you to do. So, do you have any concept of what actually happened? Just tell us, in detail, what happened."

Brian leaned forward, clutched his hands together, and began rocking gently. Brian said something in a voice so small Darcy couldn't hear him.

"What did you say?" Darcy said.

"I said, I'll tell you everything," Brian said.

13

DARCY TOOK A SHORT WALK down the hall to Seymour's office. Seymour Hirsh was a lawyer who did worker's compensation cases. He was a short, balding man with a gentle demeanor and a dry sense of humor. Darcy liked to drink scotch and play chess with Seymour. Really chess was a weak cover; Darcy liked to talk to Seymour. He was Darcy's sounding post and trusted confidant. Seymour was alone, reading the *Tribune*. A spoon jutted out of his favored red raspberry yogurt that sat on his desk.

"Hello, old man. You ready to play?" Darcy asked.

Seymour folded his paper and dropped it onto his desk, rising to greet his longtime friend. After shaking hands, they walked over to the chess board set on a small table.

"I thought you'd back out like a coward again," Seymour said. "I'm happy to see you can come back and take a beating. So, boychik, what's new in your life?" Seymour asked as he moved a pawn.

"Believe it or not, I've picked up two death penalty cases at the same time," Darcy said.

Seymour paused to look at him.

"Death penalty cases? That's not your gig, Darcy." There was a comfortable silence as Darcy surveyed the board and then made his move.

"Two of them," he said. "What do you think of the death penalty, Seymour?"

"How do you want me to answer that: as a man, as a parent, as a practicing Jew, or as a lawyer?"

"How about from each perspective?" Darcy said. "Enlighten me. You know the old dilemma, the Bible says 'an eye for an eye,' but it also says 'Thou shalt not kill.' It seems like a contradiction to me."

"You're still reading the Bible these days?" Seymour asked.

"I'm looking at it," said Darcy. "As research."

"Research? I think you're trying to find some meaning in your life," Seymour replied. "You're at an age when you have to make peace with God, or not. You're closer to the end than you are to the beginning. It's common for men our age to look for meaning, to evaluate what our lives have produced and to try to put it all into perspective."

"So what's the answer?" Darcy asked.

"To which question?"

"The death penalty and how you feel about it."

Seymour began. "There are times when it is justifiable for the government to kill. For example, when we went to war against Hitler, we were righteous, and doing the only thing righteous people could do. As a result, the entire country rallied for the war effort. Vietnam was a big difference. I still don't understand what our purpose was in Vietnam. Many people couldn't see a legitimate reason for the killing. As a result the country was con-flicted."

"But that's war. What about the state killing individuals? Do you give the death penalty to a serial killer like John Wayne Gacy?" Darcy asked.

"I think you do. I think you have to. I think it's the only statement that society can make in an instance where a crime is so heinous and barbaric. The problem with the death penalty is that it's overused. It should be used only in the most extreme cases.

"But where it gets bogged down is where you have prosecutors deciding to go for death on a certain case for reasons that are less clear-cut or where you have inept defense attorneys providing inef-fective assistance, which leads to the death penalty for someone who perhaps doesn't deserve it, or God forbid, in some cases, where an individual is factually innocent."

"I agree. Although the longer I do this the more I think the death penalty should be abolished. What's the difference if a guy dies in prison fifty years from natural causes or twenty years from lethal injection?" Darcy asked.

"One of my cases is a remand. It was a rape and murder of a nine-year-old girl. After the guy sits on death row for a decade, the DNA in the case comes back as being from some other guy."

"Ah," said Seymour, "that's the problem. "What do you do when you execute someone who is factually innocent? How do you rectify that?"

"It's an awfully tricky issue," Darcy agreed.

"What amazes me," Seymour continued, "is that you get these right-wing conservatives who go on and on about how wrong and sinful abortion is, and turn around and scream in support of the death penalty." Seymour sighed. He moved another pawn, then continued.

"For me, the issue of the death penalty dovetails into the question that man has been pondering since he stood up on two feet: 'What is the meaning of life?'"

"What *is* the meaning of life?" Darcy asked.

Seymour laughed.

"Plato couldn't answer that. Socrates couldn't answer that. How do you expect *me* to answer that?"

"Give me an answer," Darcy said. "What is the meaning of life?"

"Do you want a scotch?" Seymour asked.

"No," said Darcy. "Answer the question. 'What is the meaning of life?'" Darcy asked, gently prodding.

"I don't know what the meaning of life is," Seymour said. "But I think that life is a journey rather than a destination. You don't set goals for yourself and go from goal to goal. I think it's living in the moment while trying to obtain whatever goals you want. I think it's trying to find your niche. Something that makes you happy, that gives you purpose."

"Have you found it?" Darcy asked.

"I have found it in my private life," he said. "Work to me is a dull ache, something I do to provide for my family and I do it in a way that is manageable. I don't work a hundred hours a week. I come down on the same train and go home on the same train every day. I work a reasonable amount of time. I make a reasonable amount of money. I have a reasonable lifestyle. When I am with my lovely bride and my two children and my three grandchildren, that's what gives me *nachas*."

"What's nachas?" Darcy asked.

"It's Yiddish. It means 'joy, pleasure.' It's what makes my heart leap and sing and dance. What gives you nachas, Darcy?"

Darcy picked up a bishop and was rolling it in his hands. He put the piece down behind the board on the table, got up, and began to pace.

"I enjoy spending time with my daughter. Work has been better lately." Darcy was trying to think of something else.

"What about the good doctor?" Seymour said.

"Amy is great," said Darcy, "and I enjoy being with her, but I think I put up a wall between us sometimes."

"How so?" said Seymour.

"For example, she invited me for Thanksgiving with her and her kids at their house in Michigan. There's something about it that terrifies me. I told her that I didn't want to intrude on her family, but her kids are old enough that they probably wouldn't care. I imagine if I said let's go get a beer, they'd be thrilled. So I really can't lay it off on that, but something inside of me is missing. I don't know how else to say it, there's a deficiency. It's as if I could only be so happy. As if there is some quantum measure of happiness and I'm only entitled to get to a certain point. With Amy I am at that point and I can't go beyond it."

"Listen boychik, you're entitled to be happy. What can we do to get you beyond that point?"

Darcy walked over to the decanter and poured himself a scotch. He motioned to Seymour, who shook him off. He poured himself three fingers and opened the ice bucket, which was empty.

"You know, my friend, you have been hard on yourself for a very long time. You need to give yourself a break. You assume everyone else's misery and you take it on as your own. Maybe you should back off from what you are doing and do something more uplifting."

"Instead of crisis management, going from one person's tragedy to another, maybe do something that makes you feel better about things.

"You know, Darcy, I go for a walk along the lakefront and I see the beauty. I see the boats sliding out on the lake. I see birds and the sun. I see beautiful buildings and lush parks. I see people enjoying themselves.

"You see criminals. You see evildoers lurking at every corner. You see the pickpockets, the thieves, the prostitutes. You see the murderers and rapists, and you see them everywhere.

"Millions and millions of people in Chicago, statistically almost all law-abiding, yet in that small tiny segment of society are the criminals. That's where you spend your whole life. The world doesn't revolve around a courtroom, Darcy, and it certainly doesn't revolve around a criminal courtroom.

"There's a reason that the criminal courthouse is at Twenty-sixth and California. They don't want the good people of Chicago to have to be confronted with it. Can you imagine if the criminal courthouse was downtown and these lowlifes were walking into Starbucks?

"Yet this world is where you spend all your time. No wonder you can't shift gears when something good happens to you."

"So what do I do?"

"First of all, you have a beautiful woman, who appears to have one defective gene, and that's the gene that compels her to spend time with you. Be grateful for that and go to Michigan for Thanksgiving. Go for walks on the beach. Hold her tightly. Drink wine. Listen to music. Make love and enjoy yourself. When you get that feeling that maybe you're having too much fun, ignore it and have more fun."

"So that's the meaning of life: Have as much fun as possible?"

Seymour sighed. "You have to figure out the meaning of life for yourself, but what you also have to do is realize that your life is finite and because of that you have to make sure that every day you embrace it and enjoy it. There is no such thing as being *too* happy, Darcy. My suggestion to you is that you put as much effort into being happy as you do into saving some criminal's life."

14

Erin Powers rolled a cart full of boxes up the aisle in Judge Joseph Nicolau's seventh-floor courtroom. Darcy and Justin were seated at defense counsel table watching her roll up. She stopped the cart near the prosecutor's table and walked over to where they sat.

"Mr. Cole, nice to meet you. My name is Erin Powers. I have been assigned the Macklin case."

"Nice to meet you," said Darcy, rising as he shook her hand.

She leaned over the table to shake hands and then turned toward Justin.

"Hey Shitty, how are you?"

"Good Erin, how are you?" he said.

"So how did you wriggle this appointment?" she asked.

He nodded toward the judge, who gave them a look which was

basically an order to be quiet. The lawyers in front of the bench concluded their business and a defendant on bond walked away free for another thirty days. Judge Nicolau leaned to his clerk and whispered something. She then fumbled through the files and pulled out a large thick one and called, "Lavelle Macklin in custody." The sheriffs scurried back to the lockup to retrieve Macklin.

Erin Powers was a good lawyer. She had been assigned this case by the State's Attorney himself, who needed her to make sure that whatever happened, the State's Attorney's Office looked like they were doing their job in a fair and reasonable fashion. She was also a forty-two-year-old mother of three: thirteen, ten, and nine, the last two a pair of Irish twins. She was about five foot six, not heavy but not thin, with reddish-brown frizzy hair and blue-green eyes. She was wearing a skirt, blazer, and button-down shirt. Her hair was pulled back and she'd long given up contacts in favor of brown tortoiseshell glasses.

Lavelle Macklin came out of the back walking a few feet ahead of the sheriff. He surveyed the courtroom, saw no family, and strolled in front of the bench.

"Let the record reflect Mr. Macklin is present with attorneys Darcy Cole and Justin Schachter," the judge began. "The State is present by way of Assistant State's Attorney Erin Powers. This matter is back before the Court on a post-conviction petition. Ms. Powers, what is your pleasure today?"

"Your Honor, at this time I will tender to defense counsel discovery in this case. It is voluminous and takes up four boxes of materials, which includes transcripts from the trial, all investigative reports and the appellate briefs. In addition to that, we are giving all newspaper accounts and television news reports on videotape.

"In addition, all of the paperwork generated in this case, including police reports, supplemental reports, and general progress reports have all been reduced to compact disc in the WordPerfect format, and I am tendering those as well," she said as she handed over a stack of CDs. "This, I believe, completes our discovery in this case and the State is answering ready for trial."

The judge turned toward the defense.

"Mr. Cole, Mr. Schachter?"

Justin deferred to Darcy, who viewed the CDs and then looked back at the cart.

"Obviously, we are not prepared to go to trial. We acknowledge receipt of discovery and we need to set a status date."

"That's fine," said Judge Nicolau. "Give me a date. And gentlemen, I would like this to get to trial as soon as possible."

"That's understood," said Darcy. "Perhaps at the status date we could file any motions that we may have."

"You know," the judge interrupted, "this case has been litigated. By reading the transcripts and police reports you should be well prepared in a very short period of time."

"Yes, Your Honor," said Mr. Cole. "But since I was recently appointed to this case, I want to have the opportunity to review everything before I answer ready."

"That's understood," said the judge.

Darcy interpreted that to mean "let's get this moving." They set a date for the following month and then the sheriff barked at Macklin.

"Let's go, in the back."

He then reached out and pulled Macklin by the right bicep and led him away.

Darcy was writing his next court date into his date book. He closed it and walked to the back to see Macklin. Justin was a step behind him. Just to the left of the jury door in the back of Judge Nicolau's courtroom was a door to the lockup. They pushed through it and walked down the hallway. The dank odor of the lockup was overpowered only by the loud sound and buzz of twenty-seven men locked into a twenty-by-twenty cell. Darcy reached the bars.

Justin yelled out, "Macklin," and watched bodies part as Lavelle made his way to the bars.

"So when are we going to trial?" Macklin asked.

"As soon as we are ready," Darcy replied.

"Well, how about just after the first of the year?" he asked.

"We'll see," said Darcy. "Let us look through the material first before we get going and that way we can discuss a few things."

"Yeah, I know," said Macklin. "I'm just excited because I want to go home. I've been locked up a long time for this bullshit."

"But remember the only thing that counts is that you do in fact go home," said Darcy. "We need to take the time to prepare."

"What's this prosecutor like?" Macklin asked.

"She's good," said Justin. "She's smart. She'll do her homework and juries love her. All of her arguments are grounded in good common sense. She doesn't waste time. So judges love her too."

"Will she pull some bullshit to get me convicted?" he asked.

"Hell no," Justin said. "She wants to be a judge and all the prosecutors are afraid of getting hit with a prosecutorial misconduct charge that could ruin their chances of being a judge. But she's a straight shooter anyway. She'll play hard, but she'll play within the rules."

"So who's going to do it with her? They always have an army of them."

"Don't know," Justin replied, "but as soon as I find out I'll let you know."

After a few more questions and answers, they shook hands and Darcy and Justin walked back out. Darcy collected his briefcase and pulled his coat off the coat rack in the corner of the courtroom. He walked out with Justin. They pushed through the large oak doors of the courtroom and walked down the hallway, where they were immediately confronted by Pam Mazur. Mazur, who wrote for the *Tribune,* tried to take credit for having the Macklin case reversed, but it was really a public defender who was doing DNA testing for post-convictions who was responsible for the case. Nowhere in any of her stories about the Macklin case did Mazur mention the public defender's name or the work that he did. She reported only that DNA had proved that Macklin was not the person whose semen was found on the dead girl.

"Darcy, who's paying you to represent Mr. Macklin?"

"I'm surprised at you, Pam."

"Why's that?" she said.

"Because it's public record that I was appointed and I'm being paid from the Capital Litigation Fund. You would think a hotshot reporter like you would have done her homework."

"Since when do you take appointments?" she asked.

"Since this case," Darcy replied.

"And how did you get on the case, Shitty?"

Justin looked as if he had a cup of cold water thrown down his back.

"The name is Justin. Justin Schachter."

Darcy had never heard him complain about his nickname.

"I'm sorry," said Mazur. "Mr. Schachter, how did you get this case?"

"I was appointed, like Mr. Cole."

"When do you think you're going to go to trial?" she asked.

"Not sure yet," said Darcy. "Have to go through discovery."

Just then, Collata came walking up with a luggage carrier on wheels.

"So where is it?" he said.

"Erin's bringing it," said Darcy.

Collata went over to the large wooden doors and pulled one open. He watched as Erin Powers wheeled her cart outside. She smiled at Collata and thanked him for holding the door, which he let close behind her.

"Here you go," she said. "These three boxes are yours."

Collata pulled the first one off and placed it on the luggage rack, followed by the other two. She then handed a stack of CDs to Darcy, who immediately handed them to Justin.

"Erin, what do you have to say about this?" Mazur asked, pushing a small tape recorder in her face.

"Nice shoes," she said and then turned back to Darcy. "Give me a call if you need anything. Shitty, it was good seeing you."

"Same here," said Justin.

They watched her walk toward the elevator and hit a button with an empty cart behind her.

"So Justin, you going to give me anything?" Mazur asked.

He looked down at her shoes. "I'm not crazy about them," he said and then walked away toward the window.

Collata tied up the boxes.

"All set, boss," he said.

He began wheeling toward the elevator. Darcy walked over to the window to where Justin was looking out across the boulevard toward the skyline of the city.

"You okay?" Darcy said.

"That bitch wants a Pulitzer. She walks over people to get what she wants and moves on. Screw her," he said. "She's hurt a lot of people with her crusade. I'm not giving her anything."

"That's fine with me," said Darcy. "You ready to go?"

"Yeah, let's go."

Mazur followed them toward the bank of elevators asking questions, which they ignored. Finally an elevator came and Collata pulled the cart on. Darcy followed him in, but Justin stopped in the doorway. He turned around with arms out stretched on either side of the elevator so that no one else could get in.

"Can I get in?" Mazur asked.

"No," said Justin. "Have a great day."

The doors closed.

15

COLLATA'S DILAPIDATED VAN CRAWLED TOWARD the curb near a fire hydrant. He backed up, dragging his tires against the curb before dropping into park. "Let's go spread some cheer," Collata said. Al Maggio sat in the passenger seat, surveying the neighborhood.

"Is this the worst district in the city?" He asked.

Collata laughed. "That's why you're here. You're the real police." Collata ripped his door open and stepped out of the van.

He looked through the window at Maggio. "Let's go, pinhead."

Maggio pulled his badge off of his belt and clipped it to a chain around his neck so it hung in the middle of his chest. They walked toward the low-rise housing project and up a flight of stairs. Maggio was winded when they reached the second floor landing. Collata watched in silence as Maggio bent at the waist trying to catch his breath.

From his perspective, Collata could see the growing bald spot on Maggio's head, which was weakly covered by the remainder of his thinning hair. "Are you gonna make it?" Collata asked. Maggio stood throwing his shoulders back. "I need a drink, maybe a quart of vodka with a couple of lines to build up my courage. But no, you had to get me sober. Sober sucks. You added twenty years to my life, but who cares? It's not twenty good years, it's twenty years at the end, when I can't hear, can't see, and sit around wearing a diaper."

Collata looked him up and down. "Remind me again, when were your good years?"

Collata knocked on a door, which was opened seconds later by an eight-year-old boy wearing Donovan McNabb's Philadelphia Eagles jersey. "We're here to talk to Mr. Kirksey," Collata said. Little McNabb turned and yelled into the apartment without letting go of the doorknob. "Boo, the police want you." Collata walked past Little McNabb followed by Maggio. A frail black man in a wheelchair rolled toward them. Little McNabb disappeared into the back of the apartment. Collata extended his hand toward Dewayne Kirksey. "Mr. Kirksey, I'm Collata . . ."

Kirksey cut him off. "I know who you are." He reached to shake with Collata. His hand was limp inside of his fingerless black leather glove. He pivoted in his chair and nodded at Collata to follow him into the kitchen. Collata took a seat at the easy-credit kitchen set that was old enough to be paid off. Maggio drifted into a chair in the living room out of earshot.

There was a bottle of cognac on the table next to an empty glass and a full ashtray. Kirksey glanced toward the bottle. "Want one?"

"It's a little early for me," Collata said as he checked his watch. It was still before 10 in the morning.

"You working for Macklin's lawyer?"

Collata nodded and pulled out a cigarette, offering one to

Kirksey. Kirksey took it and let Collata light it for him. They got some nicotine into their systems and settled in.

"So tell me your story. What really happened?" Collata asked, as smoke billowed from his mouth and nose.

Kirksey seemed tired. The side of his face had a dent near the eye where the orbital bone had been shattered. His cheek below was a bit shallow from where it had been crushed. An eyelid covered his empty eye socket. As he sat in his wheelchair his withered legs hung motionless. There were a number of scars scattered across his face.

"I'd been up to the jets to score some weed. Right after I got my package, Five-O jumps out and I got locked up." He crushed his cigarette out. "I had a warrant for another drug case and a burglary. They put me on probation for the burglary. When I picked up the second drug case, the jail let me out on an I-bond. I knew I was going to end up in the joint so I just never went back. When I got the weed case the warrants popped, so I knew the shit was going come down." He poured himself a heavy glass of cognac and took a big gulp.

Collata waited him out. Kirksey wanted to tell him everything. It had been festering inside of him for years. It had cost him the use of his legs. It had cost him an eye. Mostly it had cost him his dignity. It now began to spill out.

"Detective Davis pulled me out of the lockup and into an interview room."

Collata leaned into him and used a quiet, deliberate voice. "What happened next?"

A tear began to crawl down Kirksey's face from his eye. He used his forearm to wipe it away. "He came at me asking about Ayisha Gibert. He told me that I was going to get the death penalty for what I did to that nine-year-old girl. I never heard of her. I freaked." He finished the cognac that was in his glass. His hands shook.

"He was in my face for hours. He gave me a real good beat down, but mostly he played with my head. He kept saying, 'You took that girl up to 1309.' I'd say no but he kept at me. He said, 'Once you got her up there you raped her; you're going to death row.'

"He just kept at me. Feeding me words, telling me what happened." He broke down crying, using a hand to cover his face. Collata poured him another cognac.

"He did it all. He beat me. He got into my face, then he'd back off and whisper into my ear how my execution was going to happen. Finally, he got me all broke down. Then he made his play. He was good. I never saw it coming." Kirksey pulled the glass off of the table and took a sip from a shaky hand. "He showed me Macklin's picture and said maybe this was the guy you saw leaving out of 1309 with blood on his shirt. I jumped all over it. Next morning he took me down to the courthouse and had me testify in front of the grand jury. I had never seen Macklin before I saw that photo. He might have been in the building that night; he might even have been in that apartment that night, but I never saw him. Davis turned me out like a bitch."

Collata felt awful. He fleshed out the rest in his mind, but he needed to hear it from Kirksey. They sat in silence as Kirksey struggled with his thoughts. "Davis told me he'd take care of me. The State offered me the witness quarters but Davis talked them into giving me an I-bond on everything as long as I tricked. I signed my bond slip, promising to come back to court, and went home. They threw out the weed case. When they were done with me they packaged my cases up for three years. If I had been in the witness quarters I would have gone home. I could have done easy time in the witness quarters. Instead, I go to the joint with a snitch jacket and a hit on me from the gangs. That's when I knew Davis had turned me out."

Collata blazed up a smoke, then handed it to Kirksey so he

could light his. Collata studied him. Kirksey looked at the floor as he smoked. He hadn't mentioned his injuries.

"Would you let me take your statement with a court reporter taking everything down, or on videotape?" Collata asked.

"Whatever you want. The shit's gotta end. It's gotta end."

Collata collected Maggio and left. They made their way back to the van. After starting the engine, Collata turned to Maggio.

"Thanks for coming with me. Thanks for watching my back."

Maggio smiled. "We must be at a turning point. You're actually being nice to me."

"Don't get carried away," Collata said, "but you may be able to do real investigations when you leave the police force. Until then you can watch my back from a distance far enough away so you don't become a witness. How's that?"

It was completely inappropriate for Maggio, a Chicago homicide detective, to help Collata do investigations for a criminal defense attorney, but Collata was his only friend, so he went when he was off-duty. He made sure to stay far enough away so he wouldn't hear what the witnesses said.

Maggio had been hurtling toward disaster when he met Collata. He was a hard-drinking alcoholic, using cocaine, and on the verge of suicide when Collata intervened. Collata was the one who took him to rehab. Collata was the one who stayed up all night in the Greek diner drinking coffee with him while Maggio sweated out the painful first months of sobriety. Maggio owed Collata a debt that could never be repaid.

16

DARCY POURED HIMSELF THREE FINGERS of Maker's Mark, dropped in two ice cubes, and then gently swirled it. He stood against the window in his living room with his forehead pressed against the glass, looking out over a dark November day. The snow was coming down in clumps and melting as soon as it hit the street below. It was so thick that he couldn't see the lake, only flakes of white pelting against his window. Amy was working all night and Darcy was happy for it. Somehow he felt good being alone. It wasn't the dull ache of loneliness that it once was. Rather, it was time to himself, which he enjoyed while sipping his whiskey.

In the morning he and Justin would be in the Skokie Courthouse for their first appearance on Brian Kern. He thought about his two death cases. The Capital Litigation Rules had changed in response to the spate of death-row inmates being exonerated. There had been a huge hue and cry in the press when thirteen separate men on death row in Illinois had been released after evidence had proved that they were factually innocent—they were not released on some technicality, as lay people would say, but were actually innocent of the crimes that had put them on death row. Afterward, a new set of rules had been put in place to ensure that this never happened again, and among those rules was the formation of the Capital Litigation Bar. Criminal defense lawyers were certified so that they could properly represent individuals in death penalty cases. Darcy had considered not getting certified, but in the end he had submitted his credentials, gone through a series of seminars, and become certified. Darcy took a long pull.

"So I'm certified eligible to kill my clients now," he thought.

Darcy had always been ambivalent about the death penalty, even years before when he was a prosecutor. He didn't have a burning desire to put anyone on death row. As a defense attorney he hadn't had a client sentenced to death. But ultimately, he wasn't so sure that a death penalty was any worse than eighty or one hundred years in the penitentiary, which in effect meant the defendant, his client, would die in prison anyway.

He didn't like either of his death penalty clients, Macklin or Kern, and that was good. If he liked them, he could become emotionally invested in the case, and that was the kiss of death for an attorney. He liked to keep a professional distance from his clients. He began to wonder if that professional distance extended to every aspect of his life. He was thinking again of the invitation for Thanksgiving dinner. Why would he hesitate? What was it about close personal relationships that scared him so? Amy Wagner had stirred feelings in him that he hadn't felt in decades, and yet, as he grew closer to her, he also held part of himself back. He didn't understand it. He imagined dinner at her house in Michigan with her two adult children, walks along the beach, maybe through the woods. Intellectually, it sounded glorious to him. Yet, emotionally he had some pangs of panic welling up inside. He finished his drink and then began to chew an ice cube. He thought of his late wife. He remembered how they had met, their courtship, their marriage, the birth of their daughter, and the disintegration of the marriage. He couldn't put his finger on what had gone wrong, but he was fairly certain it was all his fault.

His thoughts turned back to his encounters with death. He remembered how Tony Benvenuti Jr. had been killed right in front of him. Benvenuti, a client, had come to kill Darcy for losing his case, but was shot by a mob henchman at the last minute. Darcy had done murder cases over the past thirty years. He had seen dead people before, having been to autopsies when he was a prosecutor. He had seen photographs of corpses in every murder trial he had ever done. Yet he couldn't get it out of his mind, seeing the bullet crack into Tony Benvenuti and his head exploding. Over and over again it was replayed in his mind. It bothered him that the only feeling he could remember upon seeing this death was one of great relief.

He sat back in his comfortable chair and watched the snow. Some light from the street below crept into his otherwise dark apartment. He sat back, closed his eyes, and soon drifted away.

17

THE BRAVADO THAT DARCY AND Justin had seen at the jail was gone. Brian Kern looked frightened and tired as he was brought out of the lockup in his prison garb. Darcy, Justin, and Brian stood in front of the judge. Larry Stevens was at the edge of the bench. Judge Krupp sat above reading a motion that Darcy had filed.

"Well Mr. Cole," she said. "I read your motion, I'm sorry, your motion and Mr. Schachter's motion, to set a bond. As you know, by statute if the State is looking for a sentence of death, your client is not eligible for bond. So I suspect that we have to go to Mr. Stevens and see if the State has made their decision. They still have time within the one hundred and twenty days allotted by Supreme Court Rule to make that decision. So, Mr. Stevens," she said, turning toward him. "Has the State made a decision as to death?"

"We have, Your Honor," said Stevens, "we are seeking to go forward on this case under the Supreme Court Rules pertaining to death penalty cases, and we are seeking death."

The news didn't seem to faze Brian Kern, who stood there impassively with a tired and bored look.

"Well, that makes short order of that," the judge said, turning back toward Darcy and Justin. "So what about discovery?" she said to Stevens, while looking at Darcy.

"Well, Your Honor," he began, "my understanding is that this case is being assigned back to Twenty-sixth and California."

"Why is that?" she said, not masking the disappointment in her voice.

"For security purposes, I'm told."

"I see," said Judge Krupp. "Apparently, we're not capable of doing a death penalty case?"

She was used to high-profile cases being taken away from the suburban courts and transferred to the Criminal Courthouse at Twenty-sixth and California. They used security as an excuse. She took it as an insult against her and the other suburban judges.

"I don't know, Judge. The decision came from those higher up than me," Stevens said.

"Well, are you following the case?" she asked.

"I don't think so," said Stevens. "Although I haven't gotten an official word, I believe that lawyers from Twenty-sixth Street are going to do this case."

"Mr. Cole?"

"Frankly, Judge, I don't care where we try this case, but I don't see why it needs to get transferred. This is a case that arose in a suburb that has its cases heard in this building. So I'm a little curious as to why this case has to be treated differently."

"Come now, Mr. Cole," said the judge. "Death is different. Isn't that what everybody says? A death penalty case is different from all other cases, and if the powers that be want this at Twenty-sixth Street, then to Twenty-sixth Street it will go."

She thumbed through the court file searching for an order. After finding it she pulled it out and showed the lawyers.

"So, since I also have an order here in the file transferring it back, and it's from the Chief Judge of the Criminal Division, who is much higher in the food chain than I am, I will enter this order and will transfer it to Twenty-sixth Street. So why don't you and Mr. Schachter give me a good date when you both can be there."

They concluded their business in front of the court and then followed Kern to the lockup, where the sheriff opened a room so the three of them could sit and talk. Justin shook hands with Kern.

"How are you doing, Brian?"

Brian's grip was limp and cold. He had a vacant look on his face as he sat across the table from Darcy and Justin. Darcy reached across and shook hands with him as well.

"How are you?" Darcy asked.

"I want it to be over," Brian said. "I want to plead guilty, I want to get sentenced to die, and I want to be executed."

"Slow down," Darcy said, "slow down. Nobody's going to get executed around here. Not without a hell of a fight."

"You don't get it, Mr. Cole. I didn't have a life to begin with. I want this over. I want to plead guilty."

"Look," Darcy said, "you're a young man. You are in tremendous trouble, but I want to try to help you. Even if you don't want me to help you, I'm going to do the best I can. The only thing I want you to do is give me an opportunity to look at this and see if there is a way to win this case."

"Did you notice something?" Brian said. "Did you notice that neither my mother nor father was in court for me?"

Darcy had to think about it.

"You're right, they weren't in court. I was in court for you because I'm the one that has to help you. All they can do is blow you kisses, and you don't need that now. You need me. You need me and Justin to fight like hell for you."

"Darcy, let me tell you something. My father wasn't here because he's a piece of shit. He'll pay money. Yeah, he's good at that. He has a lot of money, but he's never had twenty seconds for me. Not twenty seconds, and you know what, I don't want to be here anymore, and if this messes up his perfect little life, I don't give a shit. I'm ready to go. I want you to go in there and plead me guilty, and I want to get the death penalty."

"I won't do that," said Darcy. "I want to find a way to win this case for you. You have to give me that opportunity."

"Why? This isn't about you or Mr. Schachter. This is about me and my dad," he said.

Justin leaned in.

"So did you do this just to get back at your father?"

"Just to get back at my father—there isn't enough time in the world to get back at him," Brian began to laugh. "But I did leave a little special something for him in this case."

"What's that?" said Darcy.

"Well, you see, this has nothing to do with Laura Martin. She was a nice enough girl, but she was in the wrong place at the wrong time."

"How so?" said Darcy.

"Trip is a sick fucker," he began. "He scoped this girl out and said no one would give a shit about her. He talked about us doing her."

"What do you mean?" said Justin.

"You know, fucking her and then killing her, and I thought that was a great idea."

"Were you planning on getting caught?" Darcy asked.

"I really didn't give a shit," he said. "My father and his career—dragging me to goddamn London for two years. I didn't know anybody. Everybody talked funny. I had no friends. Two years of utter bullshit and what did he care—not at all. He was never even home. My mom, every day after work, they would go to some event and I would stay home and watch TV. Have you ever seen British TV? It sucks. When I got back, the only guy that would hang with me was Trip. He told me about this girl that he had killed a few years ago. Told me the whole story. Man, it was a fucking rush. So he said we ought to do one together and I said what the fuck, why not?"

"So what did he tell you about?" Darcy asked.

"He hooked up with some little hottie. Took her to a party at Craig Cizmar's house. Cizmar's parents were out of town and they have this big house in Lake Forest near the lake. He took her back out behind the gazebo and he slit her throat. After he slit her throat he fucked her and threw her in the lake. He told me it was the coolest thing he ever did."

"Well, what happened this time with Laura Martin?"

"We took her out. Took her down to a secluded spot near the lake. He was trying to get into her pants and she wasn't going for it. Finally, she said 'take me home.' So she comes back toward the car, gets in the front seat, I'm in the back seat. I reach over, grab a tie, start choking her out, he runs around opens the front door and pulls her outside the car, drags her back, fucks her, then sticks her a couple times with the knife. He kicks her down the ravine into the lake and we take off. No one can prove anything. Except that I left the tie as a little surprise for my dad."

"How's that?" Darcy asked.

"You know the tie around her neck. My dad had it custom made on Saville Row in London. If the cops ever try to trace it back, they'll have a record of who they made it for. Even these moron cops here could figure that out. After all, it's got the label sewn on it. It was my dad's favorite tie. Make sure you let him know what happened to it."

Darcy turned and knocked on the glass. The sheriff came to open the door.

"We'll come visit you, Brian," said Darcy. "In the meantime, don't talk to anybody. Just wait for us to come and remember everybody in here is a snitch. So don't discuss the facts of your case with any of them."

Darcy shook hands with him. His grasp became firmer. The sheriff opened the door and Darcy and Justin filed out. They walked out of the courtroom and over to a corner where they could be alone.

"Holy shit," said Justin.

"Yep," said Darcy.

"I was going to thank you for bringing me into this," said Justin, "but now I'm not so sure."

"I understand," said Darcy. "In for a penny, in for a pound."

They stopped talking as a middle-aged black woman approached them.

"Who is that?" Darcy asked.

"No clue," Justin said.

When she was within ten feet she said, "Mr. Cole, Mr. Schachter." She had their attention.

"My name is Vanessa Baldwin."

Neither of them said anything, so Vanessa continued.

"I want you to know who I am," she said. "I run a group home in Rogers Park. Laura Martin lived there. I want you to know a little something about Laura Martin. Laura Martin never caught a break in her life. She was smart. She was funny. She was someone who was going to succeed. She was going to do it all on her own and I'm going to be here for her every step of the way. I understand that the two of you have a job to do, but I promise you that I will not allow you to drag her reputation through the mud. I'm going to be watching you. I'm going to make sure that her dignity is not also killed in that courtroom. Do I make myself clear?"

"Yes, ma'am," Darcy said. "But you're wrong about one thing."

"What's that?" she said.

"She did catch one break in her life. She had you."

She pointed a finger at Darcy and a smile crept across her face.

"Oh, you're good. I'm going to have to watch you."

"Ms. Baldwin, I can assure you that Mr. Schachter and I will do the very best we can for our client. I hope in doing so we don't offend you. We will keep in mind what you told us."

18

Darcy followed Justin out of the parking lot and drove for about ten minutes before Justin pulled into a place called Herm's Hot Dog Palace. It was a brightly painted building with a large parking lot. They pulled in near a back door and Justin was waiting for Darcy when he got out of his car.

"You're going to love this place," he said. "It's a great joint."

"I haven't had a hot dog in decades," Darcy said, laughing.

"You don't have to get a hot dog. They have everything here."

"No," Darcy said. "A hot dog sounds pretty good."

They pushed through the door into the restaurant and walked up to the large silver counter. Behind the counter was a tall, broad-shouldered man in his early thirties with short hair and a big smile.

"Justin, what's happening?"

"Matt, say hello to my friend Darcy."

Matt was wearing blue jean shorts, gym shoes, a white shirt, and an apron.

"Nice to meet you, Darcy," said Matt. "First time at Herm's?"

"Yes."

Darcy was studying the menu, which was on the wall behind Matt.

"You have everything here," Darcy said.

"The best beef around," Matt said.

"How's the chili?" Darcy asked.

"Even better than the beef."

"Well, I hope you're not offended that I'm going to go with a hot dog."

"Everything on it?"

"No peppers," Darcy said.

"Fries?"

"Yeah, what the hell, why not?"

"What do you want to drink?"

"You got a liquor license?" Darcy asked.

"No," said Matt. "Just soft drinks, Yoo-hoo's, and milk-shakes."

"Chocolate shake," Darcy said.

"You got it. Have a seat. Justin, your usual?"

"Yeah, double chicken."

"Okay, you got it. I'll bring it to your table."

They sat at a Formica table in front of a television that had ESPN on.

"This is your spot?" Darcy asked.

"One of them. Whenever I get out to the Skokie Courthouse, I stop here."

"How often do you get to Skokie?"

"Four times a month, you know, usually once a week. I get a lot of DUIs, do some traffic, misdemeanors, couple of felonies."

"Friendly place here," Darcy said.

"Matt and his brother, Jim, run the place. All their employees have been here forever and a day. One big family. You should see this place on the weekend. There's a million kids in and out of here on a Saturday. All wearing soccer or football uniforms, basketball, whatever the hell is in season. I bring my kids in. My wife's not big on the place. My kids love it, though. So that was some interview," Justin changed the subject.

"Yeah, that kid is twisted," said Darcy.

"We've got to keep him from giving up," Justin said. "He's got some issue with his dad."

"Can you believe that neither parent was there?" Darcy said. "They pay us a boatload of money and then they wash their hands of it. That's going to look like crap. We've got to get them there. At least for mitigation."

Justin got up and walked over behind the counter and pulled a cup off the top of the soda machine, filled it with ice, and then filled it up with soda. He came back and sat down.

"Kern's case is like the Leopold and Loeb debacle."

"You know about that?" asked Darcy. "I figured you're too young for that."

"Hell, man, I read that book when I was a kid—*Life Plus Ninety-Nine Years.*"

"So did you grow up around here?" Darcy asked.

"Not too far from here. My mom's family is from Michigan. A town called Northville. It was strange, we were the only Jews. Couldn't find a bagel or a good deli for miles."

"How did you get interested in criminal law?"

Justin took a sip of his soda.

"Did you ever hear of the Purple Gang?"

"Jewish gangsters in Detroit," said Darcy. "Of course I've heard of them."

"Very good, now have you ever heard of Morry Blue?"

"Morry Blue, yeah, he was a mobster in the Purple Gang. He

was supposed to be a tough little guy. That's way before your time," said Darcy.

"Morry Blue was my grandfather. Morris Bloomstein."

"Get out of here," said Darcy. "You're Morry Blue's grand-kid?"

"Yep, my mom went to the University of Michigan, met a guy named Schachter from up this way and got married. They moved here."

"Your grandfather was supposed to be a hitter."

"That's what they tell me. He was a big deal in the forties and the fifties, I guess," said Justin. "Then he bought a bunch of farm-land in Northville, Livonia, and Novi. He rented it out, had the farmers work it, and he waited for Detroit to move out. My mother and her brothers still had the land as those cities grew. After the riots, they got rich.

"So how do you know about Morry Blue?" Justin asked.

"Are you kidding?" Darcy said. "I used to read all the exploits of the Chicago mob, which led me to go into law school, which led me to become a prosecutor. I thought I'd be a prosecutor for-ever. I got pulled out of the State's Attorney's Office by an old lawyer who used to represent all the mob guys—and when I say all the mob guys, I mean all the mob guys—and these guys used to tell stories. They would tell me about the Purple Gang. They'd tell me about the New York families. They told me about the move to Vegas. All the old mustache Petes. The real reason I remember Morry Blue is because of his great nickname, but I remember some of his exploits. I assume he's dead," said Darcy.

"Yeah, long gone," said Justin.

Matt dropped their order on the table and then scurried back behind the counter to take another order.

Darcy had a little yellow plastic basket with wax paper that held a Chicago hot dog with everything except sport peppers, an order of fries, and a chocolate shake. Justin had a plate with two charbroiled chicken breasts and a couple of pickle wedges on it. Darcy took a bite of the hot dog, having trouble holding the pickle in place. He chewed a little bit and wiped his mouth with a napkin.

"This is good," said Darcy. "Now I know what I've been missing all these years. Tell you what Justin, the next restaurant I get to pick."

Darcy took a sip of his chocolate shake.

"Deal. About Macklin," Justin said.

"What about him?" said Darcy.

"It could be a bench trial," he said.

"How do you figure?" said Darcy.

"First of all, Judge Nicolau is devastated by this case and thinks the guy got railroaded. Secondly, the DNA's not his. Their eyewitness gave a court-reported statement to Collata recanting his prior testimony. Macklin's statement was that he raped and killed the girl. Since the DNA is not Macklin's, it is clear that it didn't happen the way his statement lays it out. That means it probably is a screwed-up confession, which means they have to have an alternative theory of prosecution from the last case. That means there's probably institutional reasonable doubt."

"Institutional reasonable doubt?" Darcy asked.

"Yeah, I just made that up. What do you think?"

"Sounds good," said Darcy. "So you think that's enough for Joe Nicolau to throw this case out?"

"I was his first chair for a long time," Justin said. "I think we could bench this in front of him. I think he's going to find Macklin not guilty. I don't think there's anything we can do to blow this one."

"Interesting," said Darcy, as he took another bite of his hot dog.

19

Darcy FINISHED HIS SWIM AND glided over to the corner of the pool, where he leaned against the wall. His heart was pounding, his pulse was racing and he was breathing heavily. The water behind him had gone still, and his breathing became regular as he slid under the rope and swam to the ladder. He toweled off, threw on a robe and sat at a table near the pool. He ordered Irish oatmeal and rye bread toast, a cup of coffee, and a glass of ice water. He finished the *Sun-Times* while waiting for his breakfast, and then began the *Tribune*.

In the *Tribune* Darcy was reading an article about a series of federal indictments for welfare fraud. Darcy had lost track of the number of U.S. Attorneys who had run the office in Chicago during the time that he was a defense attorney. Most of them fell into two categories: politically ambitious, connected people on their way up, or professional lawyers entrusted to run the office. But the current U.S. Attorney was neither. Since taking over the U.S. Attorney's office nine months earlier, this guy had impressed Darcy as someone who made every decision based on a hatred for defendants. As far as Darcy could tell, that hatred was equally strong toward the lawyers who represented those defendants. Darcy guessed that in this U.S. Attorney's mind there was no distinction between lawyer and client. There had been a number of defections from the office. Experienced lawyers were leaving to go into private practice, which led Darcy to believe that those prosecutors who indeed were professional, conscientious lawyers felt that it was time to move on rather than work for someone whom they did not respect.

Gary Galen was appointed U.S. Attorney in spite of the fact that no one had mentioned him as being a possible successor to the prior U.S. Attorney. He was a bit of a mystery among the Republicans who controlled that job and from whom he was appointed. He was short and stocky and wore round glasses. He had short, dark hair and an emerging bald spot. He had gotten a degree in theology from Wake Forest University in Winston-Salem, North Carolina. Then he did a year of graduate school at a bible college in Tennessee before changing his mind and going to law school at Duke University. He graduated at the top of his class and went to work for the Justice Department in Washington. After that, he spent four years in a Task Force Unit in Chicago before heading back to Washington. A number of local lawyers had lobbied the senior senator from Illinois for the appointment of U.S. Attorney. Gary Galen was the one who got the nod.

Prior to his confirmation hearing, the Chicago press was rabid in its quest to find personal information about Gary Galen. After exhaustive investigations, the press came to the conclusion that he had no personal life. He never dated, female or male. He didn't have any interests or hobbies and spent sixteen to eighteen hours a day at work. On the weekends he spent twelve to fourteen hours a day at work. During his confirmation hearing, a Senator from Tennessee who thought he was doing a favor to Mr. Galen asked him why he gave up the ministry for law. Galen's response was that he believed as a federal prosecutor he was doing God's work. He was affirmed anyway.

Darcy hated zealots. He viewed Galen as an overly ambitious, heartless man who would destroy people's lives without remorse. Sooner or later, Darcy knew the two of them would tangle. Darcy threw the paper on a chair and headed to the showers.

Half an hour later, he walked into his office, expecting it to be dark and empty. His secretary, Irma, was on vacation, and a law clerk whose name he couldn't remember was supposed to come in and answer the phone while she was gone. Looking down the hall he saw a light on in Kathy's office. He hung his overcoat in a hall-way closet, walked into his office and threw his suit coat on a hook behind his door. Kathy was at the threshold of his office when he finished.

"Good morning," he said. "You're getting an early start on the day."

He could tell by the look on her face that she had news and it wasn't good.

"I need to talk to you," she said.

"Come on in."

He walked around and sat at his desk. She shut the door behind her and took one of the client chairs.

"I have to tell you something," she began, her voice cracking.

Darcy watched as tears began to build up.

"I'm leaving you. I'm leaving the firm," she said with a small burst of energy.

Darcy was thrown for a loop. He wasn't quite sure he had heard her correctly.

"I've been with you one way or another since I was twenty-three," she said. "I'm forty-two. In that time, I've gotten married, had children, and became a partner. You and the firm are really important to me," she said.

Darcy was shocked and deeply hurt. He was having trouble following her words.

"I just can't do this anymore," she said. "I can't go from crisis to crisis watching peoples' lives self-destruct. The practice of criminal law is seeing people at their worst every day. It beats you down. I don't know how you do it. You know my friends, Megan and Rachel? They've been practicing together for two years, medical malpractice and plaintiff's personal injury. I'm going to join them.

"I don't want to do criminal anymore," she said. "It's as if we're doctors in the trauma center at County Hospital. I want to go to some suburban hospital and practice dermatology instead of trying to sew someone back together who has been shot, stabbed, or beaten. I'm going to be getting girls ready for the prom, working with zits and psoriasis. I love you dearly, Darcy, and I always will, but I just can't do this anymore. I have thought long and hard about it. I know I'm walking away from something great, but it's killing me. It's destroying my soul."

Darcy had learned long ago to choose his words carefully when he was emotional. He was trying to choose those words and coming up blank. Kathy couldn't fight it anymore, she was crying.

"I'm giving you as much time as you need to replace me. I will finish all the briefs that I am writing and all the cases I am working on, but I would like to be out of here in four to six months so I can get on with the next phase of my life."

Kathy stood to leave. Darcy leaned back.

"I need to think about this," he said. "I want to say and do the right thing, but I don't know what that is. I'm shocked. I'm going to miss you like crazy."

Kathy came around the desk and kissed Darcy on the cheek.

She put her arms around him and squeezed him. "Darcy, I'm going to miss you too, but we'll have some time to get used to the idea."

Darcy patted her on the shoulder.

"I know, kiddo."

20

COLLATA'S VAN WAS PARKED ON the Boulevard near the courthouse. The snow was coming down in thick, puffy flakes and piling up everywhere. Collata's wipers were keeping up, knocking the snowflakes off the windshield. Darcy was watching people walk down the stairs of the courthouse. Collata had his window cracked an inch to let the smoke from his cigarette escape. Darcy sat in silence, watching Justin Schachter coming down the stairs and walking toward the part of the jail that contained Cermak Health Services. Darcy pulled up the handle, popping the door open.

"I'll call you on the cell when we're done," he said.

Collata pushed the butt of the cigarette out of the window and then chased it with the smoke from his mouth.

"Okay, boss, I'll be around."

Darcy climbed out in the snow and carefully crossed the boulevard, waiting for Justin to join him. Justin was wearing a black knit hat, a blue Gore-Tex winter coat and big boots. His suit coat and tie were completely covered by the coat and his pants were tucked into the top of his boots. The briefcase hung by a strap over his shoulder and was behind him. His hands were in his coat pockets. Justin's face lit up when he saw Darcy.

"Hey, old man, great weather, huh?"

Darcy liked the snow—fresh and white, it covered all of the filth around the courthouse complex. They shook hands and Darcy grabbed hold of Justin's shoulder.

"Well, let's go see him," he said.

"How bad is it?" Justin asked.

"Pretty bad, I guess," said Darcy.

At one point in the history of the jail, Cermak was known as a hospital. Somehow over the years it changed to Cermak Health Services, which was a good clue as to what type of health services this place was actually providing.

"What do you know?" asked Justin.

"Apparently, he got a razor blade. Sliced his wrists pretty good," said Darcy. "They had him in County for two nights. Now, he's back here."

"When did you hear about it?" Justin asked.

"This morning," said Darcy.

They were escorted by a guard to a room on the third floor. It might have passed for a hospital wing at a military base or some other institution, except for the bars on the window.

Brian Kern looked tired and pale in his bed. Darcy noticed the leather restraints on his wrists and legs. Only part of his left arm was free and it was hooked up to an IV. There were large, white gauze bandages on each of his wrists. Justin pulled his hat off and stuffed it into the pocket of his coat, then unzipped his coat and pulled that off. Darcy took his overcoat off as well and the scarf that was around his neck. He laid them across the chair, with Justin's. Darcy edged toward the bed.

"You know, Brian, some people could interpret what you did as a complete lack of confidence in your lawyers."

Brian didn't react. He was working hard to look away from Darcy and Justin.

"Look, Brian, you may think things are bleak now, but let me do my job and see if I can help you," Darcy said.

Brian cut him off.

"You don't get it, do you?"

"Help me understand it," said Darcy.

Brian shot a glance over at Justin and back to Darcy.

"Do you have any idea what my life was like and what my life will be like?"

"I don't," conceded Darcy. "Explain it to me."

"Utter neglect and indifference," he said. "Do you know what I'm talking about?"

Darcy shrugged.

"Utter neglect and indifference, that's what my parents have shown to me my whole life. I never understood why my mother and father had me," he said. "They never had any time for me and my father's answer to everything was to throw money at it. His sole purpose in life was to achieve more and more success. Kids don't care about success, Darcy. They want their father to pay attention to them. They want to believe that their mother loves them. My mother didn't love me and my father didn't have ten minutes for me in a decade."

"So, you'll show them," Darcy said. "The ultimate fuck you: kill yourself, make a big mess, and embarrass them. I don't get it," Darcy said.

"What don't you get?" Brian asked sarcastically.

"Your parents have money. You're mad at them. Help us win your case. Then go to college, take eight years to graduate, get your Ph.D. in some archaic, useless subject, spending another twelve years soaking up all their funds, smoking pot, drinking beer, chasing girls, why don't you get even with them like that?"

"Oh, so you subscribe to out-of-sight-out-of-mind," Brian said, anger building in his voice. "You think . . ."

Darcy cut him off.

"Absolutely not. That's not what I am saying. I am saying why don't you take what you can get and build your own life."

"It's too late for that," he said. "My life is over."

Justin stepped into the conversation.

"If what you say is true and you kill yourself or let the government kill you, then your parents are going to get exactly what they want, to be free from you. But on the other hand, if you fight this case and win, and you're out, they really have to deal with you, don't they?"

It was obvious that Brian had never considered that point before.

"We can't win this," he said.

Darcy could tell that he was now thinking about it, which was good.

"I don't know," said Darcy. "We got one guy blaming you. Why can't we turn around and blame him? What makes him so goddamn believable? Because he cut a deal and puked first?"

Darcy began to pace.

"Do know how many cases have come back where people were found to be actually innocent? They were convicted because of some snitch wrongfully testifying against them. Every juror in there will have read the *Tribune* and the *Sun-Times* and seen *60 Minutes* and all the stories of wrongful convictions. What's the number one factor in common on all those cases? Bad testimony. Testimony from someone trying to save their own neck. There isn't anybody in the world that's going to like John Henry Phillips III. Fuck him, let's win this case."

Darcy thought he had rallied the kid, but then it turned again.

"Do you know what?" he said, his voice going dead. "I was here on Christmas alone in Cook County Jail and my mom and dad didn't come visit me."

"Guess what?" Justin responded. "You go to any trial, any day of the week, any courtroom at Twenty-sixth and California, and you're going to find a defendant all alone in the courtroom— no mom, no dad, no brother, no wife, and no girlfriend, just him all alone with his defense attorney, usually a public defender socking it out, trying to help the guy. You can boohoo all you want, but you got two damn good lawyers here who are going to bust their asses for you. If your parents don't want to be there, fuck them too. We're going to win this case, then we're going to drive you home, drop you off at your fucking doorstep and we're going to watch mom and dad have to deal with you then. How about that, Brian?"

A very, weak smile briefly flashed on Brian's face and then disappeared.

"Yeah, how about that?" Brian asked.

21

DARCY WAS SCANNING THE ROWS of empty shelves that lined the walls of the law library as he waited for Lavelle Macklin to be brought in. He turned to Justin.

"Why are there no books in the law library?" he asked.

Justin glanced up at the empty shelves. "I never noticed," he said. "It is amazing that there are no books in a room called the law library. But what's really pitiful is that I never noticed it before and I've been here at least ten times in the last two years."

Macklin was in good spirits when he walked into the library to meet his lawyers. Macklin shook hands with them, then took a seat at the table. "What's up?" he asked.

"Well," Darcy began, "we're ready for trial but we need to go over a few things with you."

Macklin's face lit up with a wide grin. He threw his hands up and exclaimed, "Finally I'm going home."

Darcy leaned toward Macklin. "We have some very strong things for us in this case. As you know, Boo has recanted his original testimony against you."

"About time! Fuck his punk ass," Macklin yelled, as he slammed his hand on the table. The library door opened up and a sheriff poked his head in and studied the people inside before backing out again.

Justin put his hands out in a calming gesture. "You have to chill out. We can't have you going off," he said.

"I'm cool," Macklin replied.

Darcy gave Macklin a stern look. Their eyes locked for a moment and Macklin eased back into his chair. "We think that this should be a bench trial," Darcy said. He paused to gauge his client's reaction. There was none, so he continued. "We think that the State's case is damaged beyond repair. There are certain cases that are jury trials and others that are benches. In a bench trial the judge decides if you are guilty or not guilty."

"I know that," Macklin said.

"Right," said Darcy, "but here you have a judge who knows a lot about this case. He has a doubt now even before he's heard any of the evidence."

Macklin interrupted. "He's already heard the evidence and sentenced me to die."

"That's right," said Darcy, as he shifted in his seat. "But now he knows that the DNA is not yours. He knows that in your so-called statement you confess to the rape and murder. Obviously, there is a flaw in the statement. Boo's recant blows his credibility as a witness against you and explains what Davis did in this case."

Macklin held his hand up, signaling Darcy to stop. "Can you trust this man? Can you trust this judge to follow the law and cut me loose?"

Justin stood and began to pace. He stepped forward and leaned in close to Macklin. "I've known this judge for years. I was in his courtroom every day for fifteen months. In this business you have to go with your gut sometimes. This is your life. This is our case. With every fiber in my body I believe Joe Nicolau is an honorable man. I believe that Joe Nicolau is afraid that he may have put you on death row for a crime you didn't commit. This is his chance to right a wrong. With this new evidence I believe he will acquit you. There are no sure things in this business, but if I were betting on this case, I'd bet big on us to win this on a bench trial."

Macklin leaned back and was processing what he heard. He crossed his arms across his chest. "Would you bet my life on it?" he asked.

Justin gave him a faint smile. "I'd bet my life on it."

22

THERE MAY BE NOTHING WORSE than February in Chicago. Although it's a short month, the weather is nasty and the people's spirits are beaten down at the end of winter. Amy Wagner had refilled her wine glass and was walking through the dark apartment trying to find Darcy on the couch near the window overlooking the lake. Darcy was thinking about the Thanksgiving weekend he had spent with Amy on the other side of the lake. He had been filled with apprehension beforehand, but he'd ended up having the best weekend of his life. He remembered waking up Friday morning and watching Amy as she slept next to him. He watched her stir, then open her eyes. She focused, saw Darcy and pulled him closer. Darcy remembered how warm and soft she was.

For the first time in recent memory, Darcy was happy. When Amy reached him at the window, she placed her glass on the coffee table and snuggled up next to him.

"So is this what you do?" she asked. "You sit out and watch the snow fall."

"Often," said Darcy.

"What happens the rest of the year, when it's not snowing?"

Darcy smiled.

"I watch the lake, the boats, or the waves—or nothing at all, just the cool blue expanse of water."

"Do you think great thoughts? Do you ponder the smallness of man compared to nature?"

"Sure," said Darcy, "that and much more."

The winter had been difficult. Although the temperatures weren't bad, the snowfall was heavy, the third or fourth most snow of any Chicago winter, and they weren't even out of February yet. Today there was yet more, snow coming down so fierce and thick that Darcy could not make out the street below.

"Do you have work tomorrow?" Darcy asked.

"Not until six in the evening," she said.

"I think you're stuck here. Snowbound with me tonight."

"I can think of no place I'd rather be," she said.

For no particular reason, Darcy was drinking Jameson Irish Whiskey. The ice was melting and his glass was getting dangerously close to empty. He swirled it once and then finished it. He put the empty glass down on the coffee table near Amy's wine glass.

"Why don't we open the blinds in the bedroom, climb into bed and watch the rest of the snowstorm?" Darcy said.

"It's a wonderful idea," she said.

Darcy was in his T-shirt and boxer shorts as he slid into bed to join Amy. The sheets were cool, she was warm, and the comforter was outfitted with a flannel duvet that Amy had given him. Darcy was on his side, and Amy's hand was under his shirt rubbing his back.

"Darcy," she said, "there's something I want to talk to you about."

"Please," said Darcy. "The last time a woman said that to me was when Kathy told me she was leaving the firm."

"You know I'm turning fifty," she said.

"I do," said Darcy, "and I have plenty of time to come up with an appropriate plan for that momentous occasion."

Amy didn't laugh.

"I have a plan of my own," she said.

"Is that right?" said Darcy. "And what is that?"

"Have you ever heard of a group called Doctors Without Borders?" she asked.

"Sure," said Darcy. "A bunch of doctors who go to some disadvantaged country and volunteer their services."

"That's right," she said. "I think for my fiftieth birthday I want to give it a shot."

"Give what a shot?" he said.

"Doctors Without Borders, or some other medical group that helps people around the world."

"You mean you'd go to some godforsaken hellhole?"

"No," she said hitting him in the shoulder. "Not some godforsaken hellhole, but some country in need. I would go there with a group of doctors and do some work for a period of time."

"How long a period of time?" Darcy asked.

"I don't know," she said. "I'm kind of thinking about six months."

Darcy shot up, and turned to face her.

"Six months? You're going to leave me for six months?"

"I'm not leaving you," she said. "I would be going on a mission of mercy. I'm going to help people. I'm going to do something to make me feel good about myself and give something back."

"But you'd be leaving me for six months?" Darcy asked again.

"First of all, I'm not leaving you. Second of all, who said you can't come with me?"

"I'm not a doctor," said Darcy. "What the hell am I supposed to do?"

"You could share the adventure with me," she said. "We can meet somewhere and travel a bit. Take some vacation time."

"When would you be going?" Darcy asked. "Would you quit your job at the hospital?"

"I'm thinking of doing it this spring," she said. "I'll take a leave of absence. It's a humanitarian effort. It's something that's encouraged by the hospital."

"Are you asking for my input?" he said. "Or have you already decided this and you're telling me now?"

"Well," she said, "I have decided I want to do it. I don't know which country I want to go to. I don't know what I want to do there, and I don't know exactly how long I'm going for. So I would suggest that you treat me really, really well so that you have more input on these decisions."

Darcy knew it was time to back off. He gave her a slow, gentle kiss on the neck.

"How's that? Is that a good beginning?"

"It is," she said, "but it's only a beginning."

23

JUSTIN WAS READING THE SPORTS pages when Darcy walked in.

"What's new?" he asked.

"Cubs are in spring training. They have pitchers, very little power, no speed—and I'm still going to go to as many games as I can."

"Is that right?" said Darcy. "A real Cub fan, are you?"

"I am afraid so," said Justin. "You know Cub fans, ninety-five percent scar tissue."

Justin had a large bottle of water and was eating a protein bar.

"What is that?" Darcy asked.

"Protein bar, low carbs."

"It smells terrible," Darcy said.

"That's funny," said Justin, "because it tastes like shit too."

"You ready?" Darcy asked.

"Absolutely," said Justin.

They loaded three bankers' boxes onto a luggage cart and tied it off.

"Let's roll," said Justin, pulling it behind him.

Justin wheeled the cart out of the office to the elevator and then out onto Van Buren, where Collata was waiting in the van. He threw the boxes one by one into the back of the van and slammed it shut, and they headed off to Twenty-sixth Street. They passed by the Metropolitan Correctional Center, a triangular shaped building that housed federal inmates. They took a left and then a quick right and headed out on the Congress Expressway toward the court- house. As they looped around to 94-South, Darcy looked out the window. A new community, University Village, had sprung up near the intersection of Halsted and Maxwell Streets in an area that was once known as Jewtown. Further to the south, the gentrification continued, pushing into Pilsen and then into Chinatown.

"Where does all the money come from?" Darcy wondered. "All these young people buying expensive condos and town- houses."

Collata veered onto 55-South and was soon approaching the Damen exit, which he took. The new bridge gave a beautiful view of the river. Darcy watched a barge being pushed down the river. He saw a worker on the tugboat. March had crept in but the weather was still cold and nasty, and he watched the worker walk- ing across the back of the tugboat looking at something and turn- ing around before disappearing into the cabin on the ship.

Another job I wouldn't want, Darcy thought to himself.

Collata stopped the van just north of the crosswalk in front of the courthouse. Justin jumped out and reloaded the luggage cart with the files.

"We'll be up in Judge Nicolau's," Darcy said.

"I got it," said Collata. "I got to run and do a few things. I'll meet you up there."

Collata gave Darcy a hard look. Darcy looked tired.

"You okay, boss?"

"Yeah," said Darcy. "I'm okay."

"Are you sure?" said Collata.

"Yeah, I'm sure," said Darcy. "Thanks for asking."

Erin Powers had enlisted Randy Edwards to help her try the Macklin case. Randy was a thickly built African-American man about five foot ten inches tall with a firm handshake, short cropped hair, and a neatly trimmed goatee. He also was a mainstay on the State's Attorney's softball team. He extended his powerful hand and gave Darcy a firm grip. Erin nodded her head to direct Darcy and Justin to the back of the courtroom. They followed her to the empty jury room.

"I have all my witnesses upstairs," she said. "I also have a lab tech from the ME's office and the DNA expert that you asked me for. They are upstairs as well, although the DNA guy is coming this afternoon."

"That's all right," said Darcy, "I don't expect to get to him today."

Judge Joe Nicolau ran his hand over his silver gray hair and adjusted his round wire glasses. He had left the bench and gone into chambers, then wandered out to the back of the courtroom and into the jury room.

"Okay boys and girls, are you ready for showtime?" he asked.

"We are," said Randy.

"We're just ironing out a few last details," Erin said.

The two of them spoke in flat, tired voices. Neither one of them had had anything to do with the original prosecution of Lavelle Macklin. Neither one of them had any responsibility for the conviction, and yet they were here now, faced with the task of retrying him. They were two talented, hardworking, honest, ethical prosecutors. They had been selected for this case because of their abilities. The State's Attorney himself knew that they would work hard and represent the office well. The State's Attorney also knew that it was a case with significant problems. It was those problems that had beaten them down. Now they had to recover. They had to channel their energy to get ready for this trial. It was, however, a very strong indication of the strength of the case that the defense had waived a jury and was submitting it to Judge Nicolau to decide.

Erin knew very well that this case had caused the judge much pain—the idea that perhaps he had sent an innocent man to death row. It was a difficult position to be in for her as a prosecutor. Prosecutors are supposed to be good guys. The ones wearing the white hats, the ones working for justice, trying to make a bad guy pay for the evil he had inflicted upon an innocent victim. But this was different. Today the prosecutors themselves were on the defensive.

Clearly, their theory of the case was irrevocably changed by the DNA test done long after Macklin had first entered death row. They now had to try a case with an alternative theory for their prosecution. In another words, they had to use the same evidence and argue a different conclusion—which was going to be a very tough sell.

24

ERIN POWERS ROSE FROM BEHIND counsel table and stepped through
the well of the courtroom to a podium that was next to an empty
jury box.

"Thirteen years ago this April 7, a nine-year-old girl named
Ayisha Gibert was playing happily outside her building. She lived
in an apartment at the Stateway Gardens Housing Project with her
mother, Tamika Kimmons. At some point while Ayisha was outside playing she encountered Lavelle Macklin."

As she said his name she walked toward counsel table and
pointed toward Macklin, who was seated between Darcy and
Justin. Macklin sat expressionless as she continued.

"Mr. Macklin lured her to a vacant apartment. Once inside, he
savagely attacked her—raping her, beating her, and ultimately
killing her. He then fled from the scene. Soon Tamika Kimmons

began to look for her daughter. When she couldn't find her, she called the police. The police arrived and after a while began a systematic search of the building, which ultimately led to the discovery of Ayisha's body. The apartment where Ayisha was found was vacant. The police sealed off the crime scene and waited for the crime lab to come work up the crime scene and remove the body. The body was taken to the morgue where an autopsy was performed. There were bruises on Ayisha's face, neck, forehead, chin, and chest, and vaginal trauma including a torn hymen, blood, and internal injuries, which you will hear from expert medical testimony were caused by sexual intercourse. Semen was recovered inside the vaginal vault as well as other points on the body and on the scene.

"During the course of this investigation, police interviewed all the residents of the building whom they could find. They developed information that Lavelle Macklin had been in the area where Ayisha's body had been found. Lavelle Macklin was well known to the police as being a leader of the gang that controlled the building, that being the Black Gangster Disciples, who sold drugs in the building. A witness, Dewayne Kirksey, told police that he saw Lavelle Macklin exit Apartment 1309 that night, and that Macklin had blood on his clothes.

"A short time later, Mr. Macklin was found driving a car in the area. At the time he was driving the car, his license had been suspended for a series of traffic offenses. The police officers knew that his license was suspended, placed him under arrest for a suspended license, and transported him to the Second District. The Second District is housed at Fifty-first and Wentworth, as is the Area One Violent Crimes Headquarters. While being processed for his driver's license problems, the detectives brought him up to Area One Violent Crimes. After being advised of his Miranda rights, the defendant gave a statement in which he admitted raping and killing Ayisha Gibert. The defendant was placed under arrest and processed for that murder. You will hear through the detectives that the confession that he gave to the police was sufficiently detailed and contained information that only the killer would know.

"At the conclusion of all the evidence I am going to ask that you find this defendant guilty of first degree murder, guilty of aggravated kidnapping, and guilty of aggravated criminal sexual assault."

Erin sat down and whispered something to her partner Randy Edwards. They began to talk softly. Darcy rose and stepped across the courtroom to the podium, where he set his legal pad down. Darcy began in quiet, measured tones.

"April 7 will mark the thirteenth year that Mr. Macklin has been incarcerated for a crime he did not commit. This was a heinous crime. A nine-year-old girl was kidnapped, raped, and murdered. The Chicago Police Department wanted to solve this case in the worst way—and unfortunately, they did solve it in the worst way. Rather than developing the evidence and following the leads, they rounded up the usual suspects, they squeezed a confession out of Lavelle Macklin, and they convicted him based on that confession.

"What's changed is that we now have irrefutable scientific evidence that Lavelle Macklin did not rape Ayisha Gibert and thus, logically, did not kill Ayisha Gibert. What we also know is that his so-called confession is a fabric of lies, and the pulled string that unraveled it is due not to police work, not to anything the State's Attorney's Office did, not to any fact-finding function of the court, but to advances in scientific evidence.

"When Lavelle Macklin was arrested, DNA testing was not in use. So at that time there was no way for Lavelle Macklin's attorneys to prove that Lavelle Macklin did not rape this girl. But luckily for Lavelle Macklin, and all the other Lavelle Macklins out there, DNA testing has proved to be a tool the legal system can use to get to the truth. The truth in this case is that the police coerced a confession out of Lavelle Macklin based on what they believed happened. As in so many other cases before this, they forced this defendant to say whatever it was they needed him to say to secure a conviction."

Randy Edwards shot to his feet.

"Objection, Your Honor, argumentative."

"This is a bench trial," the judge said. "I'll only consider relevant competent evidence and I will not be swayed by any emotion or improper argument."

Edwards slowly sank to his chair, not quite satisfied with the judge's ruling.

"Thus, Your Honor, this case comes down to this: It could not have happened as Mr. Macklin's confession states, because Mr. Macklin's confession is in effect that he raped this girl and killed her. Well, we know he didn't rape her. We know that he asserted that the so-called confession was fiction created by the police and that he was compelled to utter it to the court reporter in fear for his life. At the conclusion of the evidence, Your Honor, you may or may not believe that Lavelle Macklin is innocent of this crime. Perhaps that's left to a higher power at a later time, but you will certainly have reasonable doubts as to what happened here and you will have more than reasonable doubt that Lavelle Macklin raped and killed Ayisha Gibert. At the conclusion, you will be compelled by the evidence, the facts and the law to find Lavelle Macklin not guilty. And you will be doing that without reservation. Thank you."

Darcy sat down and the clerk called the first witness.

Tamika Kimmons walked into the courtroom. She was conservatively dressed. She raised her right hand, was sworn in, and was seated in the witness box to the right of the judge. Tamika was forty-four years old, approximately the same age as Erin Powers. She had given birth to three children, two boys and Ayisha. Ayisha was the youngest of her children. Erin brought her through her testimony slowly until she got to the point where Ayisha went missing. She then showed Tamika a photograph of a smiling, chubby, nine-year-old girl with pigtails and little pink plastic barrettes in her pigtails.

"Do you recognize this photo?"

Tamika was crying.

"That's Ayisha."

"And was this photo taken when she was alive?"

"Yes, that was taken in school. The October before she died."

Erin walked back to counsel table and put the photograph down. She picked up a photograph of the same nine-year-old girl lying on a silver table at the morgue. She walked toward Darcy and Justin. In a quiet voice she leaned in.

"Do you want to stipulate to the death photo?"

"Absolutely," said Darcy.

Justin nodded in agreement.

"Your Honor, at this time there would be a stipulation by and between the parties that Peoples' Exhibit Number 2 for identification purposes would be a photograph identified as Ayisha Gibert taken at the Cook County Medical Examiner's Office."

She turned back toward the lawyers.

"So stipulated?"

"So stipulated," agreed Darcy.

After a few more questions Erin tendered Tamika for cross-examination, which Darcy and Justin declined.

"No questions of this witness," Darcy said.

"Very well, Ms. Kimmons. You may step down," said Judge Nicolau. "I give you my deepest condolences on your loss."

"Thank you, Your Honor," she said, as she clutched a tissue and walked through the well of the courtroom and out the doors.

Detective Tommy Davis was next. He was a black man about five foot eleven, stocky, about to turn fifty. When he caught the case he had been thirty-seven years old. Davis now had gray hair around the temples. He took the witness stand and glanced briefly toward counsel table. Macklin was staring intently at Tommy Davis. He remembered Tommy Davis. In Macklin's mind Tommy Davis was responsible for taking thirteen years of his life.

Randy Edwards stood at the podium. He looked impressive in a blue two-piece suit, three buttons, with a white buttoned-down shirt and a yellow, flecked tie. He began with Davis receiving the initial call and responding to Apartment 1309. Davis described in detail the crime scene and the investigation that followed. He testified to bringing Lavelle Macklin up the stairs and into an interview room at the Area Headquarters. He testified to taking the handcuffs off of Macklin and sitting across the table from him and calmly explaining Mr. Macklin's rights. He explained how Mr. Macklin waived those rights and agreed to talk to him. He then described Mr. Macklin's eagerness to help the detectives with the case, and he pointed out that at no time did Macklin ever protest or ask for a lawyer. When Davis had begun to question Macklin about Ayisha Gibert's murder, Davis said he was suspicious that Mr. Macklin was not surprised to be asked about the case. This was very unusual, he asserted. Davis told how Macklin gave a full confession within an hour to two hours of first meeting him. They then began to explain away the thirteen hours that passed from when Macklin allegedly first confessed until he gave a court-reported statement.

"Mr. Macklin was trying to help us and he wanted to make sure we had all the details straight," Davis began. "We took him out and had him show us different things in the neighborhood, then we came back and we fed him. We told him we needed to get Felony Review, and it took a long time for Felony Review to show up. After Felony Review Mr. Macklin wanted us to get his statement correct and opted for a court reporter. We had to get a court reporter out to Area One."

At the beginning of the trial, the spectator's gallery had been three-quarters full. As Davis droned on there were seven people left. Three of them were from the press, including Pam Mazur, who sat in the front row scribbling notes.

Finally, Darcy began his cross.

"Detective, this was a high-profile case. Isn't that correct?"

"I'm not sure what you mean by high profile," answered Davis.

"Well, a nine-year-old girl was raped and murdered, and there was a lot of interest in the press in this case."

"There was a lot of interest in the press," Davis agreed.

"And you and your fellow officers felt pressured to solve this case quickly."

"There was no pressure put on us," said Davis. "This was just another case."

"What evidence did you have that Lavelle Macklin was involved when you sat down to talk to him?"

"We had gotten some information from individuals that lived in the housing project and other individuals that we knew."

"What was the information?" Darcy asked.

"Well, different people said different things, counsel."

"Well, did any of them say that Lavelle Macklin murdered this girl?"

David let out an inappropriate laugh.

"No, nobody said that Lavelle Macklin murdered this girl."

"Did anyone say they saw Lavelle Macklin with Ayisha Gibert on the day that she was murdered?"

"No," Davis said, "we had a number of people that said Macklin was in the area near the apartment."

"How many is a number?"

"I can't tell you precisely," said Davis.

"Estimate for us," Darcy said with rancor in his voice.

"Objection," said Edwards, jumping to his feet.

Judge Nicolau sustained the objection.

"Tell us one name of one person who told you that Macklin was in the area of Apartment 1309 on the day that Ayisha Gibert went missing."

"Dewayne Kirksey told us that he saw Mr. Macklin exit Apartment 1309 that night and that he had blood on his clothes," Davis said.

"He told you that more than twenty-four hours after Macklin was under arrest. Isn't that true?" Darcy asked.

"Yes, that's true," Davis conceded.

"Kirksey was in custody when he told you those things, correct?" Darcy asked.

"No, he was not in custody. He was at the police station at the time, but he had volunteered to come down to the station to help us. He was free to leave at any time," Davis said.

"Did you ever tell him he was free to leave?" Darcy asked.

"I don't remember," Davis said.

"Wasn't he at the police station because he had been arrested on a drug case and had an active warrant for his arrest?" Darcy asked.

Davis was wounded. "I don't . . . I'm not . . ." he stammered.

"I'm sorry, I didn't understand your answer," Darcy said.

Davis rebounded quickly. "It was thirteen years ago. I don't remember why Kirksey was there. A uniformed officer introduced me to him as someone with information. I didn't care about any drug case or warrant he had. I was working this homicide case."

"Other than Mr. Kirksey, can you tell us the name of any other witnesses who placed Mr. Macklin near Apartment 1309 or even in the complex near the time of this incident?"

"I don't have any names handy," said Davis. "This was thirteen years ago."

"Are there names of witnesses in any of your police reports?"

"No," conceded Davis.

"Were you doing that to protect their identities?"

"I don't recall," said Davis.

"You testify that Mr. Macklin, during a friendly conversation with you, gave a full confession. Yet, he did not sign this court-reported statement until some thirteen hours after he allegedly gave you his initial confession, is that right?"

"If that's what you say," said Davis.

"No," Darcy interrupted. "That's not what I say, I'm asking you if that's accurate."

"I'm not sure," said Davis.

"Well, let's try and clear this up. May I approach, Your Honor?"

"You may," said Judge Nicolau.

Darcy walked up and handed Davis a copy of the court-reported statement taken from Lavelle Macklin some thirteen years earlier.

"Do you recognize this?" asked Darcy.

"Yes," said Davis.

"Is this the statement you took along with a court reporter and an assistant State's Attorney from Mr. Macklin some thirteen years ago?"

"It appears so," said Davis.

He then pointed out the time that the court-reported statement started and the time that it ended.

"Does that refresh your recollection as to the time the court-reported statement was taken?"

"Yes."

"And is that accurate?"

"Yes."

"And is that roughly thirteen hours from when Mr. Macklin allegedly gave you his first statement?"

"Yes."

"And during those thirteen hours was Mr. Macklin held in custody?"

"Yes," said Davis.

"And that's because after confessing he was now, in your mind, going to be charged with this murder, is that right?"

"Yes."

Darcy then showed him the arrest report.

"Yet your arrest report has the time of arrest as being after he makes the court reported statement, is that true?"

"Yes, that's just when I did the paperwork," said Davis.

"Well, when you do the paperwork do you try to be accurate as to the time certain things happen?"

"Yes."

"And so according to this you didn't place him under arrest until after you had the court-reported statement?"

"Well, that would be the formal arrest," said Davis.

"I see," said Darcy. "You testified that it took a long time for a Felony Review Assistant to respond to the Area Headquarters, is that right?"

"Yes."

"How long did it take?"

"I'm not sure. It's just my memory is that it took a long time," he said.

"Felony Review is a unit at Cook County State's Attorney's Office, is that correct?"

"Yes," said Davis.

"And that's staffed 24 hours a day, 365 days a year, is that correct?"

"Yes."

"And their sole responsibility is to respond to cases and help prepare cases for prosecution, is that right?"

"I don't know if that's their sole responsibility, but that's one of their functions," agreed Davis.

"What time did you call them?"

"I'm not sure," said Davis.

"But did you call them immediately after Mr. Macklin gave you a statement, or did you wait until shortly before he gave the court-reported statement?"

"I'm not sure what time I called them," reiterated Davis.

"You also testified it took a long time for a court reporter to respond, is that right?"

"That's right."

"Who called the court reporter?"

"I'm not sure," said Davis.

"Well, the court reporter works for the State's Attorney's Office, is that correct?"

"That's correct," agreed Davis.

"And like Felony Review they have court reporters available 24 hours a day, is that right?"

"I believe so," said Davis.

"So what you're trying to tell the judge is that in spite of this being an extremely important case you got no cooperation from the State's Attorney's Office Felony Review Unit or the court reporter. In fact, they left you hanging and waiting for them on this extremely important case, is that right?"

"Objection," said Erin Powers.

"Overruled," said the judge. "You may answer."

"I'm not sure what you asked me," said Davis.

"Basically it's what you're telling us, Officer Davis."

"That's Detective Davis," he interrupted.

"Excuse me, Detective Davis. What you're telling us is that, in spite of this being an extremely important case, you got no cooperation from the State's Attorney's Office and the Court Reporter's Office?"

"That's not true," said Davis.

Darcy was finished with Davis. He sat at counsel table and watched Detective Davis disappear through the back door.

Dewayne Kirksey rolled his wheelchair toward the witness bar and stopped next to it. The Judge immediately saw that Kirksey could not get up the two steps to the witness box.

"Sir, why don't you just put your chair in front of the witness box. Keep your voice up so we can hear you," he said as he stood leaning over the bench.

Kirksey was sworn in and began his testimony. Randy Edwards had copies of transcripts on the podium before him. He had Kirksey's prior testimony and a copy of his recently recanted testimony. After a few preliminary questions, he finally got to the point. "Did you see Lavelle Macklin exiting Apartment 1309 that night?"

Kirksey gathered his strength. "No sir, I did not."

"Sir, did you testify that you saw Mr. Macklin exit that apartment that night?"

"I did say that before," Kirksey said.

"Did you say you saw blood on his clothes at that time?"

"I did testify to that before, but I did not see that," Kirksey insisted.

Edwards picked up a transcript and scanned it, looking for a specific passage. "Did you in fact on two prior occasions testify that you saw Mr. Macklin exit Apartment 1309 with blood on this clothes?"

"Yes I did," conceded Kirksey.

Edwards had done the best he could so he sat down. Darcy shot up. "On those two prior occasions when you testified that you saw Mr. Macklin exit Apartment 1309 that night with blood on his clothes, was it true?"

In a loud, firm voice Kirksey recanted his earlier testimony. "No sir, it was not true. I never saw Mr. Macklin in person until I testified at his trial. Detective Davis showed me his photograph."

"Why did you testify to something that wasn't true?" Darcy asked.

Kirksey slumped in his chair and tears flowed from his eyes.

His voice cracking, he began. "I was afraid. When I went to the police station I knew that I was going to prison. I had never done no time before." He stopped to wipe the tears off of his face. "Detective Davis came in to see me. I was in a little room, handcuffed to a steel hook. He came in and punched me, slapped me and kicked me. He started telling me that I was going to get the death penalty for what I did to that little girl. He then beat me some more. Each time he beat me, he'd give me more information. He'd say you killed Ayisha Gibert. Ayisha was only nine years old. You raped her. You killed her in Apartment 1309." Kirksey seemed like he was getting stronger, as if telling the tale was helping him get it all behind him. "Each time he'd come back at me stronger. Beat me harder. Yelled louder. Finally I was about to confess. He had me to where I would say whatever he wanted me to say. Then he shows me a picture of him," he said, pointing to Macklin. "So Davis says, 'Is this the guy you saw coming out of 1309?' I jumped all over it."

"What happened next?" Darcy asked.

"He said, 'He had blood on his shirt, right?' So I said right, he had blood on his shirt."

Darcy let the words hang in the air. Judge Nicolau was writing notes.

"Then what happened?" Darcy asked.

"Everything changed. He put his arm around me and said, 'See, all I wanted was the truth.'"

"How were you treated from that point on?" Darcy asked.

"Better," Kirksey said. "They gave me food, let me sleep, and then Davis drove me to the courthouse. He told me that I'd have to tell the lawyers what I saw and then I'd go home. He promised that he'd take care of me."

"Did he?" asked Darcy.

The prosecutors jumped to their feet. "Objection," they said in unison.

"Overruled," the judge said as he motioned for them to sit down.

Kirksey laughed bitterly. "They dropped a weed case and packaged up two cases for three years. I went into the joint healthy and came out in a wheelchair with only one eye. Yeah, Davis took care of me."

Edwards and Powers took turns calling the rest of their witnesses, including beat officers describing the area, an assistant State's Attorney who was present for Macklin's statement and someone from the Medical Examiner's Office, who gave a full extent of the injuries and cause of death.

The prosecutors rested. Darcy made a motion for acquittal at the close of their case, which was denied. Then Darcy and Justin presented their defense. Justin called a lab technician from the Cook County Medical Examiner's Office, who testified to the collection of bodily fluids from the victim. There were stipulations to the chain of custody for those fluids. Then Darcy called a DNA expert who did the analysis of those fluids.

Dr. Paula Angotti was approximately sixty years old with a slight build and jet black hair. Although both sides agreed to her expertise, Darcy still walked them through her impressive array of degrees, training, authored articles, and various other credentials. She explained what DNA was and how it worked.

"DNA is basically a genetic fingerprint," she explained. "In this case, we were able to test the DNA material that was forwarded to us and compare it against a sample taken from the defendant, Lavelle Macklin, and we were able to conclusively determine that the DNA material that was given to us, and which we tested, came from a source other than the defendant, Lavelle Macklin."

Erin Powers didn't have much on cross for the doctor.

"Doctor, could someone rape a nine-year-old girl and not leave DNA material behind?"

"It's possible," said the doctor, "if he didn't ejaculate or secrete, perhaps if he wore a condom. There is some possibility that an individual could have sexual intercourse with a nine-year-old girl and not leave DNA material. Although it seems that we would be able to find something."

Darcy next tried to call a lawyer from Cincinnati who had worked in the Innocence Project throughout the country.

The state objected.

"He's trying to call this witness as an expert to testify about DNA being used to prove people have been wrongly convicted," said Erin Powers.

Darcy didn't put up much of a fight. He had made his point. With that, Darcy and Justin rested.

"The defense having rested," the judge began, "does the State have any rebuttal?"

Erin Powers conferred briefly with Randy Edwards and then stood.

"No, Your Honor, we would be resting at this time as well."

"Okay," said the judge, "this would be a good time for a ten-minute break, and then we'll go right into argument."

He stepped off the bench and floated down a couple of stairs and disappeared into his chambers. The sheriff led Macklin back to the lockup, and Darcy and Justin stood talking.

"Are you ready?" said Darcy.

Justin had a notepad with him.

"You letting me close?"

"That's what we agreed to," said Darcy.

"Yeah, I'll be ready."

"I'm going to take a leak," said Darcy.

"I'm going to go back and talk to our boy," said Justin.

• • •

Darcy walked back into the courtroom just as Judge Nicolau was stepping onto the bench. Nicolau looked around.

"Are we ready?"

"Yes," said Darcy as he walked over toward counsel table.

Macklin was seated next to Justin, who was writing notes. Justin shot up.

"May I have a moment, Your Honor?"

He grabbed Darcy by the arm and walked him down the aisle. They walked to the last row and then Justin pulled him in a little bit.

"I'm not going to close," said Justin.

"What are you talking about?" said Darcy.

"I'm not going to close."

"Five minutes ago you were going to close," Darcy said. "What happened?"

"I'm not going to close," said Justin. "You're going to have to close."

Darcy shook his head in disbelief.

"Fine. I'll close," Darcy said, and walked back to the counsel table.

Justin slinked behind him and sat at his chair. Randy Edwards rose to give the State's first closing argument.

"Your Honor, the evidence is quite clear. Lavelle Macklin gave a statement to the police that contained details that only the killer would know. You heard from the defense DNA expert that an individual could have raped Ayisha Gibert and not left DNA material. This entire DNA issue is a red herring in this case because Lavelle Macklin raped that little girl, or stood by while someone else raped her, and he was the one who killed her. As he said in his statement, he beat her, he raped her, he strangled her and finally he killed Ayisha Gibert. Don't let the defense throw you off of that. You see, Your Honor, they want to you look at everything except the facts that we do have. They point to what we don't have. We don't have the individual identified whose DNA material is left there. We do have Mr. Macklin with the opportunity and the confession that he killed Ayisha Gibert. Your Honor, it's time for justice—and I'm talking about justice for Ayisha Gibert."

He walked toward the defense counsel table and pointed at Macklin.

"Mr. Macklin killed Ayisha Gibert. We want you now to continue to hold him responsible. Hear Ayisha's voice screaming for justice and find Lavelle Macklin guilty, once again, for the murder he committed."

Darcy shot a glance over to Justin. Justin's teeth were clenched and he was doodling on a notepad, drawing little boxes over and over again. His legal pad blackened under the ink of boxes on top of each other.

"Your Honor, how dare Mr. Edwards talk about justice? How dare he point to Lavelle Macklin and today tell you someone else raped Ayisha Gibert, but that Macklin should be held responsible? For thirteen years, the government's position was that Lavelle Macklin kidnapped, tortured, raped, beat, and strangled this girl, and it wasn't until the DNA test came back that they're saying that perhaps there was someone else.

"Doesn't 'perhaps' mean reasonable doubt? How can they tell you that you are to take a leap of faith and rely on a confession that is based on a lie? We now have scientific evidence that tells you that it is absolutely not true that Lavelle Macklin raped this girl.

"And they wanted to solve this case. Detective Davis is disingenuous when he tells you that he had trouble getting people like the State's Attorney and the court reporter there on time. He needed that time to work on Mr. Macklin to get the confession through the court reporter. The reason that the confession came out as it did is because that's what Davis believed happened. Davis was wrong, and now Davis is stuck with the confession that he created.

"What about Dewayne Kirksey? He told you all about

Detective Davis and his methods. He was credible. Detective Davis destroyed Dewayne Kirksey's life to nail Lavelle Macklin. He coerced a false statement from Mr. Kirksey.

"Somebody else raped this little girl, and whoever raped her, killed her. Perhaps Ayisha Gibert does cry from beyond for justice. But justice is not convicting the wrong man. Justice is forcing the police to find a DNA match and find the person who tortured and killed this little girl. The last face Ayisha Gibert saw on this earth was that of her killer. Bring that face to justice, Your Honor. The first step is to do the right thing here by acquitting Lavelle Macklin. Tell Detective Tommy Davis and his cohorts at the Chicago Police Department to get out there, get the right man, and bring him in here. Then Ayisha Gibert can rest in peace."

Darcy sat down, stealing a glance at Justin. Justin stared at his notepad.

Erin Powers rose to give the State's rebuttal closing argument. She stood looking at Lavelle Macklin. Staring at him. Quietly she began. Strolling toward the judge in the well of the courtroom.

"Your Honor, Lavelle Macklin confessed to this crime. He wasn't beaten. He wasn't coerced. He confessed. But Lavelle Macklin is a bit of a soft-shoe artist. Dancing around. Told some of the truth, maybe not all of the truth. We don't know who was with Lavelle Macklin when he killed this girl. Lavelle Macklin did admit to killing her. He had the opportunity. He was in the area, and you know Judge, innocent men don't confess to crimes in such detail on specific levels unless they were there.

"Mr. Cole talks about the right thing to do. There is only one right thing to do, and that's hold Lavelle Macklin responsible. Don't let him dance away from this, Judge. Don't let him play the victim of the system, because he's not. The police knew him because he was an active criminal. He was in the area and when confronted he confessed. You know, the interesting thing is, when we get a confession they point out what's missing, but if Mr. Cole thinks that Detective Davis set up Lavelle Macklin and created this whole-cloth, that he conspired with others to put this case on Lavelle Macklin, wouldn't Detective Davis have done a better job? Wouldn't he have made the confession flawless so that Mr. Cole would be saying 'isn't it a little bit too good?' You see, Judge, Mr. Cole wants to sit back with thirteen years' hindsight and take pot shots at a hardworking, honest detective and say look, Judge, he did this wrong and did that wrong.

"But do you know what Detective Davis did, Judge? He followed the evidence. It led him to Lavelle Macklin. He interviewed Lavelle Macklin. He didn't beat him, he didn't threaten him, he didn't trick him, he just questioned him, and Lavelle Macklin told him 'I killed her,' and Judge, let's not let that go lightly. Lavelle Macklin admitted he killed Ayisha Gibert. There's no conspiracy here, there's no frame-up, there's only one uncontroverted truth, and that is Ayisha Gibert was killed, Lavelle Macklin killed her, and we know he did because he told us exactly how he did it and the way that he said he killed her matches with the way she died. How do we know he killed her? Because when he gave his confession, the medical examiner had not completed the autopsy. So Detective Davis couldn't have fed those facts to Mr. Macklin. Mr. Macklin knew because Mr. Macklin is guilty."

She walked toward counsel table and pointed with two fingers toward Macklin.

"Your Honor, find Lavelle Macklin guilty."

She made her way over to her seat and sat. She looked straight ahead at the judge. He was reading his trial book and then closed it, gathered up some notes, and stood up.

"There'll be a brief recess. I'd like to review a few notes."

He then stepped out.

25

COLLATA WAS SMOKING A CIGARETTE in the hallway when Darcy and Justin stepped out. Darcy grabbed Justin by the arm and walked him to the stairwell, pushed through the doors and stood on the landing. Pam Mazur tried to follow, but Collata stood in the doorway blocking her access. She turned and walked back toward the courtroom looking for someone else to talk to.

"Okay, what the fuck?" said Darcy.

Justin was shaking.

"I couldn't do it."

"What do you mean you couldn't do it?" said Darcy.

"I couldn't do it," he said. "You know what that sonofabitch said to me?"

"Who?" said Darcy.

"Our client, Lavelle Macklin."

"What are you talking about?" said Darcy.

"When you went to take a leak, I went back to talk to him. Do you know what he said to me?"

"No idea," said Darcy.

"He started laughing. He told me that he snatched up Ayisha and took her to 1309. Apparently, his cousin Marvin Gillum was waiting in 1309 and they took turns with the girl, but he was worried about getting the clap from his cousin Marvin, so he used a condom."

"Jesus," said Darcy.

"Yeah. He was laughing. That piece of shit. Apparently, his cousin got whacked a few years after that so he never had to pay for it either and now this shit-for-brains is going to walk. I never ask these assholes," said Justin. "Never ask them if they did it. Don't want to know, and this sonofabitch tells me. That's why I couldn't get up there and argue for him, Darcy. Hope you understand."

Darcy put his hand on Justin's shoulder.

"Look Justin, I don't have any great words of wisdom for you here. I understand what you did, but you can't ever do it again. You're a lawyer. It's about evidence. You argue the evidence. This isn't about the truth. This is advocacy. You're fighting for your client and you can't choose to fight for him harder or lay off depending on what he tells you. Innocent guys get convicted in this building, guilty guys walk free. It's not perfect. In fact, a lot of times there seems to be no justice to it at all, but you have to do the best you can, and sometimes it sucks, like today."

Collata pushed open the door.

"The judge is ready."

"Do you want to come in for this?" Darcy asked.

"Do I have a choice?"

"Not really."

Darcy put his hand behind Justin's back and pushed him through the door.

"Come on, we'll get through this."

Judge Nicolau opened his trial book and spread out his notes. He had a glass of water to his right and he was using his pen to mark off a few last notes. Pam Mazur and three other reporters had the visitor's gallery all to themselves.

"This is a troubling case," began the judge. "A horrific crime committed on an innocent victim. There's nothing that I can say or do which will minimize the unspeakable horror around this case. This girl died as no young child should ever, at the hands of a heartless, subhuman predator.

"The defendant waived a jury trial and placed this case to be heard before this court. Thus, this court has to make the findings of fact and the rulings of law and return a verdict. The court is now prepared to do so.

"This case boils down to a confession. A confession given by the defendant over a period of thirteen to fourteen hours in police custody, perhaps more, it's not quite clear. In any event, the confession that he gives says that he himself raped and killed this child. The confession, as the State wants me to believe, has details that only the killer would know. Yet, the State also wants me to believe that the glaring omissions and/or diversions from what actually happened should be *de minimus*. The fact is, they asked me to pick and choose which elements of the confession to believe.

"How do I reconcile the idea that he committed the crime alone with the fact that none of his DNA is found here? In fact, DNA from an unidentified man was found in various areas, including the victim's vaginal vault as well as other places on her body, her clothing, and in the apartment. This lies in direct contradiction to the statement given to the police by the defendant— assuming you believe Detective Davis that this statement was voluntary.

"The testimony of Dewayne Kirksey was devastating. The law requires me to be skeptical of witnesses who recant their testimony over time. I'm well aware of a number of cases where witnesses have recanted their testimony, and DNA results then corroborate the witnesses who recanted. Mr. Kirksey is a compelling witness who tells two different stories at two different times. I can't, as a matter of law, pick and choose parts of a witness's testimony, or parts of a statement, to believe or disbelieve. There were motions to suppress the statement that were litigated and denied. Thus, Mr. Kirksey's statement is admissible. The question is: What weight do I give this statement, how much credibility is vested in this statement? When compared with DNA, that question is something that becomes more difficult to answer.

"I don't know if Lavelle Macklin raped and killed this child. I don't know if Lavelle Macklin was with someone who raped and killed this child. I don't know if someone else raped and killed this child. I presided over the first trial, and the evidence at that time was quite different. However, science has advanced, even grown exponentially. No one knew that DNA would be a tool that not only helps convict the guilty, but also helps clear the innocent.

"I'm afraid I will never know whether this is a crime that Mr. Macklin did not commit and should therefore be cleared of, or whether Mr. Macklin is catching a break because the DNA— coupled with Mr. Kirksey's recanted testimony—raised more than a reasonable doubt as to Mr. Macklin's guilt. I feel, based on the facts in front of me, based on the law, and based on the evidence, that the State has failed to meet its burden of proof to sustain the charges against Mr. Macklin. Therefore, this court will enter a finding of not guilty as to all charges and Mr. Macklin is hereby discharged."

Macklin shot two fists into the air and leaned back with a big smile. Justin stared straight down at the notepad, which was now blackened by little squares. Darcy began packing his things into his briefcase. He shot a glance over at the State, who sat dejected, staring straight ahead. The judge walked off the bench and disappeared into chambers. Macklin was led back to the lockup by the sheriff to prepare to be brought over to the jail and, hours later, to be discharged, to walk out a free man. Collata walked to counsel table and began helping Darcy gather his things. Darcy put both his hands onto counsel table and leaned over toward Justin.

"Tell you what, give me your car keys. I'll get you drunk and I'll have Collata drive you home."

Justin said nothing. He reached into his pocket. He rummaged around and flipped his keys onto the table.

"That-a-boy," said Darcy.

26

Darcy and Justin walked past Pam Mazur, ignoring her questions, and got in the elevator. They left the building followed by Collata, who was rolling a couple of boxes of files on a luggage cart. Darcy, Justin, and Collata rolled the boxes down the wheelchair ramp in front of the courthouse and across the street to the van in the garage. Collata dropped Darcy and Justin at a small hotel off Rush Street and went to park the van. They walked into a dimly lit bar with a piano player on the far end. He was playing a sad song.

"What will you have, Justin?"

"A beer," he said.

"Come on, it'll take you all night that way."

"Fuck it," Justin said. "Double Jack Daniels rocks with a Rolling Rock chaser."

The waitress appeared and Darcy gave her Justin's order and followed with a double Maker's Mark rocks for himself and a Maker's Mark neat with an ice water chaser for Collata. The waitress was depositing the drinks as Collata walked up and took his seat. He pulled his glass of Maker's Mark up.

"Congratulations. It was a nice win, boys."

Darcy reached out to Collata's forearm to stop the toast.

"We're not toasting this one," he said.

Collata took a quick swig.

"Oh yeah, why's that?"

"Seems our boy is guilty as sin," said Darcy. "He and his cousin did the girl. Only he wore a rubber."

"Jesus, Darcy," said Collata. "No one calls them rubbers anymore."

"What's the difference?" Justin asked. "Didn't you hear what he said? Who gives a shit—rubber, condom, what's the difference? He did it and we walked him."

"Listen," said Darcy. "I had a kid who I was representing on a murder. A bunch of gangbangers drive through a neighborhood, yell gang signs and empty a gun, a guy ends up dying. The only witnesses were gangbangers. They tell the police that my guy, Arturo Sanchez, was the shooter. The police swing by Arturo Sanchez's house and force their way in. They grab him and place him under arrest. Never found the gun. Three gangbangers get up there and say 'yeah, he's the one who did it.' Lying assholes, piece-of-shit gangbangers, but the jury bought it and convicted him. The judge gave him fifty. I did the appeal. The appellate court said hey, the jury made its call. You lose. But I knew the kid was clean. Honest, good kid, never got into trouble. A few years later, two of the witnesses give us recants. Tell us that the third guy told them to put it on Arturo because he wouldn't join the gang. The third guy gets whacked, and they came forward. We're all excited. We call the family. Turns out our guy died in prison. Things don't even up," Darcy finished. "Bad things happen. Sometimes you win when you should lose, sometimes it's the other way around. You can't go to pieces on it."

"Let me tell you something, Darcy," said Justin. "Someday this piece-of-shit Macklin is going to kill another little girl, and do you know who's going to be an accessory to that? Me. The girl that he rapes and kills is going to be my fault."

Darcy knew how he felt. "Look Justin, I know how you feel. We fought for our client and he won. He should be rotting in jail. Detective Davis had the right guy, but he took shortcuts. Innocent guys get convicted. Guilty guys go free. It's an imperfect system, but we have a role to play. If everybody does their job to the best of their ability, maybe there will be fewer mistakes made."

"Nice speech, but I'm not buying. We helped him get away with murder because we're smart, experienced lawyers. I want to puke."

"If you want to take on the sins of the world, then go ahead," said Darcy. "You'll end up being an alcoholic, sticking a gun in your mouth one day, and blowing your own head off."

Justin made a point of looking at all the drinks on the table.

"So what's missing, the gun?"

"Listen kid," said Collata. "I've been doing this a long time. It's going to hurt for a while, but you got to grab the next file and keep going. It's kind of like when you lost big cases in the State's Attorney's Office, right? What did they tell you? Grab the next file, try the next case."

"This is different," he said.

"How?" asked Darcy. "Because you need to recover from winning?"

Justin thought about it. He couldn't come up with an answer right away.

"I don't know. It's really getting to me this time."

He drank the Jack Daniels in one powerful gulp and then

chased it with the Rolling Rock to kill the fire. He then set the beer down.

"Fuck Pam Mazur, fuck DNA, fuck the system, tonight we howl at the moon," said Darcy. "Tomorrow, let's get back to work."

He flagged the waitress down and gave her a circular motion to order another round.

27

Darcy went down to Seymour's office a little early. He had a lot on his mind. He found Seymour alone. He gestured to the secretary's desk.

"Vacation," Seymour said.

Seymour walked over to the chessboard and sat behind white.

"So," he said.

"What do you want to drink?" Darcy asked.

"What are you having?"

"Ice water."

"Ice water," Seymour repeated. "A little dehydrated?"

"Long night."

"Yeah, what happened?"

"We won a trial."

"Ah, celebrating."

"No," said Darcy. "Actually drinking away our sorrows."

"Sorrows that you won?" asked Seymour.

"Apparently, our guy is guilty. Although the judge saw it otherwise."

"Brilliant lawyering," said Seymour.

Darcy filled up an empty coffee mug with water from the water cooler. He paused to read the mug—Art Institute of Chicago.

"How about you? You want something, old man?"

"No, I'm good," he said, waving him off, and they began to play.

"So what happened?"

"Police screwed up the confession. DNA came back inconsistent. The guy walked," said Darcy.

"Better to be lucky than good," said Seymour.

"Yeah, this kid that was trying the case with me took it real hard."

"Who's that?" said Seymour.

"Justin Schachter."

"Don't know him," said Seymour. "Good kid?"

"I like him. I'm impressed with him," said Darcy.

"How's the lovely doctor?"

"Ah," said Darcy, "bad news on that front."

"No, you blew it already?" asked Seymour.

"Not quite. She's turning fifty."

"And?" said Seymour.

"And to celebrate, she's going to leave the country for a while."

"Extended vacation?"

"No," said Darcy, "Doctors Without Borders or some other group. She's going to go to some poor country with huge problems and work with a bunch of doctor do-gooders."

"Ah, the heart and soul is the beauty of this woman," said Seymour.

"Who said that?" Darcy asked.

"I did," said Seymour.

"It sounded poetic," said Darcy.

"So what are you going to do about this?" Seymour asked.

"I don't know," said Darcy, "but I realize that I am a huge coward. She wants me to join her when she goes. I'm scared of losing her, and yet I'm scared of my relationship with her."

"Maybe it's one and the same," suggested Seymour, "perhaps because you're scared of losing her, you're frightened that as the relationship goes on you might do something to screw it up and lose her."

"When Ann Landers died did the *Tribune* ask you to take over her column?" Darcy asked.

"No, must have been an oversight," said Seymour.

"Kathy Haddon is leaving the firm."

"Where is she going?" Seymour asked.

"She's going into practice with a couple of her friends. Three women, girl power—they're going to try med mal and personal injury plaintiffs' cases. She's fed up with criminal law."

"How do you feel about that?"

"I'm going to miss her," he said. "She's a very important person in my life. For the longest time, she was the only woman in my life besides Irma."

"Did you tell her that?"

"No," said Darcy.

"What did you say to Amy about going with her?"

"Nothing yet. I'm not sure what to say."

"And thus you feel like a coward."

"That's right," said Darcy. "I feel like a coward."

"Well it seems to me," said Seymour, "that you're still hiding your feelings, and then you assume all the problems of these other people. That way you get to avoid facing your own feelings."

"It took me a while to figure this out, but I hide my feelings because I'm afraid of love. I mean a fearlessness that comes from passion, reckless abandon, and trust, and I have to figure out a way to let myself go and put my trust in Amy."

"And boychik, here's the million-dollar question," said Seymour. "What if you're hurt?"

Darcy took a drink of water and leaned back.

"If I am hurt," he began, and then it trailed off. He thought about it some more. "I suppose if I'm hurt, I'm hurt and I feel it then, but I realize that I am never going to get beyond where I am now without taking a chance. A huge chance maybe, but I have to take that chance. I think that the only way for me to get there is to get there with Amy. I have to figure out a way to let her know that."

"Funny isn't it," said Seymour. "You get paid a lot of money to communicate, to express yourself, to talk and plead peoples' cases, and here you are seemingly unable to plead your own."

Darcy finished his water.

"It's a bitch, isn't it?"

28

JUSTIN TOOK THE SEAT ACROSS from Darcy's desk. Darcy looked at him over his reading glasses.

"So how are you?" he asked.

"I'm okay," Justin said intensely.

"So," Darcy said, putting his hands together. "Are you going to be able to represent Brian Kern?"

"Absolutely," Justin said. "Do you have any doubts?"

Darcy rocked back in his chair and swiveled so he could look out over the lake. He gathered his thoughts.

"Lavelle Macklin told you that he was guilty and you fell apart," Darcy began, "and Brian Kern told you that he is guilty and wants to die, and you're okay with that—why is that?" Darcy asked.

The question threw Justin off balance.

"I'm not sure," he said, "but I am."

Darcy turned back around and cracked open the humidor and pulled out a cigar. He offered one to Justin, but Justin declined. Darcy cut the tip and rolled the cigar around in his mouth before using a lighter to blaze it up.

"I need you with me a hundred percent," he said through the smoke. "Are you going to be able to do that?"

Justin stood and began to pace. He put his hands on the back of his chair and leaned toward Darcy.

"One hundred percent," he said. "I'll be there."

Darcy took a couple of puffs on the cigar and blew smoke up into the air.

"Good, I need you," he said.

Justin was still frustrated.

"Let me ask you something, Darcy. How is it that you don't lose sleep over a scumbag like Lavelle Macklin?"

Darcy rolled the cigar between his finger and thumb.

"I hate the thought that a jagoff like Macklin is out. Given the chance, he'll kill somebody else."

Justin exploded. "Then how can you live with yourself? I hate myself and I know I'm going to hell."

"Lavelle Macklin," Darcy said, "is going to find justice. Maybe it's not going to be justice in a courtroom at Twenty-sixth and California, but justice will come to Lavelle Macklin."

"He walked away from a murder. One of the most horrific murders I have ever seen," said Justin. "Where's the justice in that?"

"You have to stop thinking like a prosecutor," Darcy said. "Justice doesn't only come measured by lawyers and judges at a courthouse. There are other forms of justice."

"What? Like when he meets his maker?" said Justin sarcastically.

"No," said Darcy. "Sit down."

Justin took his seat.

"Let me explain something to you," Darcy said. "Do you wonder why Ayisha Gibert can be murdered in the most heinous and brutal fashion and no family members were there? Did you see any family members there at all after her mother testified? The courtroom was empty, wasn't it?"

"Yeah," said Justin. "So, she's from a dysfunctional family. Her mom is a single mother. No one else there. That's no big surprise."

Darcy took a deep tug on the cigar and blew the smoke up, watching it trail away from him.

"Let me ask you this," said Darcy, "when you were in the State's Attorney's Office, did you ever work gang crimes?"

"No, mostly just courtrooms, but friends of mine were in gang crimes."

"Okay, you understand that the gangs have certain rules, right?"

"Yes," agreed Justin.

"You know that the Black Gangster Disciples and all the other gangs that make up the Black Gangster Disciple Nation report to the Supreme Leader, who is in the Illinois Department of Corrections, right?"

"Yes," agreed Justin.

"And then you know that underneath the Supreme Leader, the guys on the street that make the day-to-day decisions are the Board of Governors, right?"

"Yes," said Justin.

"Did you ever hear of a guy named Keydell Flowers?" Darcy asked.

"Nah, I don't think so," said Justin.

"Keydell is one of the Board of Governors, heavy guy, o.g.," Darcy continued, "and I don't mean o.g. like in the movies, some punk ass, rap singer, gangbanging wannabe. I mean original gangster for real."

"Yeah," said Justin.

"Anyway, do you know who Keydell Flowers's sister is?"

"Not a clue," said Justin, getting interested.

"Tamika Kimmons," said Darcy blowing more smoke out. "Ayisha Gibert's mother, Tamika Kimmons, is the younger sister of Keydell Flowers."

Darcy took another tug on the cigar and flicked some ash into the ashtray on his desk. He continued.

"Lavelle Macklin was a Black Gangster Disciple. So let me ask you this, how do think Keydell Flowers is going to feel about Lavelle Macklin being on the street? Do you think he's going to put him back to work? Think he's going to introduce himself and say I understand that you savagely raped and murdered my niece, but don't worry because there wasn't enough evidence to prove you guilty beyond a reasonable doubt. I'm going to acknowledge the finding by the court and give it full faith and credit, like Canada and the United States in a treaty. Please!" said Darcy.

"So Keydell Flowers and his boys do some vigilante job on Lavelle Macklin and you call that justice?" asked Justin.

Darcy crushed out his cigar.

"I like it better than having Macklin running free where he can grab a victim anytime he's in the mood to rape and kill."

Justin looked defeated, shot up and began to pace.

"Look, Justin, I know you want to run over and tell Joe Nicolau the truth behind this case and I'm telling you, don't do it."

"Why? He should know," said Justin.

"No, he shouldn't," said Darcy in an angry voice. "Listen to me. Joe Nicolau has spent his whole life trying to do the right thing. Joe Nicolau appointed me to this case because it was killing him. He thought that he had put an innocent man on death row. Do you understand that? Do you have any idea what that must mean to Joe Nicolau? All those years being a judge—trying to do the right thing, trying to protect society, while balancing constitutional rights for individuals. Think about it. The guy could have made a fortune being a trial lawyer. He could have done what we do, or he could have done personal injury or civil litigation and made a lot of money. He loves his job. He loves being a judge. He has had a distinguished career. Then this came up. He dragged me into this case because he needed to know that the right thing was done.

"And the right thing was done. He knew Macklin might be guilty, but he found reasonable doubt. He made his ruling according to the law. The administration of justice meant letting Macklin go. Now what? You're going to tell him that he has acquitted a guilty man? Bullshit. He did the right thing. You let him ride off into the sunset. When he retires and he's in Florida at the racetrack with his buddies, and they're talking to him about being a judge, he can let his chest swell up with pride at the brilliant career that he had. He deserves it.

"Besides, I don't think I need to point this out, Macklin told you that during the attorney-client relationship. It's privileged. So you go shooting your mouth off and you violate that privilege. You might as well hand in your ticket now."

"Maybe I *should* hand in my ticket. No wonder Kathy wants to get out of criminal law," Justin said, as he slid back into a chair. Darcy let a small smile creep across his face.

"Let me ask you this: you still haven't said why is it that you could fight like hell for Brian Kern, but Lavelle Macklin's walking is bothering you."

"Do you have some answer for me?" said Justin.

"Try this out," said Darcy. "You're okay with Brian Kern telling you that he did this horrible act, raping and killing an innocent girl. You're okay with his telling you he wants to die. You'll fight like hell for him. But Lavelle Macklin, he got over on you. You believed he was innocent and then when he pulled the rug out from under you, you were pissed."

Justin said nothing, thinking about it. Finally, he stood up again and began pacing. "I got a lot to learn," he said.

"Yeah, but you've got a good foundation," said Darcy. "Now can I change the subject? I have a question to ask you."

"What's that?" said Justin.

"How did you get the nickname Shitty?"

Justin walked over to the window put his forehead against the glass and looked down toward the street below.

"I was the first chair in Judge Nicolau's courtroom," he began. "My second chair was one of these lifetime prosecutors trying to do the least amount of work possible. Take as much time off as possible, grab a check and work toward a pension. You know, a guy who is hiding from life. My third chair was a nasty alcoholic bitch. Couldn't trust her to do anything. A simple drug case or auto theft case would have her gone all day preparing for it. You know, one of those cases where you put the cop on and say were you on duty on this day, at this time and location? What did you see and what happened next? That takes her all day to work up. She was pretty much useless and couldn't show up on Mondays because she had a snout-full on the weekends. Also in the courtroom was this Public Defender, a woman that I came up with through the system. We got along pretty well. She's a good person, worked hard for her clients. You know, she's one of these—I don't know, for lack of a better term, hippie-type broads.

"So this case comes into our courtroom. No big deal, a robbery, except the victim is the niece of an alderman. So the State's Attorney sends the First Assistant down to see me. He says you got to win this case. So I meet with the victim and her witness. They are both total flakes, but the paper on the case is good. The reports look real solid, and the coppers do grab the guy with some proceeds. He's got one prior hit, but my witnesses aren't all that hot, and I'm a little apprehensive. So we set it down for trial while the hippie Public Defender is gone for three days at a seminar. During those three days, her nitwit partner, who doesn't give a damn, sets seven other cases for trial on the same day as the alderman's niece's case.

"So the day comes around and the hippie P.D. is panicked. She's got eight cases set for trial. I answer ready on every one of them. I have got witnesses coming out of my ears. So I pull her aside and said, 'Look, I'll give some offers on these cases and we'll do them in order.' The first one is the alderman's niece's case. The P.D. has no idea the victim is the niece of an alderman. Anyway, I offer five. The guy has a prior probation for a robbery and five is a pretty good disposition. So she talks the guy into taking it, then we get rid of all the other cases. It wasn't a big deal, but she was pretty stressed out. So I forget about it.

"We're at the courtroom Christmas party, and the third chair is three sheets to the wind, and she's a bitter, angry drunk. You know, her hips are getting a little big, she's in her forties, and her husband ran off. She's got no kids, all she's got is this job, which she hates and she's not where she wants to be in life. So she gets wasted and she starts talking smack. She pulls the hippie P.D. aside and starts teasing her, saying I scammed her. She tells the story of the case, but she's so fucking loud that pretty soon everybody at the party is listening to it, and the Public Defender is furious. She walks up to me and she's acting like I betrayed her. Like I built up years of trust with her just to betray her on this one case. I didn't do anything wrong. I just put some pressure on her. She looks at me and starts pointing her finger at me, but no words come out. Finally, she just looks at me and she goes, 'You, you, you, you are shitty!' and walks away. That was it. Everyone started calling me Shitty."

"Does it bother you?" Darcy asked.

"The story or being called Shitty?"

"Being called Shitty."

"Nah, that doesn't bother me if people are being friendly.

Except I'll be damned if I'm going to let Pam Mazur call me by my nickname. Fuck her."

Darcy chuckled.

"So tell me about your life. I don't know much about you outside of work."

"What do you want to know?" said Justin. "I'm married, two kids, two girls, Emily and Grace."

"Grace?" said Darcy. "That was my wife's name."

"Oh yeah?" said Justin. "You still married?"

"Nah, we divorced and then she passed away."

"I'm sorry," said Justin.

"Yeah, me too," said Darcy. "So tell me, what's your wife's name?"

"My wife's name is Challen Dwyer."

Darcy smiled.

"Don't you love Chicago? Nice Jewish boy, Justin Schachter, marrying a nice Irish Catholic girl."

"She went to Mother McCauley," added Justin.

"Where else would a nice Irish Catholic south side girl go?" said Darcy. "Let me guess, her dad's a cop?"

"Accountant."

"A big family?" Darcy asked.

"Huge family."

"How long have you been married?"

"Twelve years."

"How old are your kids?"

"Emily is ten and Grace is seven."

"So is Challen a stay-at-home mom?"

"No, she does corporate communications for Sara Lee. You know, cheesecake. Enough about me, what about you?"

"Divorced, one kid, she's an adult. She's great. I'm also seeing a wonderful woman. Other than that, I do my job. I drink a lot and I go home and look out the window."

Darcy paused, then fell silent. Justin changed the subject.

"So what do you think about Brian Kern getting the needle?"

"Oh, we're talking seriously," said Darcy. "Brian Kern is not going to get the needle as long as I'm representing him."

"So is that the company line or are you one of those guys who's morally opposed to the death penalty?"

"I am ambivalent about the death penalty," Darcy said. "There are certain crimes where the death penalty seems appropriate. The trouble is we have made such an awful mess of it. I mean in the larger counties they are more experienced in handling homicide cases. Some of the smaller counties, they think any homicide is a death penalty case. Then, in Cook County you could get the same facts with five different defendants and they choose to go forward on death on one of them. I don't know, it's a real strange thing," said Darcy. "But I know this, even if Brian Kern did everything that he said he did, even if he's completely guilty of this, even though he's a malignant human being, I'm going to save his life, and you know what, you're going to help me."

Darcy glanced at his watch.

"Well, come on. It's time for the office meeting."

He picked a notepad off his desk and led Justin down the hall to the conference room. Justin shook hands with Patrick and Collata and then took a seat at the table. Darcy had walked toward the door to pull it shut when Eddie Jozwiak came screaming toward them with Irma right behind him.

"Darcy, my man," said Eddie before he enveloped Darcy in a big bear hug slapping his back. He released Darcy, walked over and pulled Patrick up from a handshake into an embrace.

"Patrick, you saved my life, buddy."

As he was hugging Patrick he looked toward Collata, who had his boots on the table.

"Hey, Mr. Happy, good to see you again."

Collata pulled a cigarette from behind his ear and popped it into his mouth.

"Hey Eddie, good to see you."

Patrick pushed back from Eddie and introduced him to Justin. They shook hands.

"Did you catch a case?" Eddie said to Justin, mistaking him for a client.

"He's a lawyer," Patrick interjected, "and he's working with us on a case."

"These guys are great," said Eddie. "They won my case for me. Hey, listen, I was in the neighborhood doing a job and I thought I'd stop by and see if you guys wanted any tickets?"

He pulled out a stack of Blackhawks tickets, seventy-five dollars a piece. He had two dozen.

"I've got some good ones for tonight if anyone wants them."

Darcy declined, but Patrick was clearly interested.

"What do you say Justin, do you want to go?"

"Yeah, I'll go," said Justin.

"How about you, Collata? Do you want to go?"

"Nah, I'm tied up," he said.

Eddie thumbed through the tickets, found the two best he had and gave them to Patrick.

"Enjoy the game, guys. Here, hold on."

He opened up his jacket and unzipped an inner pocket. He fumbled for something and pulled out a parking pass.

"This is the parking lot right next to the gate. You're going to walk by the Michael Jordan statue right into the game. The best parking you could get. I'm talking rock star parking."

He handed the pass to Patrick.

"Enjoy the game, my man. I gotta fly. I'm triple-parked out there."

Darcy shut the door after him and they began the meeting.

29

THE BILLY GOAT TAVERN ON West Madison wasn't the original, but the food was just as good and it was far more convenient to the game than Lower Michigan Avenue. After a couple of double cheeseburgers and a few beers, Patrick and Justin headed to the stadium. Justin pulled into the parking lot, and, as promised, they walked right by the Michael Jordan statue into the stadium.

"Nice parking pass," said Justin. "What's that all about?"

"Eddie caught a case for syndicated gambling. We beat it for him. He's a very friendly guy."

"Oh yeah? What's he doing when he's not gambling?" Justin asked.

"He works for Streets and Sanitation."

Justin laughed. "So the cliché is true? If you need a bookie in Chicago, find a Streets and San truck?"

"Listen," said Patrick to Justin. "There's something I want you to know, because I don't want it to create a problem between us, and I guess if it does, let me know now."

"Yeah, what's that?" said Justin.

"Well, I'm gay," said Patrick. "And I don't usually come out and tell people like that, but you know, we're at the game and I don't want to run into anybody and have something said or whatever. You should know now."

"I don't care," said Justin. "Besides, I pretty much figured it out already."

"Oh, yeah?"

"Yeah, my best friend in law school was gay. He told me all about you guys. Twinks, jocks, daddies, queens, bears—I'm guessing you're a bear," said Justin.

Patrick laughed. "I'm a bear. Big hairy guys like me are bears. I used to try to be a jock, but I'm five hundred beef sandwiches past that." They watched the game for a few minutes before Justin leaned into Patrick.

"Listen," Justin said, "since we're talking, I kind of had a meltdown in that trial with Darcy."

"Darcy didn't say anything, but I could tell something happened."

"I was supposed to do the close on a bench trial and the client told me something that made me not want to do it. I couldn't handle it. So I told Darcy I wasn't going to do it, and he had to do the close even though I was the one who had prepared it."

"Big deal," said Patrick. "I'm pretty sure Darcy represented Cain when he killed his brother Abel. That's how long Darcy's been doing this. Darcy loves this stuff. He is very understanding. Darcy's got a second-chance rule. He's never told me but I know it's true. I'm sure Darcy doesn't care if you melted down in this case—as long as you never do it again. You know, he doesn't expect you to be perfect, but he does expect that you would go to war with him and that he never has to worry about his back because you got it. So make sure you cover his back from now on. You know, Darcy saved my ass," said Patrick.

"How'd he do that?" Justin asked.

"I was with the U.S. Attorney's Office. Somebody outed me. I was young, I was sure I was gay, but I wasn't at all sure about how to be gay and live in Chicago and be a professional. I was pretty confused and vulnerable when somebody outed me. It pretty much put a brick on my career. I wasn't going to get promoted again. I was floundering professionally. Darcy and I had tried a case together. I didn't know who told him, but one day I'm in my office and he called me and said 'Hey kid, meet me for lunch at the Union League Club. I want to talk to you.' He offered me a job and I took it. I walked back after lunch, walked into the U.S. Attorney's Office and tendered my resignation to his empty desk. Then I gave a copy of my resignation to the First Assistant and said 'thanks for everything, I'm out of here.' Darcy's been there for me ever since through thick and thin, personally and professionally. I was in a very close relationship and my partner was murdered. Darcy got me through that too. He told me not to worry about work—that they would cover everything and just take as much time as I wanted. He even offered to buy me a ticket to go to Europe and just hang out, drink wine, and soak up the sun. If he's on your side, there's no one better."

Patrick ordered a couple of beers and Justin rushed to pay for them before Patrick could.

"Listen," Patrick said. "Did you know Kathy's leaving the firm? You'd probably be a really good fit here. I don't know what Darcy's thinking but we're going to need somebody. Think about it."

Justin pocketed the change and took a sip of his beer.

"I will," he said. "Definitely."

30

DARCY SET THE COFFEE MUG down. His empty oatmeal bowl was in front of him, a pile of newspapers on the chair next to him. He glanced out over the empty swimming pool. It was here at the club that Darcy was able to think best; alone, without phones ringing or people interrupting him. Kathy was leaving him. Over the years, he had come to rely on her, not just professionally but emotionally as well. He could not quarrel with her reasons for leaving. Professionally, he thought it was a good move, but it left him vulnerable. He could find another lawyer to do her work. Good lawyers are a dime a dozen, but he would find no one who could replace her in his heart. He needed her. He had relied on her all those years.

If that wasn't bad enough, Amy Wagner was leaving him also. He understood. She was reaching a milestone in her life and she wanted to do something that would feed her soul. That left him feeling selfish because he was upset that she was leaving. Intellectually, he knew that she would be back and that this was a hiatus in their relationship, but somehow he felt like he was being abandoned. He didn't know what to do about that.

Amy had brought out feelings in him that he did not believe he was capable of. In a courtroom Darcy knew what to do. He could identify a problem and create a plan of attack. Sometimes it worked and sometimes it didn't. Sometimes he won and sometimes he lost, but at least he knew what to do. He could be proactive. He could be in charge of the situation. It was outside the courtroom that Darcy felt he failed miserably. There was nothing that he could think of to do to be proactive. He was at the mercy of Amy and her desire to do something meaningful. He got a bit more depressed when he thought that being with him was not meaningful to her. He then chided himself for wallowing in self-pity. Of course he was meaningful to her. She just wanted to do something professionally to contribute and inject significance and purpose into her life. He knew that if she did that she would be happier and their relationship would be better. So, he was stuck again with trying to figure out what to do.

He heard somebody entering the pool and expected it to be his friend, the bankruptcy judge, coming for his morning swim. But it was a stranger. The judge did not appear. An employee carrying towels scurried by, gave Darcy a slight nod and then disappeared in the distance. A waiter came to replenish Darcy's coffee mug, but Darcy waved him off. Darcy cinched his robe a bit tighter, and walked to the steam, hung his robe on the hook outside the door and sat on a fresh towel. He leaned back against the wall and shut his eyes. His thoughts turned to work.

On the last day of Governor Ryan's administration, he had commuted all the sentences of all the prisoners on Illinois' death row to natural life, thus emptying death row.

Since that act, prosecutors around the state were seeking to meet the self-imposed challenge of filling death row with a new generation of heinous murderers. Darcy was trying to visualize Brian Kern on death row. Darcy felt that he was at a crossroads with Brian Kern. If he blew it, Brian Kern could be sentenced to die, and Darcy believed that Brian would want to waive all his appeals. He could end up being the first person executed after the Ryan commutations. Darcy had no intention of letting one of his clients play that role. But he needed Brian's cooperation if he were to have a chance at winning. Darcy was convinced that if he pushed the right button, Brian Kern would crumble and be willing to fight for his life. But Darcy had yet to find the right button. Brian wanted to get back at his parents and this was his grand statement. Darcy had to figure out how Brian could get his point across without actually having to die.

31

PAUL KERN SAT IN A client chair across from Darcy's desk. Darcy leaned toward him.

"Paul, we have some problems. I'm trying to save your son's life. Your son seems to be conflicted as to whether or not he wants to live. That's problem number one. Problem number two is that neither you nor his mother have been to any of these court proceedings. It sends a bad subliminal message to the judge."

Kern exhaled loudly and then stood up. He paced and then ended up behind the chair with his hands on either side. He seemed to be gripping it for strength.

"Things are a little bit complex in that regard," he said. "I'm not sure Brian wants us there. You see, neither his mother nor I have ever been particularly close to Brian. He's always been a bit of an odd kid."

As he spoke his voice was tinged with anger and frustration. "No matter what opportunities we gave him, Brian never really followed through."

"What does that mean?" Darcy asked.

"Well, whenever he wanted to do something, he wanted it until we would let him have it. And then he'd give up. For example," he said, "he wanted to play Little League Baseball. So we signed him up. He went three times and then he quit. Music, he wanted to play the guitar. He's going to be a rock star. Again, we get him a guitar, we sign him up, and he quits. His life is replete with examples of his quitting things. He is a weak kid."

"So," Darcy said, "what did you do?"

"I'm not proud of this," Kern said, pacing now uncomfortably. "But we kept giving him more and more space until—well, he pretty much coexisted with us. Any chance for a normal parent/child relationship was gone. Look, I'm not proud of it. We made mistakes as parents, but. . . ." His voice trailed off and he looked away.

Darcy thought he was having trouble composing himself.

"We weren't good parents," Kern said finally. "But, well, it sounds horrible to say, but he was not a good son, either. He wasn't a good child. He's not a good person."

He continued. "I had my work and that kept me busy and that kept me basically happy. Janet filled her time with charitable events and volunteering."

Darcy was frustrated. He wasn't sure Kern understood the urgency of the situation.

"Paul, they want to put your son on a gurney, strap him down, put a needle in his arm, and deliver fatal doses of chemicals. Do you understand that?"

Kern looked defeated. He came around and sat in the chair.

"I understand it better than you think," he said. "What do you want me to do?"

"I want you and Janet to be there for each and every court date. I want you to look like this is the most important thing in your life."

Kern interrupted. "It is the most important thing in my life. I just don't know how to deal with this. That's why I am paying you, you're an expert. You've been down this road before. I wanted the best—that's you. You tell me what to do and I'll do it."

Darcy nodded. "That's all I ever wanted," he said. "I want you and your wife to be at every court date and I want you to sit in the first row in the spectator's gallery right behind defense counsel's table and I want you to look lovingly at your son every time he comes in. You got it?"

"Understood," Paul said.

"We need to get your son to help us fight for his life. He needs to follow through, no quitting."

32

OPART THAI HOUSE WAS A storefront restaurant on Western Avenue overlooking the L-stop. Because it was Amy's favorite restaurant, they dined there frequently. Opart's did not have a liquor license, but they allowed you to bring your own and a liquor store was conveniently located two storefronts to the north. Darcy had purchased a bottle of Kendall-Jackson Chardonnay and the waiter was kind enough to uncork it for them.

Darcy looked at his wine glass and leaning toward Amy said, "To us," and they tapped their glasses.

"To us," she said and they each took a sip. "Interesting toast," she said. "Is there something you want to tell me?"

It was like Amy to get right to the point. Darcy was uncomfortable but happy to have it out on the table.

"Yeah, I'm worried," he said.

"About what?" she asked.

"About us disintegrating."

"Why would that happen?" she responded.

"Because you're going halfway around the world with a band of doctor do-gooders to try and save some starving kids in Somalia or somewhere."

"And that's a bad thing?" she asked.

"No, it's not a bad thing," Darcy conceded. "It's actually an honorable thing, but it certainly scares the hell out of me."

"Why?"

"Because I'm afraid that something bad will happen to you in a poor, war-torn country. I'm afraid that I won't be there to protect you. I'm afraid that even if I were there, I wouldn't be able to protect you. And lastly, I'm afraid that when you spend a significant amount of time away from me, you're going to find that preferable to spending time with me."

She reached across the table and held his hand.

"I'm not going to give you up," she said. "At least not without a fight. I told you that you could come with me, but I know that's not practical. So we have to come up with some sort of compromise, don't we?" she said.

"I like the sound of that," said Darcy.

"But I want to know some things. I want you to take your time and think about those things," she said.

"Okay," Darcy agreed.

"First of all, I want to know what you're feeling. I want to know what's in your heart. If this is companionship, I want to know that. If this is something else, I want to know that, too."

Darcy began to speak and she held her hand up, stopping him.

"Don't say anything now," she said. "I want you to take time and I want you to think about it, because you have to be accurate and precise."

Darcy lowered his voice so that no one in the restaurant could hear him.

"So are you saying that if I told you that I loved you and wanted to marry you, you wouldn't go?"

She gave a short laugh. "No, I'm not saying that," she said. "You are confusing my motives here. I want to know what we're doing, where we're going. You are concerned about my feelings for you. Well, I want to know how you feel about me, too. We need to talk about us independently of what I'm going to do with this leave.

"I'm going away to do something with this leave. I'm going to do something for myself. You may think that that's a selfish thing and you're right. I need to do something that makes me feel good. That makes me feel noble and important."

"And saving lives in Chicago doesn't do that?" he asked.

"Yes, it does do that, but I need more. You see," she said, "I'm part of the world community. I'm a doctor, a healer, and I need to contribute my share toward healing the world. There are plenty of doctors in Chicago, and when I'm gone there will be enough doctors to cover the emergency room without missing a beat, but if doctors like me don't contribute to the wider world, then a lot more people are going to die. They're going to die just because they lack the wealth that we have.

"There's a doctor that I work with, Dr. Fred Mendelson. Fred goes away every year with Doctors Without Borders. He does it for himself because it makes him feel important. No one is suing you for malpractice; no one is asking you testify in a car accident case. You're just treating people who need to be treated. I'm not going to make a career out of this; I'm not going to do this every year. But I do need to do it now. I'm going to do it. Now, I want to know what we're doing, what our relationship is about because quite honestly, I'm going to consider that when I figure out where I am going and for how long."

Darcy smiled. "How about a week to Hawaii? Would that work?"

"Nice try," she said. "But at least it's a beginning point in our negotiation. I promise you I'll find a way to nurture my soul without destroying our relationship," she said. A waiter appeared and dropped a plate of Chicken Satay and Shrimp Puffs on their table.

Amy put a shrimp puff in her mouth and ate it quickly. She dabbed her lips with the napkin.

"I love this place," she said.

33

Brian Kern was wearing his jail khakis with white socks and white plastic shower shoes as he shuffled down the hallway of the Residential Treatment Unit at Cook County Jail. The RTU was a hospital wing. It was for patients who needed constant medical treatment, were suicidal, or needed to be segregated from other prisoners for some special reasons. The guard who had been two steps behind Brian stepped in front of him and unlocked an attorney conference room. Darcy, Brian, and Justin went in and sat around a wobbly table.

"How are you doing?" Darcy asked.

"Better," Brian said in a timid voice.

"Did your mom and dad come and see you?"

"Yes, thank you."

"Don't thank me."

"Please," he said, "they would have never come to see me if it wasn't for you. I know you talked to my dad. I had to get arrested for murder to get their attention. We had a long talk. My father apologized for his shortcomings. Imagine that. My dad talked to me, not at me, for the first time that I can remember."

"So where do we go from here?" Darcy asked.

"I guess we fight," said Brian.

"Good."

"So, where do we begin?" Brian asked.

"I guess we begin at the beginning," said Darcy reaching into his briefcase and pulling out a legal pad. "Tell me everything you know about Trip."

Brian got to his feet and began to pace.

"I met Trip when we moved back from England. I had gone to New Trier High School before we moved to England. Didn't have any friends, didn't connect with anyone. I think I was kind of a joke there. So we go to England and did two years there and I come back. Well, I didn't want to go back to New Trier. So my dad got me into Longwood Prep. Figured I finish the year there and then go off to college someplace. Anyway, when I went to Longwood I met Trip."

"So you guys became friends?" Darcy asked.

"Not at first," said Brian. "See, Trip was kind of a sick fuck and had no close friends. He was pretty much the only one who was a bigger loser than me. So we hung out sort of by default because no one else was going to hang with Trip. No one was going to hang with me. Two losers wasting time together is more like it, but you could say that we became friends."

"So what would you do together?" Darcy asked.

"Are you kidding?" Brian responded. "You know what they say: rich kids have the best drugs. We used to get high all the time."

"What kind of drugs?" said Darcy.

"We would blow some weed. Do some coke, ecstasy, that's pretty much it. Although we dabbled in everything. So one day we were at Craig Cizmar's house and we're there with a couple of girls and this one girl passed out drunk as can be. So Trip takes her into a back bedroom."

"How did he do that?" Darcy asked.

"Well, I helped him carry her into the bedroom," he said.

"Then what happened?" Darcy asked.

"Well, he stripped her down and Trip did pretty much everything he wanted to with her."

"Was she responding?" said Darcy.

"No, she was out."

"So what were you doing?" Darcy asked.

"I was kind of watching," he said. "I was freaked out; I didn't know what to do."

"So what happened?" said Darcy.

"Well he's in the middle of his business and he won't stop talking. He was talking to me while he's doing her."

"What's he saying?" said Darcy.

"He's asking me if I want to help him kill her. I said, 'Man you're fucking crazy.' But he's telling me that a year and a half ago he had a girl at Cizmar's party just like this and he took her out and killed her. I'm freaking out and I'm like, 'No way, you're full of shit, you're bull-shitting me.' But he's going on and on and I'm starting to believe him."

"So what happens next?" Darcy asked.

"So he finishes his business and then he takes his pants up and when he takes his pants up he reaches into his pocket and pulls out a seal and then cuts up a couple of lines and we do some blow. He tells me all about killing this other girl."

"What's the girl doing?" Darcy said.

"She's just flopped out, man. She was out."

"Let me ask you something," said Darcy. "Was she drunk or do you think he slipped her something?"

From Brian's reaction, Darcy could tell that he hadn't thought about this before.

"I've seen a lot of chicks drunk," he said. "I've never seen anyone out like that."

"Do you think he put something in her drink?"

"Ah, now that I think about it, she was really out. I mean it was something that I have never seen before. I mean you could have lit her feet on fire and she wouldn't have come to."

"And then what happened?" Darcy asked.

"Well, we're sitting there in the bedroom. She's on the bed and we're doing coke and he's telling me about he killed this chick about a year and a half ago."

"What's he saying?"

"He's telling me everything about it."

"Then what happens?"

"Well, at some point Craig came to the door."

Darcy interrupted, "Is that Craig Cizmar?"

"Yeah, he's knocking at the door. He said, 'Yo, we gotta go.' So after a little while we left."

"Where was the girl?" Darcy asked.

"On the bed," he said.

"Did you ever see her again?"

"Not that night."

"Have you ever seen her again?"

"I might have seen her at a party after that. I don't really remember that well."

"Did you jump in and get anything while you were there?"

"Naw man, I was too freaked out and besides I can't get naked in front of a guy like that. That would wig me out. I couldn't rape anyone. So is any of this going to help?" Brian asked.

"Maybe," said Darcy. "We've got to run it down. Check everything out."

"Can you win my case?" Brian asked.

"I don't know yet," said Darcy, "but at least now we have a fighting chance."

34

IT WAS COOL FOR THE middle of May, and Darcy wore a light jacket while Amy was wearing a sweatshirt and jeans. They were heading to Sherman's Ice Cream. In southwest Michigan, Sherman's Ice Cream was well-known. Amy made a point of stopping in most weekends that she was in South Haven. They grabbed two pints of ice cream, butter pecan and black cherry, and ran back to the car. Amy gave Darcy directions and he drove the car back toward the lake. Once inside the house, Amy lit the gas fireplace and stood close by, rubbing her hands. Darcy took his coat off and hung it up in the closet just to the left of the front door. He walked up behind Amy and put his arms around her.

"Can I help you warm up?"

She put her hand on his hand and said, "I'd like that; give me a few minutes in front of the fire."

Darcy pulled a case from his pocket that contained four cigars and put it on the coffee table in front of him along with a lighter and cigar clip. Eventually Amy wandered over and sat next to him, leaning against him. Darcy picked up the lighter and started tapping it, turning it over and over again nervously as he began to speak.

"I've come to a conclusion," he said, "and that is, I'll follow you to the ends of the earth."

She smiled.

"I've come to a conclusion too," she said. "I'm not going quite to the ends of the earth. I came up with a destination that I think that both of us could live with. There's a hospital called Hadassah Ein Karem in Jerusalem," she said. "It's famous. Have you heard of it?" she asked.

Darcy was drawing a blank.

"Sorry," he said.

"It's famous because it sits in Jerusalem. It's an Israeli hospital but it treats all people, and as you can imagine, its expertise is in trauma work. All the victims of violence in the area are brought to Hadassah and are treated by great doctors. There are Israeli doctors and Arab doctors who within the walls of the hospital work with only one purpose, and that's to heal and treat all those who have been injured."

She took a deep breath and then exhaled.

"So what I've decided is that I'm going to go to Jerusalem and work for Hadassah. They're in dire need of doctors, and with my background in emergency room trauma care I would be a tremendous asset to them. I'm going to be treating people who are victims of this insanity and hatred that has plagued the Middle East and the world for generations. I'm going to go there and make a difference. It won't make much difference in the whole configuration of the Middle East and the generations of war, but it will make a difference with me and I can save some lives."

"There's no question for me," said Darcy. "When I finish my trial, I'll follow you to Israel."

35

DARCY FINISHED HIS SWIM AND floated under the ropes to the ladder. He climbed out, toweled off, pulled his suit off and wrapped himself in a robe. He took his usual table with a *Tribune* and *Sun-Times* on one of the chairs and sat down to his usual Irish oatmeal, rye bread toast, unsweetened grapefruit juice, glass of ice water, and a cup of coffee. Every day the waiter in uniform dutifully would ask him what he wanted and everyday he ordered the same thing. Both the waiter and Darcy knew that the order was going to be the same each and every day, but the club had its protocol and the waiters were trained and expected to give the highest level of service. After taking the order the waiter scooted off as a busboy poured a cup of coffee for Darcy.

Darcy finished the paper, showered and got dressed, and headed into the office. He took a stack of messages from Irma's hand as he walked by. She was on the phone picking up the rest of the previous evening's voicemail. Darcy threw his coat on the hook behind his door and strolled over to the window. Looking out over the Harold Washington Museum, beyond Buckingham Fountain and Grant Park, and to the lake, Darcy's mind began to drift. On the other side of that lake, he had just spent a glorious weekend with Amy at her house in South Haven. His thoughts were interrupted by a knock on the door.

"Darcy, can I come in?"

Kathy Haddon was standing there.

"Absolutely," he said.

She slid into a chair across from Darcy's desk.

"Guess who died?" she asked.

"Give me a hint—are we happy or sad?"

"Oh, we're happy," said Kathy.

"That category's too large. Who died?" Darcy asked.

"Remember Jose Salazar?" she said.

Darcy thought about it.

"You mean the witness in the Betancourt case?"

"Bingo," she said.

"What happened?" Darcy asked.

"Got blown away."

Darcy turned around and looked out over the lake.

"That's no surprise," he said. "Rival gang members?"

"Yep," she said.

The silence lingered between them. Darcy thought that he should feel bad that another human being was killed, but then again, he didn't think Jose Salazar was much of a human being. Jose Salazar was a gang member who seemed to have only two options in life: jail or death. He had been to jail a few times and now he was experiencing death. Armando Betancourt was a young man who Darcy had represented in a murder case. One of the crucial witnesses against Armando was Herlinda Salazar, Jose's mother. Armando Betancourt had been an honor student at St. Ignatius High School. He was a freshman at the University of Illinois-Chicago and his father had helped him get a job at a restaurant along the father's restaurant-supply delivery route. His father was also named Armando, so the younger Betancourt was known as Armandito. There had been a shooting in the neighborhood. One gang had fired shots from a moving car at a group of people who were standing on the corner that belonged to a rival gang. One of the gang members was killed. Two of the remaining gang members told police that it was Armandito who did the shooting. The police drove by Armandito's house. He was standing outside talking with two neighbors when they came up and placed him under arrest. They subjected him to a gunshot residue test which proved negative. Armandito told them that he had heard the shooting, but at the time of the shooting he was standing across the street talking to Herlinda Salazar. Instead of going home that night, Armandito was arrested and subjected to trial where to his surprise Herlinda Salazar had testified that she had not seen Armandito at the time of the shooting but saw him running behind an abandoned garage where police later found the murder weapon. That along with the two gangbanger eyewitnesses had been enough for a jury to convict Armandito. Kathy had tried the case with Darcy, and wrote the briefs and argued the appeal, but the Appellate Court affirmed the jury verdict in the Circuit Court, and Armandito Betancourt was now looking at the next fifty-five years in jail. The two gangbanger witnesses, Raoul Perez and Pablo Escobedo, had been in and out of trouble themselves.

"Do you remember the detective on this case?" Kathy said.

"Tony Fields," said Darcy.

"That's right," she said. "He's a complete scumbag. I know that he forced Herlinda to testify against Armandito or he was going to put the case on her son Jose."

"You know that," said Darcy, "or you believe that?"

"Trust me when I tell you. It's a mother thing. I saw her testify. I know what her motivation was, and now I can prove it."

"How's that?" said Darcy.

"Her son's dead. She's not going to protect him anymore. Now she can worry about someone else's son. I'm going to send Collata out to talk to her and see if she'll tell us the truth about Armandito."

"To what end?" said Darcy.

"If Collata takes a statement from her and we run down Perez and Escobedo and they give us statements, I'm going to go in and try to get this case reversed."

"I thought you were leaving," said Darcy.

"I was," she said. "I might be. I don't know. I'm not leaving right now. I keep getting ready to go. The new job is a great opportunity—yet I don't want to go," she said. "Now this. I'm not going to let Armandito be another Arturo Sanchez."

Darcy came out from behind his desk and sat in the chair next to Kathy. He put his left hand up the top of her back toward her neck and rested it there.

"Listen kiddo, you can stay here forever, but stay here for the right reason. Don't look for excuses to stay here. Stay here because you like what you're doing. If you don't like what you're doing and you think that you're going to like trying civil cases, go do that. If that doesn't work, you can always come home."

"I don't know if I'm just having cold feet," she said. "But I just don't think that I want to do depositions on accident cases."

Darcy smiled.

"Okay, let's not make that decision now. How do you want to handle this case?"

"I want to whistle Collata in, give him an assignment, and send him out to talk to Herlinda, Perez, and Escobedo. Is that okay?" she said.

"It's okay with me," said Darcy. "We're just going to do this pro bono, huh?"

"Pro bono," she said.

"You know that's Latin for 'no money,'" said Darcy.

Kathy smiled.

"I think the translation is a little bit closer to 'for the good.'"

"Huh," said Darcy. "So now you're the do-gooder. Where do you want to begin?"

"Well, I think what I'm going to do is try to get the recants and if I do, I'm going to leak something to Pam Mazur at the *Tribune*."

"Pam Mazur?" Darcy said. "She's despicable."

"You're right," said Kathy. "But you know that's she been really effective and she certainly has the same agenda."

"Her agenda is to get as much publicity for herself as possible," said Darcy.

"Right, and my agenda is to get Armandito out of jail. I promise you I will control the relationship with her. She won't control me."

"Be careful," said Darcy. "Make sure that whatever you have is rock solid because as soon as she gets involved, the State's Attorneys are going to have their backs against the wall."

"I'll see what Collata comes up with first," said Kathy.

36

Darcy took a sip of Glenlivet and then slid his pawn.

"I see you're opening with the Helsinki move," began Seymour.

"Please," said Darcy. "I'm not going to fall for that line of crap. Make your move," said Darcy.

Seymour chuckled.

"So, boychik, what's new?"

"I'm going to Israel," said Darcy.

"Really," said Seymour. "To the land of milk and honey. What's going to send a fine Gentile like you to Israel?"

"Dr. Amy Wagner," said Darcy.

"She's Jewish?" asked Seymour.

"No. She's going to work at a hospital called Hadassah in Jerusalem."

"Ah," said Seymour. "She's working at Hadassah."

"You know of it?" said Darcy.

"Of course. Hadassah is not just a hospital but a ray of hope. Do you know that the hospital, while primarily Jewish, also has Arab doctors? Working side by side, they treat all comers: Palestinian, Jew, Muslim, it doesn't matter. They give them the best medical care possible. In the Middle East if there's one place that is a sanctuary, it's not a church, it's not a temple, it's not a mosque—it's Hadassah hospital. It is off limits to terrorists because the terrorists' daughters, sons, nephews, and nieces are treated by the doctors at Hadassah."

"I'm going to finish a trial and then I'm going to get on a plane and go to Israel and join her," Darcy said.

"Good for you," said Seymour.

"I'm going to meet her in Jerusalem and then we're going to travel somewhere as long as we can as long as we're enjoying it."

"Are you telling me you're taking an extended vacation?" Seymour said in a surprised tone.

"That's right," said Darcy. "I'm going to follow this woman around the world."

Seymour smiled broadly.

"I think that's great. I think you're going to have a great time. Can Patrick manage the practice alone?"

"Well, that's another thing," said Darcy as he slid his rook out. "It seems that Kathy's not leaving as soon as she said she was. In fact, she's not sure if she's leaving at all."

"Second thoughts," said Seymour.

"Well, she's kind of on a mission. We did a case a long time ago and we lost. It left a bitter taste in our mouths and circumstances have changed and now she thinks she might be able to do something on a post-conviction motion. You know the law was always skeptical about recants. But over the years, with all these cases that have turned around on actual innocence after the

Appellate Court has affirmed the convictions in the lower court, these recants have taken on a whole new life. Kathy thinks she can get recants on this case."

Seymour slid a bishop to the center of the board.

"How's the Leopold and Loeb case?"

Seymour slid his queen into position to force checkmate.

"I think we got the kid turned around. I think he wants to win. I got him talking to his parents and his parents talking to him. They even went to visit him at the jail, which couldn't have been easy. So we'll see. Maybe his parents will continue to see him. Maybe his spirits will stay up. Maybe he'll let me save his life."

Darcy moved his knight.

Seymour slid his rook into position.

"Checkmate."

"Sonofabitch," said Darcy as he tipped up the glass and let the Glenlivet slide down his throat.

37

Justin walked into Darcy's office, taking the chair across from his desk.

"So did you see Brian?" Darcy asked.

"Yeah, just came back," said Justin.

"How's he doing?"

"He's pretty fragile," said Justin. "But for now, he's hanging with us. We'll see if we can get him through this trial."

Darcy glanced at his watch.

"They're probably waiting for us in the conference room."

Justin popped up and followed Darcy down the hall. Collata had a briefcase on the table that looked like it might have been used by the Pony Express. He pulled out an accordion file full of smaller files. Patrick was seated across from Collata with a bottle of water in front of him on the table and his hands in a bag of beef jerky.

"Hey, Shitty, what's up?" Patrick said.

"I'm good, how about you?" said Justin.

"Not bad."

Justin nodded toward the bag.

"Atkins?" he asked.

"Yep, phase one. All protein, no carbs."

"I got a better diet," said Darcy.

"Yeah, what's that?"

Darcy smiled.

"Eat less, eat better, and work out more."

As they sat down, Collata slid a couple of files toward Darcy.

"Here's what we got on Brian's friend Trip," Collata began. "I ran down the rape victim. Her name is Margaret Heming. Margaret's at a college in Vermont that caters to the rich and troubled."

"Do you think she'll be willing to come back?"

"Yes. She never reported it to the police because she thought her actions contributed to the rape, but over time she's become convinced that Trip slipped a drug in her drink that knocked her out. She's pissed and wants everybody to know what kind of an asshole Trip is. So I think she's on board. The homicide that Trip told Brian about is a little different. A girl named Brittany Wilson. She disappeared about the time of that first party Trip was talking about. No father in the picture, her mother's kind of a bust-out. Didn't report her missing for a week. Apparently mom thought Brittany was out slutting around. Brittany got hooked up with the Longwood Prep group because she liked to get high and they always had a steady supply of cocaine. We got it narrowed down to a time frame in which we could prove beyond any doubt that our boy was in England going to school at the time. So Trip has a rape and a homicide that the government probably doesn't know about."

"Yeah, well, he gets immunity anyway," said Darcy.

"So we ask him about it. He admits it and he never pays for it," Justin said.

"Could be," said Collata, "but as far as I know, when the state gives him immunity it's for all the crimes he commits in their jurisdiction. Brittany Wilson was killed and her body was dumped in Lake County and they don't give immunity for cases in other counties."

"So we get him to admit all this on cross so he's talking himself into a murder case in Lake County?" Justin said.

"That's right," said Darcy.

Justin clapped his hands together.

"Beautiful. I guess sometimes we can bring some justice to the world."

Kathy came in and took a seat at the table.

"So how solid is this Margaret Heming?" Darcy asked.

"Pretty good," said Collata. "She's going to testify that she was drugged and that she believes that she was raped. She's going to explain why she believes she was raped and she's going to talk about the humiliation. She's also going to testify that she confronted Trip a couple weeks later after she put it all together and he laughed at her. Told her she wasn't that good, but next time when he fucks her, she'll be awake. She slapped his face and walked away."

"That's good," said Darcy. "Anything else?"

Collata emptied the contents of the accordion file on the table.

"It's all here," he said. "Read it and if you need me to go out on anything else, let me know."

Justin collected all the file folders.

"I'll read them first," he said.

"Anything else?" Darcy said.

"Yeah," Collata pointed to Kathy. "I ran down that case for the princess here and I got some good results. Herlinda Salazar has flipped on her testimony. She gave me a full recant. She told me that Detective Fields laid it out for her and said it's either our boy or her son. So given that choice, she rolled over on Armandito. Said she feels real bad about it. Also told me that she knows that Raoul and Pablo lied."

"Great," said Kathy. "How does she know they lied?"

"Because they told her that they lied. Apparently the three of them were sitting in an office in the State's Attorney's Office before trial and Raoul, Pablo, and she talked about everything and Raoul and Pablo gave it up to her that Fields told them that they were going to do what he said or it was going to be bad for them."

"Were you able to talk to them yet?" asked Kathy.

"Not yet. I know where Raoul is, he's locked up in Pontiac doing a ten ball on an attempted murder. Pablo is in the wind, but I've got some feelers out there and I think we're going to locate him."

"That's great," said Kathy. "Can I have a copy of the recant?"

"Absolutely," he said. "I have it in my briefcase and I'll run down Raoul and Pablo as soon as I can."

"You're the best," she said.

"Good, tell your boss to give me a raise."

38

THE DAY THE BRIAN KERN trial was to begin was a typical rainy July day in Chicago. Hot with a steady rainfall, it made the windows in the courtroom steam up a bit. Larry Stevens had ended up staying on the case, following it from the Skokie courthouse to Twenty-sixth and California. His partner in the trial was Olga Cepeda.

Olga had grown up a few blocks from the courthouse. Her father, an immigrant from Mexico, had worked hard. Olga had attended Catholic schools and went to Rosary College on a scholarship. After doing everything well in college, she went to Loyola University's law school at night on a scholarship while spending her days teaching English as a second language in the Chicago public schools. Besides English and Spanish, she also spoke fluent French. Larry Stevens was thorough and deliberate in his approach. Olga was compassionate and bonded well with juries as she led them through trials in an efficient manner guided by common sense. She was of medium height, slender with dark hair and brown eyes. She looked younger than her thirty-seven years but carried herself with the dignity and maturity of someone older. The rumors around the courthouse had her making judge in the next round of appointments.

Judge Robert Wolfe was in his late sixties with thinning gray hair and glasses. He was smart and strict and had a quick temper. He ordered his sheriff to begin bringing in prospective jurors. Darcy and Justin studied each and every person who walked through the door and assumed a seat on the hard benches that made up the spectator gallery.

Wolfe made a show of shuffling the jury cards with the questionnaires filled out by prospective jurors. He called fourteen names and had them seated in the jury box. The judge methodically asked follow-up questions where appropriate. After a short break the lawyers were allowed to ask their own follow-up questions of the prospective jurors. Darcy asked questions of a few people before zeroing in on a woman named Karen Donaldson. Donaldson was from Winnetka and she had two daughters close in age to Laura Martin.

"Ms. Donaldson, have you heard anything about this case prior to coming into court today?"

"I don't believe so," she said, "but I don't really remember."

She was a well-groomed woman in her late forties. She wore diamond stud earrings and had a diamond pendant. Her hair was silver and black and she was conservatively dressed.

"Ms. Donaldson, you're going to hear testimony that the victim in this case was roughly the same age as your two daughters. Is that going to affect your ability to be impartial in this case?"

Her hands were in her lap and she was nervously pushing her left thumb into the palm of her right hand.

"I suppose it's possible," she said, "but I don't know why it would. I would do my best to not have it enter my mind during any of the proceedings."

It was a good answer. A good answer for everyone except the defense. After a few more questions, Darcy sat down and the judge then ushered the lawyers into chambers. He threw his robe on a coat hook and then sat behind his desk. He took a quick glance at the cards before handing them to Darcy.

"Okay Mr. Cole, what do you have?"

"I'd ask that Ms. Donaldson be stricken for cause."

"Denied," said the judge.

"Do you want to hear argument?"

"No, move on."

"That's all for cause," Darcy said.

"State, any for cause?"

"No, Your Honor."

"Okay, preemptories? You've got the cards, Darcy."

Darcy and Justin went through the cards, looking at them very carefully, trying to find clues to the jurors' character. On the front was the person's name and address and on the back were a series of personal questions: Whether they were married, where they worked, had they ever been a victim of a crime, etc. Darcy tapped his pen on the card by Ms. Donaldson's name and address and then flipped it over and used his pen to point out the ages of her daughters. Justin nodded. They would use a preemptory challenge to keep Donaldson off the jury.

"We'll excuse Donaldson."

"Are the others acceptable?"

Darcy excused two more jurors and handed the cards to the judge. The judge leaned over and gave them to the state.

"Okay, boys and girls, what do you want to do?"

The state went through the cards and then excused two more. Five prospective jurors had been stricken. They went back into the courtroom. The judge took the bench as the lawyers sat at table.

"Ladies and gentlemen, with thanks, I'll excuse the following jurors."

He then read five names.

"Those of you who remain in the jury box, please go with the sheriffs in the back of the jury room. We'll get back with you shortly."

They called another fourteen names and filled the jury box. The process began again.

Four and a half hours later, Darcy, Justin, Olga, and Larry stood at counsel table and watched as fourteen people took the oath to serve as jurors. After the jurors were seated, Judge Wolfe addressed them.

"Ladies and gentlemen, you have been selected as jurors to hear this case. Twelve of you are jurors and two of you are alternates. The alternates will be with the jury at all times up until the point that deliberations will commence. If one of the jurors becomes unavailable for deliberations, then the first alternate will move up in their stead. If two become unavailable, then the second alternate will also move up in their stead. It's very important that all fourteen of you listen very carefully. I will give you instructions on the law and you are not to discuss the facts of this case or the witnesses during the course of this trial until I give you this case for you to deliberate. You are not to speak with anyone during the course of this trial about this case. You have those jurors' stickers, which we call juror badges. You are to wear them at all times in the courthouse.

"In the morning, if I am doing things in court when you walk in, please do not hesitate to sit down. Walk right through this courtroom through that door to the jury room," he said as he pointed. "Walk right through. I cannot emphasize that enough. We will be conducting court business on other cases and you might be nervous about cutting through. Don't be. Just walk right through the court and to the jury room. If you have any problems at all, talk to one of the sheriffs who will be with you at all times. While in court, your cell phones and pagers must be turned off. We'll give you notepads and pens. You are not to take them home. We will collect them each evening and pass them out to you each day.

"At the conclusion of the trial, after you have rendered your verdict, we will destroy those notes so that you do not have to worry about anyone ever seeing any of your notes or work product. Finally, if you see any of the lawyers in the courthouse or anywhere else and they ignore you, it is not because they are rude. They are under my instructions not to talk to you. So if you see them and they nod and say nothing to you, do not be offended and do not hold that against them because I have told them that they cannot communicate with you in any manner, shape, or form. If anybody attempts at anytime to communicate with you about this case, bring that to the attention of the sheriff immediately.

"Ladies and gentlemen, we are going to commence tomorrow with opening statements at 10:30 a.m. Please be prepared to work full days. You are welcome to bring your own meals if you prefer, but please understand that we will provide meals and snacks for you. The food that we will provide for you will vary from pretty good to marginally edible. However, since I'm here every day I'll do the best I can to get you the best food possible."

There were a few chuckles among the jurors.

"Okay, ladies and gentlemen, that's it. Tomorrow morning be here before 10:30 and we'll get started."

With that the sheriff yelled, "All rise for the jury."

The jury was escorted to the back of the courtroom into the jury room, followed by the judge, who walked off into chambers.

39

OLGA CEPEDA STOOD BEFORE THE jury. She waited, making sure that all the jurors were completely focused on her before she began her opening statement in a slow, deliberate tone.

"Last November 4, a body washed up from Lake Michigan in Evanston which is just north of Chicago here in Cook County. The body was that of a young woman who had been in the water for a while. The body was badly bloated and there were obvious signs of foul play. Evanston Police Detectives Kelly and Johnson began their investigation. The first thing they had to do was to determine who this victim was and how this victim died. You'll hear from Dr. Sally Fitzhugh of the Cook County Medical Examiner's Office about how the Cook County Medical Examiner's Office received the body. She'll tell you the condition of the body when it was received. She'll tell you how the victim was killed and how the victim was identified. You'll next hear from a woman named Vanessa Baldwin. Vanessa Baldwin is going to tell you about the victim. She was a young woman named Laura Martin.

"Laura was a young lady who had been born into difficult circumstances, but she did not let that define her or keep her down. Vanessa Baldwin is going to tell you that Laura Martin was a ward of the state and lived in a group home in Rogers Park. Vanessa Baldwin ran that home as sort of a group mother to these girls. She's going to tell you the kind of person Laura Martin was. That is important because you need to know that Laura Martin in this case is a victim in the purest sense. She did nothing to contribute to her death."

Olga began to pace slowly in front of the jury.

"Laura went to school and worked part-time at Lincolnwood Mall. It was during the course of her work that she met a young man, a young man who you're going to meet, named John Henry Phillips III. John Henry Phillips III is also known by the nickname Trip. Trip is a young man whose circumstances are completely opposite from Laura's. Trip was born to a wealthy family. His mother, father, and he live in the north shore suburbs. Trip was a student at Longwood Prep, which is a private school in the northern suburbs. You will learn that Laura Martin met Trip at the Lincolnwood Mall. Trip began to visit Laura while she worked at the mall. By late October, Laura and Trip were spending time together, and on October 30 Laura and Trip went out together. The defendant, Brian Kern," she continued, as she walked over and pointed to Brian, and then turned back toward the lectern in front of the jury, "was a friend of Trip's. Brian Kern was also a student at Longwood Prep," she said, "which is where he became friends with Trip.

"On October 30, Trip, the defendant Brian Kern, Laura Martin, and a few other people had done some socializing. Brian, Trip, and Laura ended up alone. It was while the three of them were alone that Brian Kern devised a plan. The plan was that he and Trip were going to have sex with Laura Martin. There were two of them and Laura was not a particularly strong girl, so they figured that they would be able to overpower her and be able to rape her. At some point, Brian pounced on Laura and began yelling for Trip to help. Laura fought desperately to stop Brian Kern from raping her. You're going to hear testimony about this from Trip, and I'm going to tell you right now that you're not going to like him. If Trip had stepped up and said to his friend Brian, 'No, don't do this,' then we probably wouldn't be here today. But in this business, we don't get to choose our witnesses. You know who chose the witnesses who will come to court?" She again strolled over and pointed at the defendant Brian Kern. "He chose the witnesses because he is the one who committed the crimes. He chose the victim. He chose the place. He chose the witnesses. Trip is going to tell you that he was afraid of Brian Kern and that he did nothing to intercede and in fact, that he helped Brian Kern and ultimately participated in the rape and murder of Laura Martin. Now, I would love to be able to prove this case without using the testimony of John Henry Phillips III. But you see, we prosecutors have to make decisions, and the decision that we made was that it was more important for us to convict the worst of the two, that being the defendant, Brian Kern," she said, again pointing toward the defendant, "than it is merely to punish Trip. So Trip is going to testify, and for his testimony he's going to be rewarded with a lesser sentence. As disgusting as that may seem to you, it's even more disgusting to us. But you see, this is the only way to convict the worse culprit, Brian Kern," she said.

"In exchange for his cooperation and his pleading guilty and admitting his involvement in this case, Trip is going to be sentenced to twenty-five years in prison. But we are not going to ask you to count on Trip's word alone to convict the defendant. We're going to give you ample evidence and corroboration that proves beyond any doubt, much less any reasonable doubt, that the defendant, Brian Kern," she said, again pointing, "is in fact the person who committed the rape and murder of Laura Martin. Now, ladies and gentlemen, in Illinois the term rape isn't used in legal proceedings. In this case, the conduct which you would normally consider rape is charged as aggravated criminal sexual assault. This means that Brian Kern was armed with a knife and used force or the threat of force while armed to perform a sexual act, in this case, sexual intercourse, with the victim Laura Martin without her consent or permission. He's also charged with murder in that he stabbed and strangled Laura Martin, causing her death, and felony murder in that in the course of committing the aggravated criminal sexual assault, he killed Laura Martin. The evidence in this case is overwhelming. I'm going to ask you to listen carefully to what the witnesses say. At the conclusion of this case, after you have heard all of the evidence and you've been instructed by the judge as to the law to be applied in this case, I'm going to ask you to find the defendant guilty on each and every count."

She walked over slowly toward Brian Kern and pointed to him yet again.

"I want you, ladies and gentlemen, to tell Brian Kern that he cannot get away with this. He is responsible and he will be held responsible for the cowardly acts that he committed. Ladies and gentlemen, Laura Martin is gone. Laura Martin cannot speak here today, so we, my partner Larry Stevens and I, will give voice to her memory. Ladies and gentlemen, at the conclusion of this case you will find Mr. Kern guilty, not out of sentiment, not out of pity, not out of any feelings or emotions, but based on the cold, harsh reality that in fact he is guilty. He is guilty of sexually assaulting Laura. He's guilty of murder. While Laura Martin cannot cry out for justice, we can and we will, and you will deliver it."

The judge nodded to the defense counsel table, then picked up his coffee mug and took a sip.

Darcy walked to the podium. He gathered himself and began his opening statement. He too pointed at Brian Kern.

"Ladies and gentlemen, that is Brian Kern. Take a good look at him, because throughout this entire trial there's one thing for you to keep in your mind. That is that Ms. Cepeda and Mr. Stevens want you to sentence Brian Kern to death. To do that, to convict Mr. Kern and sentence him to death, they're going to present one key witness, John Henry Phillips III, or as he's known, Trip. Ms. Cepeda wants you to believe that Trip is also a victim in this case, that Brian Kern is the mastermind behind the rape and murder of Laura Martin. And she wants you not only to believe that, but to believe that beyond a reasonable doubt. She's going to offer very little in the way of corroboration, and the reason for that is because she has very little corroboration.

"You're going to hear that there were scrapings taken from underneath the fingernails of the victim Laura Martin. You're going to hear that what was under the fingernails was some skin, because as Laura Martin was fighting for her life she scratched the person who was attacking her. Some of the skin from her attacker lodged under her fingernails, and lo and behold you're going to learn that that skin was tested for DNA, and the DNA conclusively indicates that it came from none other than their star witness, Trip. Not Brian Kern. You're going to hear about the investigation from Detectives Kelly and Johnson and how they quickly focused on Trip and began to suspect that he had committed this crime. You're going to hear how eventually Trip was arrested, and after being arrested how this deal ended up happening. The deal will allow Trip to serve close to the minimum possible sentence as opposed to the state seeking the death penalty against him."

Darcy was moving slowly back and forth the length of the jury box making eye contact with the jurors.

"Once the deal was struck, the state was committed to proceeding in the way they are proceeding today, which is to try to sell you on the notion that Trip was manipulated by Brian Kern. I ask that you keep an open mind. You're going to be instructed throughout this case that you're not to deliberate until all the evidence has been heard. The government, by way of the State's Attorneys, Mr. Stevens and Ms. Cepeda, present their evidence first, and that's because they have the burden of proving the defendant guilty.

"You will learn and be instructed that the law says that right now you must presume that my client, Brian Kern, is innocent. So if the trial ended right now without hearing any evidence, you would be compelled to find the defendant not guilty. Now why is that important? Well, one of the reasons it is important is because in this case when you walked in through those double doors," Darcy said as he pointed to the doors leading into the courtroom, "and you sat down, you said to yourself, 'I wonder what kind of case it is.' Then you saw the defendant sitting next to his lawyers and you said to yourself, 'I wonder what he did?' I know you did that, ladies and gentlemen, because that's what everybody does. 'I wonder what he did.' In your mind you assumed he was guilty. He must be guilty because he's sitting there at counsel table. The police arrested him and the police know what they're doing. The prosecutors are trying him and they know what they're doing so he must be guilty. Now, ladies and gentlemen, I'm not going to ask you to presume that Brian Kern is innocent, even though you're required to do just that. I'm going to ask you just to hold off and not make a decision until you hear all of the evidence. Opening statements, ladies and gentlemen, are nothing more than the attorneys' opinion of what the evidence will show. Opening statements are not evidence in and of themselves. Ms. Cepeda has given her opinion on what the evidence will show. But I'm making you a promise right now. I promise you that no matter what you think at the end of the state's case you will hear evidence in the defense case that will make you think completely differently about this case and especially about their star witness, Mr. John Henry Phillips III.

"At the end of this case you're going to know that the state's star witness, John Henry Phillips III—Trip—is a rapist and murderer. Ladies and gentlemen, you will see that there is no way in the world that Brian Kern was the one who created this situation. They can point to Brian Kern fifty times, a hundred times, it doesn't matter. Pointing isn't evidence. I'm going to tell you this: John Henry Phillips III is the one who's going to convince you that he is responsible for these acts. He is the one who created this situation. He is the one who is responsible, and by selling his story to the government, he is saving his skin at the expense of Brian Kern. You took an oath. An oath that as jurors you will follow the law. And you have been instructed by the judge that the defendant is presumed innocent, and that you're not to deliberate until you are given the case by the judge for deliberation. Ladies and gentlemen, I ask you only for one thing: Wait until you have heard all of the evidence, and at closing argument I will pull it all together for you. I guarantee you that the true story is much different than Ms. Cepeda would want you to believe."

Darcy now stood behind the podium directly in front of the jury. He put his palms on it and leaned forward as he uttered his last few words.

The judge waited for Darcy to be seated and then he looked toward the state.

"Call your first witness."

Vanessa Baldwin stood to the right of the judge with her right hand in the air, and accepted the oath before being seated in the witness box. Larry Stevens was behind a lectern forty feet away from her.

"Ma'am, can you tell us your name and spell your first and last name for the record."

"My name is Vanessa Baldwin, V-A-N-E-S-S-A B-A-L-D-W-I-N."

"Ms. Baldwin, are you employed?"

"I am," she said.

"And who are you employed by?"

"I'm employed by the Sisters of Mercy. We are a charitable organization licensed through the Department of Children and Family Services to run homes for children who are wards of the state."

"Ma'am, without giving us the exact address, can you tell us where your particular home is?"

"Yes, it's not far from Sullivan High School near Bosworth and Lunt."

"Now, ma'am, in that complex did you know a young woman named Laura Martin?"

"I did," she said.

"How did you know her?"

"Ms. Martin lived in the group home that I ran."

"Can you describe her for us?"

"She was a lovely young lady."

At this point Darcy could have objected but he would have only alienated the jury. He was going to let Ms. Baldwin talk about what a lovely young lady Laura Martin was. Justin was scribbling notes while Brian sat passively. Brian's parents were looking on from the second row.

Ms. Baldwin went on to talk about Laura and how well she did in school and how she worked afternoons, evenings, and weekends at a kiosk at the Lincolnwood Mall. She said that Laura had met someone that she called Trip and that over time Trip had become a more frequent part of their conversations. She identified a photograph of Laura. Then the prosecutors and defense lawyers stipulated that she be able to identify a photograph of Laura taken at the morgue. The first photograph was known as the life photo. The second one was the death photo. With that, the state had used

Ms. Baldwin to prove that Laura Martin had in fact been alive and that Laura Martin had since been killed. The law required that these simple facts be established in a murder trial. Darcy and Justin declined to ask any questions of Ms. Baldwin on cross, and she was excused.

Stevens asked permission of the court to allow Ms. Baldwin to watch the rest of the trial from a seat in the spectator's gallery. Although witnesses were not allowed to hear the testimony of other witnesses, Darcy and Justin agreed because they didn't expect Ms. Baldwin to be called back as a witness. More importantly, Darcy told Justin "it's the decent thing to do."

Tim Kelly was next. He took the stand and settled in. The jurors were looking at a clean-cut detective in a brown herringbone jacket, tie and a white button-down shirt. He had a rubber Timex sports watch on his wrist and a thick black pen sticking out of his shirt pocket. Olga Cepeda led him through his paces, beginning with arriving at the lakefront and observing the retrieval of the body. He was precise and articulate. She led the jury through his investigation in a logical procession.

Finally, it was Darcy's turn. Darcy asked a series of questions to highlight that Kelly and his partner Johnson had had no knowledge of Brian Kern until after they had cut a deal with Trip. Darcy began to zero in.

"Detective, who was it that first broached the idea of a deal being made for Trip to testify?"

"He did, actually," said Kelly.

"And when he did this, was that in front of you and your partner?"

"Um, no actually," said Kelly. "My partner had gone out to get a soda and Trip asked me if he could help himself in any way. I told him the only thing he could do is tell the truth. We would evaluate what he had to tell us and see if there was any way that we needed his help."

"What did he say to that?"

"He asked whether or not it would make a difference if someone else was involved that we don't know about. I said absolutely."

"So that was the genesis for your deal with him to cooperate, is that right?"

"I suppose so," said Kelly, "although I wouldn't characterize it in that way."

"Well that was the time at which he proposed to you being able to give you something in exchange for your being able to help him with this problem, is that right?" asked Darcy.

"Yes, that's correct," agreed Kelly.

"Specifically, he asked you if giving you information about someone else involved in his crime could lessen his sentence."

"Not verbatim, but yes, in so many words that's what he asked," Kelly agreed.

"And so he knew at that point that if he could testify against somebody that his sentence would be reduced and that he would get a lesser sentence for this crime, is that right?"

"Yes," said Kelly.

"And at this point, this was a deal between you and him."

"Not a deal," said Kelly. "We were in preliminary discussions."

"So rather than talking specifically about the case, your conversation with him while your partner was out of the room was what he could do to help himself, is that right?"

"That's what he wanted to talk about," said Kelly.

"So that would be a yes?" asked Darcy.

"Yes," said Kelly.

"What steps did you take at that point to memorialize this agreement between the two of you?"

"It wasn't really an agreement," said Kelly. "At this point we were talking about what he could do for us and what I could do for him."

"And what did you promise him?"

"I didn't promise him anything," said Kelly. "I told him that if he could help I would let the State's Attorney know about it and the State's Attorney would have to make the decision."

"Well, is that accurate?" asked Darcy.

Stevens jumped to his feet.

"Objection, Your Honor."

"Sustained," said the judge.

"Let me put it this way," Darcy began, "did he ask you what he could get if he gave you the name of the either one or more other person or people that were involved in this criminal act?"

"He did," said Kelly.

"And at that time, did you say to him that it would help him?"

"I did," said Kelly.

"And you don't have the authority to make that promise, isn't that correct?" asked Darcy.

Stevens again shot to his feet, objecting, but this time the judge overruled him.

Kelly thought about it.

"Well, I can't make the final decision, but my experience in dealing with the State's Attorney's Office is they do give deference to the detectives on the case."

"In other words, you don't have the ability to make that promise to him," said Darcy.

Kelly agreed, "Yes, that's correct."

"Now did you tell him that you didn't have the authority to make that promise?"

"Not exactly," said Kelly.

"You were trying to get out of him anyone else that might have been involved, is that right?"

"Yes, that's right," he said.

"And then eventually he told you about my client, Brian Kern, is that right?"

"That's right," said Kelly.

"Well, Detective Kelly, you weren't able to corroborate anything that he told you about Mr. Kern before you placed Mr. Kern under arrest, is that right?"

"Not exactly," said Kelly. "We were able to corroborate his address, his age and that he was a classmate at Longwood. Things like that."

"Were you able to corroborate any of the details pertaining to the crime that Trip told you about Mr. Kern?"

"No," conceded Kelly.

"And after you placed Brian Kern under arrest, he exercised his right to remain silent, isn't that right?"

"Yes."

"In fact, that was because a lawyer was there with him, right?"

"Right," agreed Kelly.

"You knew at the time that Laura Martin's body was recovered—or I should say you learned shortly afterward at the autopsy—that some material was taken from underneath the decedent's fingernails. In other words, they had scraped the fingernails of Laura Martin and recovered some material that the medical examiner believed could be tested for DNA, is that right?"

"That's correct," agreed Kelly.

"And you did not wait to find out the results of that DNA test, is that right?"

"That's correct," said Kelly. "It would have taken at least six weeks to get the results back."

"And you know sitting here today that the DNA came back not to the defendant Mr. Kern but rather to your witness, Mr. Phillips, is that correct?"

Again Kelly agreed.

"As you sit here today, Detective, you have no physical evidence linking the defendant to this crime, is that right?"

"That's correct," said Kelly.

"And the only evidence you have against this defendant is Mr. Phillips?"

"Pretty much," said Kelly.

Darcy went back to counsel table and whispered to Justin.

"Anything else that you can think of?" he said.

Justin checked his notes, crossing off various scribblings before answering.

"No, that's cool."

"Nothing further, Your Honor."

"Any redirect, state?"

Stevens stood.

"No further questions of this witness. Your Honor, at this time we seek leave of court to call John Henry Phillips III to the stand."

"Very well," said the judge, "bring him in."

Trip took the oath and sat down. He wore a blue blazer, khaki pants, blue button-down shirt, and a regimental striped tie. His hair was cut short, but he had some bad adolescent sideburns. He looked clean cut and appeared frightened to be there. Olga Cepeda began her direct by having Trip explain the deal he had gotten in exchange for his testimony.

"I'm going to prison for twenty-five years," he began. "I have immunity for any other crimes that may be brought up here. I have pled guilty to the murder of Laura Martin and I'm going to prison for twenty-five years, assuming that I testify truthfully."

Cepeda asked, "When are you to be sentenced?"

"After this case is over," Trip replied. "If I don't testify truthfully then the court could sentence me to anything they want on my plea of guilty to the murder of Laura Martin."

She then ran him through his first meeting of Laura Martin. According to him, they slowly developed a close relationship. Finally, she brought him to the day of the crime.

"Did something unusual happen that day?" she asked.

"Yes."

"What was that?"

"I picked Laura up and we were parked by a spot where a lot of us hang out by the lake."

"And what happened?"

"Well, Brian Kern showed up," he said.

"Did you know Brian from before?"

"Yes, he was a friend of mine."

"Do you see Brian seated in court today?" she asked.

"Yes," he said.

"Would you point to him and describe what he is wearing?"

He pointed to Brian and described his clothing.

Olga continued, "Your Honor, may the record reflect the in-court identification."

"So noted," said the judge.

"So what happened when Brian came to where you were parked?" Olga said.

"He came up and knocked on the car window."

"What did you do?"

"I told Laura I'd be right back."

"And where did you go?"

"I got out of the car and we went for a walk a little distance away."

"What happened then?"

"He looked like he was wasted or something."

Justin shot to his feet, followed closely by Darcy.

"Objection," they roared.

"Sustained."

"Tell us what you saw and heard," the judge said, "not what you believe."

"He had a look about him," Trip began.

Darcy and Justin again objected.

The judge leaned in, "Sir, tell us what he said and what you saw."

Trip nodded. "He told me he needed to get high and he wanted to know if I had anything."

"And what did you say?"

"I told him that I got a little something in the car, but I was planning on sharing it with Laura."

"What did he say to that?"

"He got angry. He said, 'Fuck her, let's get high and then we can both do her.'"

"What did you say?"

"I didn't say anything. I was a little bit afraid of him at this time."

"So what happened next?"

"He grabbed me. He pulled me toward him, then he said, 'I'm serious. We're going to do her whether she wants to or not.' I tried to say, you know, dude, back off, I'm dating her, and things like that, but he wasn't having any of it."

"What happened next?"

"He pulled out a knife. It was one of those lock blades, black with gold, and he snapped it open and held it to my throat and said, 'Either you're with me or you're against me.'"

"What did you do then?"

"I was so frightened I did what he told me to do."

"So what happened?"

"He told me to go get Laura and that we were going to go down by the beach."

"Then what happened?"

"I got Laura out of the car and we went to where he was."

"Then what happened?"

"We started walking through the patch of woods that leads to the bluff that goes down by the lake."

"Then what happened?"

"He had the knife behind him. She couldn't see it. All of a sudden he came up on her and put the knife to her throat."

"Then what happened?"

"He used his leg and kicked her backwards on the ground and he was on top of her."

"What happened then?"

"He screamed at me and said, 'You hold her down or I'll kill you.'"

"What did you do?"

"I went to grab her arms. She was fighting and trying to keep me off. She scratched my arms but I was able to hold onto her arms."

"Then what happened?"

"He wrapped a tie around her mouth and tightened it real tight so you couldn't hear her screaming."

"Had she been screaming at that point?" she asked.

"A little bit," he said, "mostly she was pleading, saying 'please don't do this. Let me go. Leave me alone. Please don't do this. Let me go. Leave me alone.'"

"Who was she saying that to?"

"She was saying that to him and then she'd look at me and she'd say 'Help me! Help me! Don't let him do this.'"

"What did you do then?"

"Nothing."

"Why? Why didn't you do anything?"

"Because I believed him when he said he was going to kill me," he said.

Olga flipped over a page on her legal pad.

"What happened next?" she asked.

Trip's voice cracked then he regained his voice.

"He punched her in the face then he held the knife up to her throat and said, 'You move and I'll kill you.'"

"Then what happened?"

"And then he cut her pants off."

"How did he do that?"

"He unbuttoned the pants and tried to unzip them, then he took the knife and he pulled it just to the side of where the button was, cut it and just ran it right down the leg."

"What did he do?"

"He pulled her pants off and then her underpants."

"What was she doing?"

"She was sobbing," he said, looking down in disgust.

"What happened next?" she asked.

"He raped her."

"By that you mean, he had sexual intercourse with her?" Olga asked.

"Yes," he said.

"After a while did that end?"

"It did," he said.

"Then what happened?"

"Well, he was kind of resting for a little bit and then he looked at me and said, 'We got to take care of this.'"

"Did you know what he meant?"

"I wasn't sure, but I was afraid," he said.

"So what happened next?"

"He said to her that he would take the gag off but if she screamed, he'd stab her."

"What did she do?"

"She was just crying," he said.

"Was it loud?"

"No, it was like a whimper," he replied.

"So what happened next?"

"He had the knife in his right hand and with his left hand he reached up and pulled the gag off her mouth. The tie went just over her chin and fell down around her neck."

"Then what happened?"

"He kind of pulled one end of the tie and it tightened around her neck."

"Then what happened?" she asked.

"It was like he snapped."

Darcy objected but the judge overruled it.

"Go on," she said.

"Then he started tightening it more and more. She was choking and having trouble breathing. She let out a scream then he just jammed the knife into her somewhere in the chest between the chest and the belly-button."

"What happened?"

"She got this shocked look on her face. She was making no noise, just sort of a gurgling sound."

"What happened then?"

"He tightened the tie around her neck more. He was pulling on it with both his hands now with the knife there and I could see blood on the knife."

"What happened?"

"After a while she began twitching a little bit and then she stopped moving."

"And what did you notice about her?"

"Her eyes were open but it didn't look like she was breathing anymore."

"What happened next?"

"He cut off her shirt. It was like a cross between a sweatshirt and a T-shirt and he cut that off and the shirt underneath it, which was a T-shirt, and her bra."

"Then what happened?"

"Well at that point she just had on some socks and her shoes and her pants were hanging half off of her and he took everything off of her."

"Then what happened?"

"He told me to gather up all her clothes."

"Did you do that?"

"Yes."

"How did you do that?"

"Well, I rolled everything up into a big ball."

"Then what happened?"

"He said we had to get rid of her. He told me to hold her arms. He grabbed her ankles and we carried her to the edge of the cliff that overlooks the lake and we threw her down. Her body hit down on the ground below, then we made our way down. We brought her out and pitched her into the lake."

"Now the point where you threw her into the lake, is it a beach?"

"No," Trip said. "It's a rock wall. So once we got to the edge of the wall we pitched her in. She was in the lake, not in the shallow water by the beach."

"Then what happened?"

"We walked back up. We got the ball of clothes, then we got in my car and we began to drive."

"Then what happened?"

"There was a plastic bag in my car that I used to hold a bunch of CDs and Brian took that bag and threw the ball of clothes in there and we drove."

"Where did you go?"

"We just headed south."

"Then what did you do?"

"We went into downtown Evanston. We went to a Burger King and Brian took the bag of clothes and he threw it in the garbage can that was in the parking lot by the Burger King."

"Then what happened?"

"We went in and we had something to eat."

"Did you talk about anything then?"

"Yeah, he told me if I told anybody what happened he'd kill me."

"Did you ever come forward?"

"Not until I was sitting with the detective."

"Was that at Evanston Police?"

"Yes."

With that she tendered the witness. A few of the jurors were clearly disgusted. Olga slowly made her way back to her seat. She wanted to let Trip's testimony marinate with the jury before Darcy could respond. Darcy shot to his feet eagerly and dropped a notepad on the podium.

Darcy began.

"Mr. Phillips, Mr. Kern is a friend of yours from Longwood Prep, isn't that right?"

"Yes."

"Prior to this night, you had never seen anything from him that made you fear for your life, isn't that correct?"

"Yes," he said.

"And the two of you had done a lot together, isn't that right?"

"Yes," he agreed.

"And according to your testimony, Laura Martin was your girlfriend, isn't that right?"

"Yes," he said.

"But prior to this night, your friend Mr. Kern and Laura Martin had never met, isn't that right?"

"Yes, that's correct."

"And Mr. Kern at this time was your closest friend, wasn't he?"

"I suppose so," agreed Trip.

"Now when you were at the police station you began to talk about a deal giving up your best friend to help you in your case, isn't that right?"

"I guess," he said.

"You guess?" asked Darcy. "Aren't you sure?"

"Well, it wasn't exactly like that."

"Well, did you ask the detective or detectives if there was something you could do to help your case?"

"Not exactly," he said.

"Okay, let's start at the beginning," said Darcy. "When you went to the Evanston Police Station, who did you go with?"

"Detectives Johnson and Kelly," he said.

"And at some point did you begin a conversation with either one or both of the officers about someone else being involved in this crime?"

"Yes," he said.

"And who was that?"

"Detective Johnson," he said.

"I see," said Darcy, "and what did you and Detective Johnson talk about?"

"I asked Detective Johnson if someone else was involved in this and I told him about it, would that help me?"

"What did he say?"

"He said, 'Yes, it would help you.'"

"And what did you tell him?"

"I told him that I know what happened but I'm not telling anyone unless I know what's going to happen to me."

"So what happened then?"

"He told me that he can make a deal with me that if I tell him what I know that he could make it easier on me."

"And what did that mean to you?" he said.

"Well, originally he told me that I was going to get sentenced to die. I didn't want to die. So I asked him what we could do and he told me that if I came clean he would let the prosecutor know. That's when I asked him if someone else was involved and I told him about that person, would it help me."

"Where was Detective Kelly when you were talking to Detective Johnson?"

"I don't know," he said.

"Describe Detective Johnson for the ladies and gentlemen of the jury."

"He's about six foot one, black guy, kind of strong," he said.

"I see," said Darcy. Darcy knew the jury had picked up on his mistake. They had met Kelly. It would be difficult to believe somebody cutting a deal to save their life could confuse or forget who they dealt with. Darcy pushed ahead. "Now when you were talking with Detective Johnson about these things, did you eventually arrive at an understanding?"

"Yes," he said.

"And what was that understanding?"

"That they would go easy on me if I told them the truth."

"And so did you tell them the truth?" Darcy said.

"Yes."

"And then what happened?"

"He said he would let the prosecutors know and we would work something out but I had to be willing to testify."

"At some point did a lawyer get involved?" Darcy asked.

"Yes."

"When was that?"

"While I was at the police station a lawyer showed up. My parents hired him."

"And at that time did you finalize the details of this deal you had with them?"

"Yes, the lawyer did."

"And as part of that deal you're pleading guilty to one count of murder of Laura Martin, getting a sentence of twenty-five years in the Illinois Department of Corrections, and the Cook County State's Attorney's Office gave you immunity for any other crimes, isn't that right?"

"Yes."

"Now, that's important to you, isn't it?"

"What do you mean?" Trip said.

"Well, your lawyer wouldn't let you testify unless you had immunity for any other crimes, isn't that right?"

"Yes."

"You understand that, don't you?"

"Yes."

"And that's because there's some issues that could come up and your lawyer is afraid of you getting into any further trouble, isn't that right?"

"Yes."

"I want to bring you back to a point in your testimony where you and Mr. Kern are standing on the edge of the woods and your car is back in the parking lot, do you remember that point?"

"Yes," he said.

"At that point, according to your testimony, Mr. Kern showed you the knife and he told you that you had to go get Laura and bring her back, do you remember that?"

"Yes."

"And you went over to her where Laura was in the car, is that right?"

"Yes."

"And that was fifty to one hundred feet away from where you were, isn't that right?"

"Yes."

"And when you walked that fifty to one hundred feet toward Laura you were walking away from Mr. Kern, isn't that right?"

"Yes."

"And Mr. Kern didn't move. He stayed there, right?"

"Yes."

"And you got to your car. By the way, did you have your car keys with you?"

"No."

"Were they in the ignition?"

"Yes."

"When you left Laura, was the car running?"

"Yes."

"And you got in the car to talk to Laura, is that right?"

"Yes."

"And you talked to her and said, 'Hey, I want you to come outside,' right?"

"Yes."

"There was nothing stopping you from putting that car into reverse, backing up and driving away, was there?"

"No, just that I was afraid."

"You were afraid of this man standing one hundred feet away, correct?"

"Yes."

"And yet when you had the opportunity to escape, you got into a car that was running, all you had to do was put it into gear and drive away, isn't that correct?"

"Yes."

"And you didn't do that, did you?"

"No."

"In fact, you brought Laura, your girlfriend, into harm's way, right?"

"Yes."

"You got your girlfriend and you walked her to this person, isn't that right?" Darcy asked in mocking tone.

"I suppose so," Trip said.

"Well let's get back to you. You're so afraid of this young man that instead of fleeing, you're going to do anything he said, including murder, isn't that right?"

"Yes."

"Now, you've done some things that you're not proud of, right?"

"Yes."

"Do you do drugs?"

"Yes."

"Do you drink?"

"Yes."

Darcy suddenly shifted gears.

"I want to ask you about somebody named Margaret Heming."

"Objection," said Stevens and Cepeda in unison.

"I don't know yet, overruled for now. You'll tie this up, Mr. Cole?"

"Absolutely, judge. You know Margaret Heming, don't you?"

"Yes," Trip answered.

"And Margaret Heming is someone that you were at a party with, right?"

"Yes."

"Are you familiar with a drug that's known as GHB on the streets?"

"Yes."

"You put some GHB in Margaret Heming's drink at a party, didn't you?"

Olga shot to her feet followed by Stevens.

"Objection, Your Honor."

"Overruled," the judge answered.

Trip was uncomfortable. He looked away as Darcy reminded him.

"You have immunity and as long as you admit to any crimes on the witness stand, you can't be prosecuted for them, right?"

Trip agreed, "Yes."

"But they have to be brought up by me in order to be covered by your immunity agreement, right?"

"Yes," he agreed.

"And so by admitting to these crimes on questions that I bring up, it saves you from being prosecuted for them in theory, right?" Darcy asked.

Trip's energy level picked up.

"Yes," he agreed.

"So I am going to ask you again. Did you put some GHB in Margaret Heming's drink?"

"Yes," he said.

"And that's commonly known as the 'date-rape drug,' because it knocks the victims out. Makes them unconscious, right?"

"Yes," he said.

"And when Margaret Heming was unconscious, you took her into a room at this party. You undressed her and you had sexual intercourse with her, didn't you?"

"Yes," he admitted.

The jury was now staring daggers at him.

"And when you did this, my client didn't participate in that, did he?"

"No," he admitted.

"It was just you, right?"

"Yes."

"And you're not going to get prosecuted for that because of your immunity deal with the prosecutors, right?"

"Yes," he said.

"Well, let's talk about Brittany Wilson."

Again the state objected, but the judge waved them off.

"No, no, I want to hear this," he said.

"You know Brittany Wilson, don't you?"

"Yes," Trip said.

"You were with Brittany Wilson at a party at Craig Cizmar's house almost two years ago, right?"

"Yes," he agreed.

"And again you slipped some of that drug into her drink, right?"

"Yes."

"And again you raped her, right?"

"Yes."

"Was my client there helping you?"

"Yes, he was," he said.

"I see. And what happened that night?"

"What do you mean?"

"Well, at some point she came to, right?"

"Yes."

"And she started saying that she was going to call the police because she knew what you did to her, isn't that right?"

"Yes."

"And then you killed her by stabbing her twice, isn't that right?"

"No," Trip said.

"Well, were you there when she was stabbed?"

"Yes."

"Who stabbed her?"

"Your client, Brian Kern."

A rush went through the courtroom, and everybody was now leaning forward.

"There's a problem with that," Darcy said. "Don't you remember that my client was living in England at that time?"

A little smile crept across Trip's face.

"Oh, that's right," he said. "I guess he wasn't there."

"Well you have to tell the truth for immunity to apply, isn't that right?" Darcy said.

"Yes."

"So I'm going to ask you again, didn't you kill Brittany Wilson at Craig Cizmar's house?"

Trip waited a second.

"Not in his house."

"Well, where did you kill her?"

"In Craig's backyard."

The jury was disgusted with Trip.

"And you killed her in Craig Cizmar's backyard by stabbing her twice, isn't that right?" Darcy bore in on Trip.

"Yes," Trip said.

"Now, Craig Cizmar lives in Lake Forest, right?"

"Yes."

"And you have a deal with the Cook County State's Attorney's Office for immunity, don't you?"

"Yes," Trip said, annoyed.

"Well, Lake Forest is in Lake County."

"So?" he said.

"You don't have an immunity deal with Lake County, do you?"

It hit him like a shot in the face. He reached out and grabbed the rail of the jury box and began to stand.

"I want my lawyer," he said.

The judge looked at him.

"Sit down, Mr. Phillips."

Darcy resumed his questioning.

"Do you really expect the ladies and gentlemen of this jury to believe that you, a rapist and a murderer, were afraid of my client?"

"I'm not answering any of your questions," Trip said.

"Your Honor, I ask that you direct the witness to answer questions."

"You will answer the questions," Judge Wolfe said.

"I want my lawyer," Trip said.

"You're going to answer these questions, period," the judge said. "Or I'm going to lock you up right now."

"You weren't afraid of my client that night, were you?" Darcy asked.

"Yes, I was. He threatened to kill me."

"Was my client even there?"

"Oh yeah, he was there. He killed her."

"Just like he killed Brittany Wilson?" Darcy asked.

The state objected.

"Sustained."

Darcy turned toward the judge.

"I have no more questions."

40

THE STATE CALLED ITS LAST witness, Rick Li, an employee of Macon and Wall. Macon and Wall had been making fine men's clothing since the early 1800s. Impeccably groomed, Rick Li cut a dashing figure in a tailored pinstriped suit, silk tie, and Pima cotton shirt with French cuffs. After Li took the oath and was seated, Larry Stevens ran him through some preliminary questions. Finally, he showed him People's Exhibit Number 110, which was the tie that was taken from Laura Martin's body. Stevens handed Mr. Li a large clear plastic bag that contained the tie.

"Mr. Li, do you recognize what's contained in this plastic bag?"

"I do," he said.

"And what is that?"

"That is one of our ties."

"How do you know that?" asked Stevens.

"First just by looking at it I can tell that it's a tie that came from our shop. Further, I can see the label which is clearly visible through this bag. It is our label. And finally, I recall the fabric."

"Now this tie, do you sell them off a rack in the store?"

"No sir," said Mr. Li.

"How do you sell your ties?" Stevens asked.

"Our clients have very discriminating tastes. We show them possibilities and they tell us what they would like."

"Could you explain that a little bit more?" said Stevens.

"Yes sir. We have swatches of material that come from different bolts of fabric. Clients choose their fabric and style. They tell us what they want and we make it for them."

"Is there a limit to how many ties you will make out of the same material?"

"There is. We will never make more than ten ties from the bolt of fabric."

"I see. Well, are there other bolts of fabric of the same pattern?"

"No, we will only do one bolt of fabric of one pattern, with the exception of school ties, regimental ties, club ties, things of that nature. For individual ties we are very concerned with limiting our output."

"Do you keep records of the ties you make?"

"Absolutely, we keep records of everything that we make."

"Prior to your testimony, did I ask you to check your records regarding this specific material?"

"You did."

"And sir, I am going to show copies of your records, which I marked as People's Exhibit Number 111."

Stevens walked over toward counsel table to show Darcy and Justin the exhibit. Darcy held his hand up, waving him off to show he accepted the evidence. Stevens then proceeded.

"I have shown People's Exhibit 111 to opposing counsel. May I approach, Your Honor?"

"By all means," the judge said.

Stevens handed the records to Mr. Li.

"Do you recognize these?"

"I do. Those are the records that you showed me earlier. They are the records from my shop."

"When you went through those records, did you determine how many ties were made from this material?"

"I did. There were four," he said.

"And sir, did you learn the identities of the four people that you made these ties for?"

"I did."

"And was one of those individuals a person by the name of Paul Kern?"

"That's correct."

Mr. Stevens stood in the well of the court and addressed the judge.

"Your Honor, at this time the parties will be proceeding by way of stipulation."

"By all means," the judge said. "Is it in writing?"

"It is."

Stevens walked up and handed a copy to the judge. He then walked over and stood in front of the jury box and addressed the jury directly.

"Ladies and gentlemen of the jury, at this point the parties, the People of the State of Illinois and the duly elected Cook County State's Attorney by and through his assistants, Olga Cepeda and Larry Stevens, and by the defendant, Brian Kern, by and through his attorneys, Darcy Cole and Justin Schachter, agree that if the witness, Mr. Rick Li, were to be shown a photograph of Paul Kern or would Paul Kern have been called as a witness he would iden- tify Paul Kern as the person for whom this tie was made and who purchased this tie. Furthermore, there would be a stipulation that Paul Kern is Brian Kern's father."

"So stipulated?"

"So stipulated," replied Darcy and Justin.

Paul Kern stared at his tie. He remembered it, but had never even noticed it was gone. He was amazed that something as innocuous as a tie could be so destructive. He gritted his teeth and felt nauseous.

They then tendered the witness for cross-examination. They could have asked him if he knew for sure if the tie that he was holding was the same tie that was sold to Paul Kern. They suspected that they would only lose credibility in the eyes of the jury, however, so after a brief conversation they both agreed that it would be better to let the witness go without cross. Darcy stood.

"We have no questions of this witness. Thank you, Your Honor."

Darcy was calm. He knew that he had some ammo for his closing argument.

The state rested.

Outside the presence of the jury, Darcy made a motion for a directed verdict, which was denied. He then informed the court of his intention to call Margaret Heming to the stand. Olga and Larry leapt to their feet, screaming objections. The judge stood and looked to the jury.

"Ladies and gentlemen, this would be a good time for you to take a break, use the bathroom, and stretch your legs. We'll be back to you in just a few minutes. There are a few legal issues I need to discuss with the lawyers." With that, the sheriff led the jury out and the judge had the lawyers approach the bench. Olga Cepeda started in immediately.

"There is no reason to call Margaret Heming other than to play to the emotions of this jury. The witness in this case has admitted that he raped Margaret Heming. There is no issue in dispute. There's no reason to call her."

"I disagree," said the Judge Wolfe, "but I will limit the scope of her direct. In addition to that, are you going to try and call someone to prove up the Brittany Wilson murder?"

"I have a Lake Forest detective," Darcy said.

"And what is he going to testify to?" the judge asked.

"The brutal nature of the murder and the similarities between Brittany Wilson's murder and this murder. It's proof of other crimes in reverse."

"Proof of other crimes in reverse?" the Judge Wolfe asked. "There is no such thing."

"Yes, the state uses proof of other crimes, not to prove that the defendant had a propensity toward committing the crime, but as a *modus operandi* or fingerprint that the crimes were so similar and the method unique that it's clear that the defendant committed the crime. In this case, I am trying to show that the Brittany Wilson murder was so similar to the Laura Martin murder that in fact it was not the defendant but the prosecution's own witness who committed the Martin murder. This is the logical extension of that."

"I see," said the judge. "And that's what you would call a reverse proof of other crimes?"

Darcy smiled. "I believe we should be allowed to perfect this impeachment."

"Well, I am going to have to think about this."

After getting the jury settled in the room, one of the sheriffs walked back into the courtroom. The judge addressed her.

"Susan, why don't you take the jury to lunch?"

"If it's all the same with you judge, we ordered food and it's being brought up to them."

"That's fine." Judge Wolfe let the sheriff leave and then addressed the lawyers. "Um, ladies and gentlemen, why don't we do the jury instructions conference in about a half hour? You could grab a quick bite. I'm going to do a little research, then we'll do the instructions conference, and I'll give you my rulings on the Heming and Wilson evidence."

Justin pulled a protein bar and some raw almonds from a pocket in his briefcase and bought a bottle of water from the vending machine in the first-floor canteen. Darcy got a cup of coffee and they stood against the white Formica table in a room that was full of smoke.

"So what do you think?" Justin said.

"I think that diet is going to kill you," said Darcy.

"What do you think about the case?"

"I think they'll let us put on Heming and I think they'll let us get into the Wilson murder, but not too far."

"I agree," said Justin, "then what?"

"Then we argue the hell out of this."

Justin ate in a rush and downed the water bottle in two big gulps. Darcy finished his coffee and threw the cup in the garbage and they headed back upstairs. Judge Wolfe's chambers were sparsely furnished. He had two pictures of his family and a picture of a sailboat on an open lake. On the far wall were his diplomas, University of Illinois undergrad and Loyola University Law. There was also a photo of him with a prominent alderman, who also happened to be a committeeman and was probably the reason that Judge Wolfe was a judge in the first place.

"Okay, you can call Heming," he said, "and you can call the detective on Wilson, but I am going to give you very little latitude. I do not want this turning into a farce."

Darcy crossed his legs.

"A farce," he said, "you mean when the star witness/flipper admits to other crimes including murder and rape and has immunity for them?"

"Nice try," said Stevens, "but since you already got him to

admit to a murder that he doesn't have immunity to, the Lake County prosecutors will probably want your boy to testify."

"Then why don't we cut a deal right now?" said Darcy.

"What kind of deal?" said Stevens.

"Five years on concealing a homicidal death," said Darcy.

"You're out of your mind," said Stevens.

"Well, what do you want?" said Darcy.

"It has to be more than five and it's not on a concealing. It's got to be a first-degree murder."

"First-degree murder does a hundred percent time," said Darcy. "It's out of the question."

"Well, what do you propose?" Stevens shot back.

Justin chimed in.

"How about ten on a second degree?"

"No way," said Stevens. "He'll do four and a half and he's already been in long enough that he'll be taking a short bus ride."

"If he testifies in Lake County," Darcy said, "then he's earning his time off. You cut a deal with this scumbag and it blew up in your face. At least you know that my guy isn't involved in any other crimes."

"We don't know that," said Olga.

"Please," said Justin. "You blew it. You bet on the wrong pony."

"Bet on the wrong pony?" said Olga angrily.

Before she could finish her thought, Judge Wolfe interjected.

"Look, let's get through this trial. Do you want to cut a deal?" he said to Stevens.

"No," he said, after conferring with Olga.

"Okay, then let's finish this."

"Is there anything in the jury instructions out of the ordinary?" Judge Wolfe asked.

"No," said Stevens. "Although we are asking for an accountability instruction."

Darcy shot to his feet. Accountability meant that Kern could be held responsible for the actions of Trip.

"Accountability? Judge, they flipped that scumbag to testify that my client did the crime and now they're backing off, and they want accountability? The instruction itself says that they, or someone else for whom they are legally responsible, committed this crime. They can't have it both ways, Judge. Either they believe that my client murdered her or they disbelieve it and he should be acquitted."

"I like the passion," Wolfe said. "Of course, I'm giving them the accountability instruction anyway. So what else do you have?"

"Judge, may I be heard on this?" Justin said.

"No, I'm giving the instruction. Let's move on."

They finished the instructions conference and were ready to proceed with the defense case.

Margaret Heming stood about five foot three and may have weighed a hundred and ten pounds. She had short blonde hair, the kind of blonde hair that could be purchased at Walgreens. Modestly dressed, her only jewelry was diamond studded earrings and an angel pin that stuck to the lapel of the jacket she wore over a button-down shirt. The angel pin had been hers for approximately ten minutes before coming to court. It was in those ten minutes that Justin had persuaded her to accept and wear the pin that he had purchased for her. Margaret Heming got through most of her testimony in a firm voice until she got to the assault itself.

"And did you know what happened?" Darcy asked.

"I wasn't quite clear what was going on. I couldn't move and I was floating in and out of consciousness, but I had this sensation that somebody was on me."

"And you know who that was?"

"Absolutely," she said. "It was Trip."

"By Trip you mean John Henry Phillips III?" asked Darcy.

"Yes," she said.

"And what happened?"

"I was dazed and after a while he got off of me."

"Could you feel what was happening?"

"I could only feel it in sort of a distant way. I mean I knew something was happening but it's like when the dentist is drilling your tooth and you know that it's being drilled and you can feel a little bit of pressure, but you don't feel any pain or feel connected to it."

"Then what happened?" said Darcy.

"After a while, things started coming back to me and I got dressed, and I was so ashamed, I cried and cried."

"What happened?"

"I had to clean myself off."

"When you say clean yourself off, what do you mean?" said Darcy.

"Well, he had ejaculated and it was just a mess," she said. "So I cleaned myself off and I got dressed. I went home and showered."

"Did you ever call the police?"

"No," she said. "I was ashamed and I felt that somehow it was my fault."

"Why is that?"

"Well, I was drinking that night and I thought that I had too much to drink and that made me feel that I might have contributed to this, but after a while I realized that I hadn't had that much to drink. He had slipped something into my drink."

This is the point where the state could have objected. Olga and Larry chose instead to try and get through this with the minimal amount of damage. They didn't want to alienate the jury any further by having the rape victim of their star witness being challenged by them.

"Did you ever talk to Trip about this?"

"Yes," she said. "About a week later, I confronted him."

"And what did you say to him?"

"I said, 'You raped me.'"

"What did he say to you?"

"'Well, don't worry because it wasn't all that good so it won't happen again.'"

"What did you do?"

"I slapped him as hard I could," she said.

"Did you ever go to the police and tell them what he had done to you?"

"Yes," she said.

"And when was that?"

"After I heard that he got arrested in this case."

"And why did you do that then?"

"Because I thought they had to know what he did to me and I was no longer afraid because, well, they had him in jail."

"I have no further questions of this witness," said Darcy.

Olga Cepeda stood and approached her.

"Ms. Heming, I am very sorry for your ordeal."

"Thank you," she said.

"I have a few questions," Olga continued. "The night this happened you had been drinking alcohol?"

"Yes."

"And at that time, you were not of legal age to drink, is that right?"

"That's correct," she said.

"And did you do any drugs that night?"

"Maybe," she said. "I don't really remember."

"Well, what would you have done—marijuana, cocaine?"

"Yeah, whatever was around," she said.

"So that night you were intoxicated?"

"No, I think I was drugged," Margaret said, "and not by what I chose, but what your client chose."

"He's not my client, he's a witness," Olga said.

"Well, whatever he is, I'm talking about Trip. He put something into my drink and that's how I ended up being raped by him, your witness," Margaret said.

Olga had to backpedal. She didn't want to get into a fight with Margaret in front of the jury. She tried softening things up.

"Is it fair to say that you don't really remember this so-called assault?"

Margaret was livid.

"'So-called assault'? How about when I had the so-called semen from your so-called witness dripping from my vaginal area?"

Olga was in trouble. The jury was probably getting angry with her and she had to get a way out.

"So Ms. Heming, you didn't come forward on this for months and months and months, isn't that right?"

"I didn't come forward until after your witness was arrested and I knew then that I could come forward safely. See, I didn't want to end up like Laura Martin with your witness out there."

Olga cut her losses.

"No further questions of this young lady," she said.

Justin called Lake Forest Detective Rob Lambert to the stand to testify about the Wilson murder. Lambert walked up to the jury box and took the oath. He was wearing a short-sleeved dress shirt and a Sipowicz tie that left about four inches from the bottom of the tie to his belt. Justin took Lambert through the investigation from the discovery of Brittany Wilson's body until the investigation had stalled. The best that Lambert could do was say that Trip had been one of the last people that Brittany Wilson had been with prior to her death. It was the brutality of her murder and the similarity to the murder of Laura Martin that was important. The lingering question of proving it against Trip was made unimportant when he admitted to it during cross-examination. After milking Lambert as much as he could before the jury, Darcy tendered the witness. Thinking of Olga's walk through quicksand, Stevens declined to ask any questions of Lambert, and the defense rested. The judge asked them to go immediately to closing argument.

Paul Kern was holding hands with his wife as they sat in the hard wooden pew. He had sweated through his blue dress shirt. Darcy was calm and in control. Paul watched Darcy and marveled as confidence radiated from the seasoned courtroom veteran.

Olga Cepeda did the state's initial closing argument.

"Ladies and gentlemen, the evidence here is overwhelming. We told you in the beginning that you would not like Trip. We told you that it wasn't our choice to put Trip on, but that it was Mr. Kern's choice," she said, pointing to Brian. "You see, it was Mr. Kern who decided who the witnesses would be because it was Mr. Kern who raped and killed Laura Martin. You know, Mr. Cole has tried very hard to make you hate Trip. So hate him all you want. But you know that Laura Martin is dead and you know that the two of them were there, and that the two of them participated, which is why you're going to get a jury instruction that talks about accountability. Accountability is the legal rule that says when two people get together and work together to kill somebody, we don't have to prove if A did the stabbing or if B did the stabbing. From the fact that they worked together, A is responsible for the actions of B, and B is responsible for the actions of A. So if you want to believe Mr. Cole's theory that in fact it was Trip who was the one who delivered the fatal blow that's fine, but his client was there up to his eyeballs in guilt. Ladies and gentlemen, the evidence is overwhelming. Yes, Trip brings baggage to the stand, and God bless Margaret Heming."

"Objection," said Darcy.

"It's argument," the judge said. "The jury will reach its own conclusions."

"The Brittany Wilson murder was horrible, horrible. But let's not lose sight of the fact that these two young men were together with Laura Martin and these two worked together and these two are responsible for the death of Laura Martin. So, ladies and gentlemen, you are going to hear from the defense and after the defense argues, my partner, Mr. Stevens, will talk to you one more time, and at that time he will hopefully answer all of the questions that may remain in your mind. But make no mistake about this: this defendant," she said, pointing at Kern, "is guilty beyond all reasonable doubt. He's responsible for what happened that night because he participated in what happened that night. Ladies and gentlemen, find him guilty."

Darcy stood center stage.

"Ladies and gentlemen, whose DNA material was found under the fingernails of Laura Martin? Laura Martin struggled for her life and she struggled against her attacker. Her attacker had a lot of experience in rape and murder because he had done it before, he had raped Margaret Heming and he had raped and murdered Brittany Wilson, and ladies and gentlemen, he was doing it again. These people," he said pointing to the State's Attorneys, "gave him a deal. The deal they gave him was beautiful. They were going to give him almost the minimum amount of time possible and not even punish him for the rape of Margaret Heming and the murder of Brittany Wilson."

Stevens objected and the court sustained it. The judge told the jury to disregard it, but Darcy had rung a bell and the bell could not be unrung. He knew it and continued.

"Ladies and gentlemen, in the opening of this case, Ms. Cepeda and Mr. Stevens didn't talk about accountability. They weren't saying that Mr. Kern was accountable. They said he did the murder. It wasn't until after this trial started and they learned during the cross-examination of their star witness that they were wrong. They were wrong. They cut a deal with the devil. A young man who would rape and murder—would that man also lie to help himself cut a deal? Of course he would. If he would rape a young girl and humiliate her, if he would rape and murder another young girl, for nothing more than the sadistic pleasure of watching her die so that he could feel powerful and Godlike, would he lie? Of course he would, and he did. And you know what? We caught him. Remember what he told you? 'Oh yeah, Kern raped and killed Brittany Wilson.' And then when he learns that Mr. Kern was in England and couldn't have possibly been there, and he was reminded of his great immunity deal, he fesses up and says 'Oh yeah, I did that by myself.' It makes you wonder what else he's done that we don't know about."

Olga shot to her feet and objected, and the judge overruled it and waved her down.

"You know what else is interesting? How about that little tidbit where he can't tell the difference between Detective Kelly and Detective Johnson? Now, it seems to me that when you cut a deal to save your life, you'd know who you'd cut it with, but if you're a pathological liar, then you probably wouldn't even notice who you were lying to. I submit to you in this case, it may seem like a small thing not being able to tell Johnson from Kelly. But think if it was the most important moment in your life, wouldn't you remember it correctly? What evidence do they have that my client committed this murder? Well, if you take away Trip, the only thing you're left with is a tie. Now, a tie doesn't commit a murder. It seems to me since Trip and my client, Mr. Kern, were friends, Trip could have taken the tie from my client's home or my client's car at any time. My client doesn't necessarily have to be present just because something from his father's closet is present. Do we convict the young man for murder because a tie from his home is present at the murder scene? There's no DNA. There's no confession or statement from my client admitting anything. You have a tie and you have a raping, murdering liar. Ladies and gentlemen, that is the essence of reasonable doubt. An unbelievable witness with no corroboration. Ladies and gentlemen, we have all seen, over the past few years, the discovery of cases where people were convicted even though they were actually innocent."

Cepeda and Stevens shot to their feet with objections and the judge sustained it, and ordered the jury to disregard that comment.

"Let me say this," said Darcy, "when you go back into that jury room and you talk about this case, you have to bring your life experiences, your common sense, and your intelligence with you. Ladies and gentlemen, if you do that, I'm absolutely certain that you will return the only verdict that is fair, that is just—a verdict of not guilty. Ladies and gentlemen, if Trip, John Henry Phillips III, Longwood Prep, BMW-driving, rich monster Trip, told me that it was a sunny day, I'd grab my umbrella. Do not take my client's life from him based on the testimony of John Henry Phillips III. You know, it's interesting that his nickname is Trip. By my count, we know that he raped Margaret Heming. We know that he murdered Brittany Wilson and we now know that he murdered Laura Martin, the Third or 'Trip' in his litany of evil. Ladies and gentlemen, find my client, Brian Kern, not guilty on all counts."

Brian sat stoically watching Darcy walk toward him. Paul Kern was satisfied. He hired Darcy and Darcy did a great job. Paul Kern felt a little bit like a father. A feeling he barely remembered.

Stevens had some ground to make up, and he came out firing.

"No doubt about it, John Henry Phillips III is garbage. He is a horrible human being, but it doesn't mean that when he told you what happened that it wasn't true. How do we know it's true? Well, first of all how would he get that tie? How does Mr. Cole put the tie in Trip's hands if it doesn't come through his client, Mr. Kern?"

He then pointed to Kern.

"This man heard the exploits of Trip, Trip the amoral, the murderer, the rapist, and he said, 'I want to get in that club with you.' You see, these two were outcasts, losers, no friends, nobody to be with except each other. Kern wanted to be like Trip, and you see, he is like Trip because he and Trip got together, and together they raped and murdered Laura Martin. Mr. Schachter and Mr. Cole are great lawyers, but they're not very good magicians, because they can't make the evidence disappear. The evidence here is overwhelming. The proof is clearly well beyond reasonable doubt. Ladies and gentlemen, the task ahead of you is not difficult. The task ahead of you is to see clearly and remain focused on what the evidence is. Not what Mr. Cole wants you believe it is, but what it actually is. The evidence is what you heard from that witness stand," he said, pointing to the stand. "Ladies and gentlemen, it is clear and overwhelming, and it is your duty to find this defendant," he said pointing to Kern, "guilty on all counts."

The judge slowly and carefully read the jury instructions to the jury and sent them to deliberate. The sheriff began bringing the exhibits in after they got settled in the jury room. Judge Wolfe summoned all the lawyers to chambers.

"Well, ladies and gentlemen," he said, "quite a case."

He hung his robe up and was pacing behind his desk.

"So, are you still seeking death?" he asked the state.

"No," conceded Stevens. "I'm not going for death on this anymore."

"That's what I figured," said the judge, "when you put the accountability instruction in, you kind of killed all of your chances of frying this kid."

"Well, I have reservations anyway," Stevens said.

"Would that be because you flipped the wrong guy?" Judge Wolfe asked. "So what are you going to do? You have the flipper who has confessed to a rape and a murder in another county."

"We talked to Lake County," Stevens began, "they're going to take him after the trial and they're going to charge him with the murder."

"What about the rape? That young woman who got raped."

"I don't think they're going to proceed on that," Stevens said.

"Okay, are they interested in Darcy's client being a witness?" Judge Wolfe asked.

"Yes," Stevens conceded.

"What do you want to do about that?"

"Assuming we get a guilty verdict," Stevens answered, "I wouldn't be opposed to continuing sentencing until Lake County is done."

"You want me to carry this case three years from conviction until sentencing?"

Stevens was dejected. "What do you want me to do, Judge?"

"I don't know," said Judge Wolfe. "This whole thing stinks."

"How about if we cut a deal?" said Justin.

"You want to cut a deal now?" said Stevens. "The jury's out deliberating."

"If they come back with a guilty, the kid is going to sit for at least twenty years, hundred percent time. How about a second degree? Ten years?" said Justin.

"Can't do it. He's got to do murder time."

"Okay, how about twenty years on a second degree?"

"The office wants first degree," said Stevens.

"Look, on the first degree he does 100 percent time. That means he's going to do at least twenty years," said Justin. "You could give him twenty on a second degree and he'll do nine and a half."

"I don't know if we can do it," Stevens said.

He looked over at Olga. Olga just shrugged.

"What if we give him twenty on the second degree and five on the concealing consecutive so that he has a twenty-five-year sentence and does twelve and a half?" Stevens suggested.

"I have to talk to him," said Darcy. "I'm not crazy about it, but I have to convey it to him. It's his decision to make."

"Well, you better get cracking," said the judge, "because once the jury comes back, you're both stuck with the verdict."

Darcy and Justin went out and found Paul Kern and after a little bit of wrangling, he found his wife. Darcy began to explain the deal and Mrs. Kern walked away. She couldn't handle the discussion and left it to her husband to deal with the mess. Darcy laid it out for him and waited for him to think it through.

"I think you should grab it," Kern said. "Twelve and a half years—he'll still be a young man, he'll be able to get his life started again. I'll be able to get him back on the right track."

"Okay, come on," said Darcy grabbing him by the bicep. "You're coming back to talk to him with us."

"You think that's a good idea?" Paul asked.

"I think it's an excellent idea," said Darcy.

Brian Kern sat alone in the lockup. Darcy, Justin, and Paul walked in. He popped up and walked over to the bars.

"They have a verdict already?" he asked.

"No," said Darcy. "The good news is they're not seeking death anymore."

"Why not?" Brian asked.

"Because they're no longer convinced that you killed Laura Martin. They think you may be accountable, but they're not so sure that you're the one who actually killed her."

"Well, what does that mean?" Brian asked.

"Look kid, I'm going to give it to you straight. If you lose this case, you're going to do anywhere from twenty to sixty.

"But they have made you an offer. If you're willing to testify against Trip, they will offer you twenty-five years under a different formula. Instead of first-degree murder time, where you have to serve one hundred percent of the time, they'd take it on a second degree, where you serve fifty percent of your time, and a concealing of a homicidal death, also at fifty percent time."

"What does that mean?" Brian asked. "What does it actually mean if I took that deal?"

"What it means is you would max out at twelve and a half years before any other good time, and you get credit for the time you have been sitting in custody waiting. So the bottom line is in about ten years you'd be going home."

"Ten years?"

"Yeah," said Darcy. "Ten years."

Brian began to pace. Paul stepped to the bars.

"Son."

Brian turned and looked at him.

"Are you talking to me?" he said.

"Yes, I am talking to you. I have something that I want to say to you," Paul began. "I have been a terrible father. I realize all the mistakes I made. I thought that if I made a lot of money and became very successful that would mean I was a good father. I would give you opportunities that I never had. The best schools, never have to worry about money, you would be able to pursue your dreams without any concern about how you would get through it. I worked my ass off to get everything that I have, but I lost sight of everything that was important. I blew it. I was a horrible father and the only thing that I can tell you is that if you take this deal, I will be able to help you when you get out, and while you're serving your time, I will do everything I can to try and be a father to you. I'll visit you. And when you get out, I will help you in any direction that you want to go. Son, I'm not asking you to take this to give yourself a second chance, although that's a good idea. I'm asking you to take it to give me a second chance. I want to be your father. I want to help you. Ten years is a long time, but you know what, it will be ten years that we can work together, and up until now, we've never done that. Take this deal. Take it and I'll help you in every way that I can."

"I deserve to die," he said.

"No you don't," his father replied.

"Don't you get it? I did nothing. I stood by and did nothing while he raped and killed Laura. She was a nice person. She was kind and compassionate. If I had stood up to Trip, she'd be alive today. I'm a coward. Can you image how it feels to be a coward and know that it was Trip that intimidated me?"

He broke down in sobs. His shoulders heaved and he held his right hand over his face while his left grasped the bars in front of him.

His father reached through the bars and placed a hand on his shoulder. "Brian, don't be so hard on yourself. You're young and you never had a father around to help you. But I'm here now and will be here for you from now on as long as I'm alive," Paul said as tears built in his eyes.

"Are you serious?" he said. "You're really going to be there for me? You're not just saying this so I can go away and be out of your hair?"

"No," Paul said. "I failed you before, but I'm not going to fail you now. I'm going to be there for you, I promise."

"Okay, then. I'll do it."

Darcy pulled on Justin's arm and they left, leaving the two Kerns to talk. As soon as they got out, Darcy looked at Justin and smiled.

"You know, what if we go back and see if we can knock off five?"

"Are you kidding me?" Justin said.

"Come on, it's worth a shot. What do we have to lose?"

"All right man, I'm with you," said Justin, "but you got to play this."

"Okay, follow me."

Darcy stepped into the judge's chambers, where the two prosecutors and the judge were talking about anything other than law.

"Listen," said Darcy, "I don't know what to say. The kid's almost there, and I really want him to do this. You know, not for him, but for me. For me, can we do fifteen and five? I would feel better about all of this."

There was silence. Stevens looked at Olga. Olga looked back at Stevens. The judge stood up.

"Larry, Olga, you put a witness on who admitted to a murder and a rape, and this would be a third crime. Give the kid the twenty. My Lord, let's get out from under this. Do you really want this going to the Appellate Court? Do you really want the *Tribune* to be writing about this case for years? Cut your losses. Let's go."

Stevens nodded.

"I'll see if I can get this done right now," said Darcy.

Darcy walked into the court and dug up a jury waiver and a waiver of pre-sentence report, the two documents he needed to execute in open court to do the plea. He then went back and gave the good news to the Kerns.

"Now you're going to be fine. Make the time count," Darcy said.

The plea took about fifteen minutes. The judge allowed Brian to hug his parents before he was taken away. The jury was brought out to court and the judge thanked them for their service and told them that the case had been resolved. A number of them looked relieved.

41

Kathy was driving her minivan with Darcy in the passenger seat. They went out under the stock exchange and then under the old post office, and looped onto 94, heading toward the courthouse.

"I filed a *habeas* in federal court for Armandito."

"That's nice," said Darcy as he looked out the window.

"I was wondering, what do you think about the idea of us doing some civil rights work?"

"Such as," said Darcy.

"You know, Section 1983 work, suing the police for bad arrests."

"Hmm," said Darcy, "haven't given it any thought."

"I mean, you know a lot of lawyers who could refer civil rights cases to us."

"I suppose," said Darcy.

"And the costs aren't that expensive."

"I hadn't really thought about it," said Darcy.

"And if I did that, it might add a little balance to my work, and . . ." She didn't finish her thought.

Darcy smiled. He would be happy to have Kathy stay with the firm.

"Figure out what you want to do, and know that whatever you want to do, you have my support."

"What about Justin?" she said.

"What about him?" asked Darcy.

"Are you going to extend an offer to him?"

"Yes," Darcy said, "especially now that you'll be doing some civil work. Also I'm going to start taking a little more time off."

Kathy smiled. "Civil work for me and more time off for you, huh? Who said you can't teach an old dog new tricks?"

"Woof, woof," Darcy barked.

42

It was one of those hot, sticky days that people called the dog days of August. Justin hadn't had anything to eat since a bowl of Cheerios early that morning, and it was close to two. He had spent the afternoon trying a DUI case in Skokie and now he realized how hungry he was as he pulled into the parking lot at Herm's. He pushed through the doors and was grateful for the air conditioning, which was cranked. Matt was behind the counter wearing shorts and using a white cotton towel to wipe the sweat from his forehead.

"Justin, what's up?"

"Long day," he said loosening his tie.

"Double chicken?"

"Yes sir, couple of pickles too."

Justin walked around the counter and poured himself a soda

from the fountain. He took his usual table, picked up a *Sun-Times*, and sat in front of the Cub game on television. On page three, he read an article about the Kern trial and Trip getting charged for murder in Lake County. He shook his head and mumbled out loud.

"What am I getting involved with?"

Matt walked up and dropped a manila envelope on the table.

"What's this?" Justin asked.

"Hey, some scary-looking dude dropped this off for you."

"What did he look like?"

"Big guy, bald, goatee, muscles, kind of a gut on him. Looked like he rides a motorcycle. He had that look about him. You know, kind of scary."

"What did he say?"

"He asked me if I knew Justin Schachter. I said, 'Yeah.' He says, 'Has he been in yet?' I said, 'No.' Then he handed me this and said make sure you get it."

A customer walked in and Matt walked back behind the counter to take care of him. Justin looked at the nine-and-a-half-by-twelve envelope. On the front was a label from Darcy's office. He opened it up. Inside there were three letter size envelopes. Two of them were thin and one of them was thick. He opened the first envelope. It contained four box seat tickets to a Cubs night game and a parking pass with a note. 'If you can't make this game, call Eddie Jozwiak and switch games.' Darcy had included Eddie's pager number and cell phone number. Justin had been to enough Cub games to know that they were prime seats in the third row between the on-deck circle and the Cubs' dugout. The parking pass was next to the fire station right outside the ballpark.

He opened the second envelope. There was a check made out to him from Darcy's client's fund account for twenty-five thousand dollars, and a note that read, "The Kern family was extremely grateful for the great services you provided." This was the biggest fee he ever received. He read it three times to be sure he was counting the zeroes right.

He then opened the third envelope, the thick envelope. There was no note inside, just an autopsy report. The autopsy report was eight pages long and tri-folded. He used his hands to straighten out the fold and began to read it. He got to the victim's name, Lavelle Macklin. He threw it across the table upside down, pushed the newspaper aside and turned back to watch the Cubs.

By the time he took his wife and daughters to the game, the Cubs would probably be in fourth place. After all, it would be the middle of August, and for the Cubs it was always "wait until next year."

About the Author

Larry Axelrood is a former prosecutor in the State's Attorney's Office in Cook County. A member of the National Association of Criminal Defense Lawyers, he is a graduate of Indiana State University and the Chicago Kent College of Law. Axelrood practices law in Chicago and lives with his family in the North Shore suburbs.